T0304995

THE
UNRAVELLING

ALSO BY VI KEELAND

Worth Forgiving
Belong to You
Made for You

Other books by Penelope Ward and Vi Keeland

The Rules of Dating
The Rules of Dating My Best Friend's Sister
The Rules of Dating My One-Night Stand
The Rules of Dating a Younger Man
Well Played
Not Pretending Anymore
My Favorite Souvenir
Rebel Heir
Rebel Heart
Stuck-Up Suit
Playboy Pilot
Mister Moneybags
British Bedmate
Park Avenue Player

THE UNRAVELLING

VI KEELAND

PIATKUS

PIATKUS

First published in the United States in 2024 by Emily Bestler Books/Atria,
An imprint of Simon & Schuster, LLC
Published in Great Britain in 2024 by Piatkus

1 3 5 7 9 10 8 6 4 2

A CIP catalogue record for this book
is available from the British Library.

Hardback ISBN 978-0-349-43887-0
Trade paperback ISBN 978-0-349-43888-7

Printed and bound in Great Britain by Clays Ltd, Elcograf S.p.A.

Papers used by Piatkus are from well-managed forests
and other responsible sources.

MIX
Paper | Supporting
responsible forestry
FSC
www.fsc.org   FSC® C104740

Piatkus
An imprint of
Little, Brown Book Group
Carmelite House
50 Victoria Embankment
London EC4Y 0DZ

An Hachette UK Company
www.hachette.co.uk

www.littlebrown.co.uk

For Kennedy,
who believed in this book before I did.

CHAPTER 1
Now

We used to look at each other like that. Before *you* went and messed everything up.

The man wraps a scarf around the smiling woman's neck, then leans in and kisses the tip of her nose. I force my eyes from the store window and keep walking. Maybe another mile will do it—will clear my head so I can think properly. Figure out what to do with the rest of my day. The rest of my life.

Another block, then two. I stop behind a dozen people at the crosswalk. A woman checks the time on her phone, a child sways under the weight of his backpack full of books, a businessman in a five-thousand-dollar suit spews into his phone about some deal gone bad.

He's angry. Probably needs therapy. Most of us do. Myself included.

Myself especially.

A teenage girl smokes a joint as she bops along to the buds in her ears. A twentysomething wearing baggy jeans and a T-shirt pretends he's not freezing his ass off.

One thing stands out that makes them different from me—they all seem to have somewhere to go.

Then again, I probably look like I do, too. I'm good at pretending these days, aren't I?

But soon they'll be home with their families or their dog or their video game, and I'll still be out here walking. Searching for something, though I don't know what. I still have my wits enough to know that means I might never find it.

Maybe I should get a dog. That would at least give me a purpose for all this walking. Of course, I'd have to feed it. Drag myself out of bed early every morning to take it outside so it doesn't ruin the carpets. Give it love and affection.

I swallow a lump in my throat. I'm not capable of committing to any of those things. Especially the last one.

The light changes, the wave of people surges forward, and I let it carry me across the street. I turn a corner at random, and seconds later I'm among brownstones. I slow my pace, and another walker brushes against me, hurrying. Another person with a place to be.

A breeze ruffles through the leaves, and the yellow and orange colors of a ginkgo tree rain down around me. We almost lived here in Gramercy Park, in one of these very brownstones. With a foyer painted in sky blue and an office window facing the city. If we'd chosen this home, instead of the apartment, would things have been different? Would that one choice have made ripples through our lives, and you'd be standing next to me right now?

I let myself imagine it. It's the sort of neighborhood where people raise families. Maybe we'd have a baby by now. Maybe I'd have taken a year off. Maybe I'd have paid more attention and noticed how bad things with you really were. If you were still here, you'd probably be on the road right now—off playing a game in Michigan or Canada. My practice would be thriving, instead of crumbling. Maybe we'd have hired an au pair. Maybe . . . just maybe.

That breeze comes again, slicing through my open overcoat. I yank it closed, tie the belt tighter. I've been out for hours, and I should go home. But why?

Tree branches sway, and a fresh tide of leaves skims over my shoes. A rogue yellow one blows up and tangles into my hair. I reach up to pull it out and a cab rushes by mere inches away, creating wind that slaps me in the face. *Shoot.* I didn't even see that red light. I step backward to the curb and bump into a person behind me, nearly falling.

"Ma'am? Are you okay?"

A twentysomething in a Burberry trench, a two-year-old on her hip in a matching jacket and pigtails, and another little one tucked into a vintage pram sucking her thumb.

A ripple, a glimpse of what could have been. What will never be anymore because of *you.*

I reach into my coat pocket and rub my keychain. *Your* keychain. The one that reminds me of all our hopes and dreams. It soothes me. As much as I can be soothed these days.

"Ma'am?" The woman I already forgot about steps closer. "Are you all right?"

I look away, her little family too close to my imaginings for comfort. "Fine. Thanks."

I go back the way I came, walking faster now. *Fleeing.* Fleeing what? It doesn't matter. I stare down at the gray concrete, then up at the gray sky. A shop window reflects back at me—a pale, narrow face, too much cheekbone, too much chin. Hollow eyes, once bright green, have gone dull. They look gray, too. I should get highlights, perk up my dishwater-blond hair.

A bell jangles over the next shop door, pulling my attention. A young couple sits in the window, all sheepish smiles and hands wrapped around paper coffee cups. I duck in, file into line, lost in the anonymity of the city once more.

I blink around. I've never been here, on this corner, in this coffee shop. Or maybe it's new. The world has been changing around me over the last year, and I haven't taken notice.

The line moves forward, and I let it pull me along. You would have hated this place. The overly bright lighting, the din of thirty or so people chatting, the hiss of a barista foaming milk, the whirr of the grinder. Paying seven bucks for a coffee.

"Good afternoon. What can I get you?" A woman with a gummy smile and a blond ponytail is a little too eager to take my order.

"Coffee. Black, please." I hand over cash, accept change, and shuffle down the line, eyes lingering over a cranberry-orange scone. I try to remember if I've eaten today.

"Meredith? Coffee, black," a voice rings out.

I pull off a glove to pick up the paper cup and let the warmth seep in through my skin as I scan the room for an open table. There's only one, near the front of the shop, looking outside. It gives me something to focus on, at least. People swarm the sidewalks, tourists gaping up at the tall buildings with shopping bags in hands and locals grumbling as they're forced to weave through them. Hundreds of people come and go in only minutes. It's a sea of ambiguity, face after face after face, until they all start to blur.

But then . . . there's a flash of familiarity. A face I know in the crowd.

I lean forward, ignoring the table digging into my ribs as I stare at the man. My hand comes to my chest when recognition turns to dismay. And my heart gallops off wildly.

It can't be him.

Can it?

Olive skin, dark beard, lean build. He smiles—lips curled up as he talks into his phone. Then *laughter*, the sort that rocks his whole chest as he tilts his head up, smiling at the sky. This man wouldn't laugh—*couldn't* laugh. After all, he's been through worse than I have.

I squeeze my cup too hard and coffee sloshes over the edges, scalding my hand. Pain radiates across my skin, and I look down at my pink flesh.

It feels good. The sting floods me with an odd sense of relief.

It's not a normal response. I'll probably spend hours overanalyzing it at some point. But right now . . . my attention is back to the window. *He's* way more interesting.

I'm out of my chair, dumping my barely touched coffee into the nearest garbage, and through the jangling door in seconds. The man strides down the sidewalk, walking between gaps in pedestrians, making it easy to track him. Easy to—I jolt forward—follow him.

It's akin to following a ghost.

Except he's not the one who died.

They are.

We are stuck here. In limbo.

Me. And him.

Gabriel Wright. The last time I saw him, I felt almost exactly as I do now. Numb. Distant. Unbelieving. *That night.*

I slip my hand into my pocket again, reaching for your keychain to help shake away the bad memories. But there's no time to soothe myself now because I'm falling behind. So I speed up, give chase. Gabriel turns a corner, hands stuffed in his pockets. He's leaving Gramercy, heading south toward the East Village. We're not the only two striding this way. I step behind three women, oversize shopping bags hung over elbows like trophies they're bringing back from a hunt. Tourists. They're the perfect blind for my own hunt.

I want to know what he's doing, where he's going. Why he's *here* of all places, and most of all—I flash back to his face, laughing, smiling—is he *really* happy? Happy enough to laugh. To feel joy, after what *you* did.

Gabriel stops at a newsstand up ahead. A rush of suited office workers flood the sidewalk coming out of a building. It's after seven now. I've been outside since noon, wandering. I should go home. Order in some food, find a way to spend my time—

But I can't force myself away from *him*. I press my phone to my ear to block my face as he scans the sidewalk, waiting for his turn. He holds up a hand, uses his phone to pay for a pack of cigarettes—some brand in a white package—and shoves them into a pocket.

An urge to get closer hits me. He probably wouldn't recognize me. We never met, not formally anyway. No. We just went through hell together, several rooms apart.

You in one room.

His wife and child in another.

I swallow the acid rising in my throat, the consequence of coffee on an empty stomach and stressing while speed-walking down the sidewalk after a man I should steer clear of.

Gabriel stays at the newsstand a moment longer. Smiling again. Chatting up the man who works behind the counter.

I step back, lean against the brick of a building, and pull out a tiny notebook, the one I keep my to-do list in. I haven't written in it in weeks, maybe months. No point in a to-do list when there's nothing to do. But now, I scribble.

Gabriel Wright.

I double-check the time on my phone like it's a critical piece of information and go back to writing.

Thursday, 7:13 p.m.

Walking on East 15th Street. Stops at newsstand on corner.

Smoker.

Laughing. Smiling. Happy?

That last word gives me pause. These days, the idea of happiness is like a fable or a fairy tale. A dream every little girl growing up in a screwed-up house wants to be a part of, but knows deep in her heart is just make-believe.

Gabriel offers a warm smile to the newsstand man and turns his back to saunter off in a loose amble, like he hasn't a care in the world. I want to grab him and scream, "Are you really happy?" or maybe, "I know you're pretending. You're just better at it than me. It's not possible you're whole again. Not after what *we* did to you."

It doesn't make sense.

He doesn't make sense.

My breath catches in my throat as his strides quicken. I have to keep following. No, I *need to* keep following. I'm suddenly driven by purpose for the first time in months. A craving opens up wide inside me, something that could swallow me whole. *How? Why?*

I glance behind me as I step back into the crowd and lock eyes with a young woman with long blond hair and an armful of books. She looks like she's going to say something, but then I realize she's probably just hoping I'll get the hell out of her way. Like everyone else except me in this city, she's in a hurry. Though now I have purpose, too.

For the first time since *you*.

I don't know where I'm going, or what happens when I get there.

But I know I must follow him.

CHAPTER 2
Then

"I almost forgot—I have a surprise for you." I slipped out of bed and pulled open my dresser drawer.

"Get back here." Connor's voice was gruff. Playful. "I want to give you a surprise, too. A *big* one."

I chuckled and tucked *my* surprise into my palm, hands behind my back. "I know how upset you were when you lost your Gretzky jersey keychain a few weeks ago."

"My coach gave that to me on my sixth birthday. I showed it to Wayne himself when I met him the night I was drafted into the pros. He told me someday, people would be carrying around keychains with my number on a jersey."

I smiled and brought my hands from behind my back, opening my fist. "Well, Mr. Gretzky is a smart man."

Connor sat up in bed. "Holy shit. Where'd you get that?"

"I had it made."

My husband's eyes welled up. He took the tiny replica of his blue and red New York Steel jersey, lucky number seventeen, and ran his finger over it.

I pointed. "There's a tiny mistake. See on the bottom, how the red paint bled too high into the blue section? I'm going to ask him to remake it, but I couldn't wait to give it to you."

Connor smiled. "That's not paint. That's my opponent's blood. Don't have it remade. I love it just the way it is."

"There's more to the surprise. The guy who made it wants to license the rights to distribute them. I gave him your agent's number, and they're already negotiating a contract. He would make a *half million* to start. Imagine all the six-year-old boys walking around with this keychain, with dreams of being *you* someday."

Connor pulled me to him, cupping my cheek. "I love it. Thank you."

I rubbed my nose with his. "You're welcome."

"I have something I want to give you, too, Mer."

I smirked and playfully rolled my eyes. "Been there. Done that."

"Oh yeah? Is that so?" Without warning, I was lifted off the bed and hoisted into the air. I yelped and Connor settled me back down on his lap, my legs straddling him. "Do you remember what I said when I proposed?" he asked.

"What?"

"I said that my entire life, I'd only ever wanted one thing: to win a hockey championship. But since the day I met you, it wasn't enough anymore. I needed three things: You. A championship. And a family. I was lucky enough to get you to marry me. Six months ago, my dream of winning the championship came true. All I need now, for my life to be complete, is a family. I want to have a baby. I know I travel a lot for games, but I'll be all-hands-on-deck whenever I'm home. I promise. Will you have my baby, Mer?"

I covered my mouth with my hand. "Really?"

He nodded. "Really. I know you just built your practice to where you want it. So if you want to wait, I'll understand. But I'm ready when you are, babe. I'm more than ready."

Connor was right. I'd busted my ass the last few years since going out on my own. Working at two hospitals and the psych center, picking up the worst on-call shifts just to get patient referrals. It wouldn't be easy to take a step back now. But was there ever a good time to have a baby?

"I can find a part-time psychiatrist to help out. Maybe another mom who wants to go back to work but can only do half days or something." I nodded. "I'll make it work. We'll make it work."

Connor's lips curved to a giant, boyish smile. "We're gonna have a baby," he whispered.

The thought left me a little breathless. I swallowed. "We're gonna have a baby."

"I want a boy first. Then a girl. Then maybe three or four more boys."

"Uh . . . slow down there, big guy. That's five or six kids. How about we try one and see how it goes? It's going to mean a lot of change for us."

"Whatever you want, beautiful." He pushed a lock of hair behind my ear. "It'll be a good change. I see nothing but happy days ahead, for the rest of our lives."

CHAPTER 3 *Now*

alking in the first time is the worst part.

Weaving through the hallway of closed doors—people like me hiding behind them, ready to diagnose what's wrong with someone who was a complete stranger only an hour ago. MD, PsyD, PhD, all sorts of fancy-sounding letters tacked on after names. I knew coming in was intimidating for my patients, but I don't think I comprehended just how bad it could be. Until now. When the doctor became the patient.

I ride the elevator up to the third floor. It's like every office building—cheap, rough carpet, neutral walls, heavy fire-resistant doors, and too much silence. I stop outside my destination, 302b. As I contemplate going in, my cell rings. *Jake* flashes on the screen. My brother. I hit ignore, telling myself I'll call him back later. Though I know I probably won't. He wants to make sure I'm doing okay, like everyone else who checks in on me occasionally. Except my brother knows me too well. So I try to answer on the good days, when it's most believable that I'm happy. Though lately those are few and far between.

I take a deep breath and tuck my phone into my coat pocket, going back to staring at my new therapist's office door. Inside waits a man I've never met. A stranger I'm supposed to tell how I'm feeling. *Keith Alexander, PhD.* Nausea works its way from my stomach to my throat, and I haven't even opened the door yet. My hands are damp and sweaty. I wipe them on my jeans, wishing the turbulence of my thoughts would slow down, just *slow down* already.

Yesterday my thoughts *were* slow. Painfully snail-like. It took me twenty minutes to fix a cup of tea, an hour to get ready to leave the apartment. Even putting on my shoes was an effort. And now I'm buzzing like I've downed a dozen cups of coffee.

Gabriel. I saw Gabriel Wright.

And he was happy.

But I can't think about that now. I need to be somewhat normal for this man. He'll scribble in his notebook and say, "Uh-huh," and, "Let's talk about that." I can see him now—fifties or sixties, gray hair, playing the part.

My hand touches the doorknob—a polished chrome, not original to the dingy building. It's cold. I hesitate, my stomach gurgling. I'm *hungry*.

I can't remember the last time I felt much of anything, much less hunger. Until yesterday.

I push through the door, and a midtwenties or early thirtysomething man looks up. He's no older than me. Dark blond hair, tanned skin, and a welcoming, open smile. It must be dress-casual Friday, because he's in jeans and a blue T-shirt that fits him well enough that it's hard not to notice it fits him well. A notebook lies open on his broad desk, appointments by the look of it. He must be Dr. Alexander's assistant.

"Hello. I have a six thirty appointment."

"You must be Meredith Fitzgerald."

"Meredith McCall," I correct him. "I'm using my maiden name, but it wasn't changed when . . ." I let my voice trail off. If Dr. Alexander's assistant doesn't know the details, I'm not going to be the one to provide them . . . when I made the appointment," I conclude.

"Ah." He straightens, offers a kind smile. "Well, Dr. McCall, come right in, then."

It's not until I step past him and into the inner office that I realize no one sits behind the desk in the corner. Dr. Alexander is not perched on the leather couch or the matching armchair. Because the young man I mistook for an assistant *is* Dr. Keith Alexander. Heat works its way up to my face.

How many times had I been mistaken for an assistant because I was young and attractive? Too many to count. Furthermore, he is not what I was expecting. How am I supposed to talk to *him* about the crushing guilt I feel or how much I miss my husband while simultaneously wishing I'd never met him?

I blow out a breath, sitting tentatively on the edge of the couch. Instead of the creamy white walls my office has, his are alternating blue and gray. A modern white-and-wood coffee table sits atop a Persian rug. A frosted-glass window calls my attention from a few feet away. During the day, it must bathe his patients in sunlight.

"I'm Dr. Keith Alexander. I'm glad to see you this evening." He sits across from me and crosses one leg over the other, hands folded in his lap.

Dr. Alexander gives me an open, welcoming smile, but I'm not seeing him—I'm seeing myself, doing the exact same thing with my own patients. Except I don't get to do that anymore. Not after what happened. For the time being, my office goes on without me.

He clears his throat, snapping me back to the moment. "Can I offer you herbal tea? Water?"

"No, thank you." I set my purse beside me and work my jacket off my shoulders. I find the clock behind him. 6:32 p.m. Only fifty-eight minutes to go. I press my lips into a smile that probably looks more like a grimace. "Oh, before I forget." I unzip my bag and pull out the paper I'd folded in half. "I have this for you to sign."

He leans forward and takes it. "What is it?"

"It's for the Office of Professional Misconduct. You enter the date I've started therapy and sign. I'm required to start by next week, so I guess this just tells them I've complied with their punishment."

Dr. Alexander takes a pen from the end table next to him. He pushes his glasses down his nose and reads the document over before scribbling today's date and his name at the bottom.

"Here you go." He hands it back to me and smiles. "And I'm sorry you think of coming here as punishment. I promise to do my best not to make it feel that way."

"I . . . I didn't mean . . ."

He waves me off. "It's fine. I understand. I'd probably feel the same way if I was mandated to do something instead of coming voluntarily."

"Thanks for saying that. But I really didn't mean to use the word I did."

"It's fine. Let's move on."

"Okay."

We stare at each other for a long time. It's definitely not a comfortable silence.

"So . . . this is awkward, isn't it?" I say. "A therapist getting therapy."

"Not at all. I'm of the opinion that all therapists should go to therapy, at least occasionally. Just like we get a physical checkup once a year, we should get a mental one, too." He taps his head. "How's your day going?"

I force another nervous smile. "Fine. Yours?"

"Very good, thanks. Any weekend plans?"

I hold back a sigh. He's making small talk. Trying to make me comfortable before he jumps into the real stuff.

"No," I say. "It's hard to . . ." *Do anything after what happened. Plan a life without my husband. Get out of bed before noon.* ". . . make plans these days," I finish.

"I see." In my peripheral vision, he shifts, then switches tacks. "Well, I'll get right to it, then. How are you doing following the tragedy you endured seven months ago?"

My tragedy. Like my life is a Shakespeare tale instead of the train wreck it is.

Static fills my head. I'm still trying to wrap my head around the simple fact that I wake up alone every morning. Dr. Alexander's leap into the deep end is too much, too fast. I need to make sure I can keep my head above water before I begin to swim.

I swallow. "Do you think we can talk about something other than my husband to start?"

There, a simple request. An easy-to-respect wish. If my patient said that to me, I'd nod and move on. And Dr. Alexander does exactly that.

"Okay, well, what did you do today? Can you run me through it?" The timbre of his voice is soft, kind. It grates at my nerves, and my gaze drifts toward the clock again. 6:35 p.m.

Fifty-five minutes to go.

"What's a day in the life of Dr. Meredith McCall like?"

"Well, earlier I went for a walk," I say, "a long walk. I pretty much do that every day lately."

"And how was that? Go anywhere interesting?"

"The park," I say. "And I got coffee." I stop myself before I say the rest of it—*where I saw Gabriel Wright for the second day in a row and followed him for another hour. Maybe longer. Long enough that I nearly didn't make it here in time.* "Then I did a little shopping," I finish, wrapping up my day with a lie.

"Oh? Grocery shopping or . . . ?" Dr. Alexander tilts his head to show interest.

"Just window-shopping, mostly." Another forced smile. I catch my leg jiggling and press a hand over my knee to still it.

He holds a pen in one hand, a small bound notebook in his lap. I haven't seen him jot down anything yet, unlike me when I see patients. I take lots of notes.

Is he not writing because he knows I'm lying?

Maybe it's a bad idea to lie. Maybe, like me, he can almost surely *tell* when someone is lying. And lying is half of what got me into this mess in the first place, isn't it? Pressure builds inside me until I find myself asking, "Is what I say here confidential? I mean, obviously I know about doctor-patient confidentiality rules. But do you have to report details of our session to the medical board, since my visits are mandated by them?"

Lord knows I signed a bunch of papers at the hearing without reading them. Maybe I've lost my right to privacy—like so many other things I've lost because of *you*. Perhaps that notebook on his lap isn't so much our session notes but where he'll write notes on what he has to report back. Maybe—

"What's said in this room is confidential." His voice interrupts my ruminating. "I do have to tell the medical board if you don't come to your sessions, but what you tell me here is covered by patient confidentiality, the same as any other patient we would treat."

My hands unclench. I take a deep breath and let myself sink back on the couch.

"Okay." I make the split-second decision that truth is the best policy. At least here, where these words will only echo within the walls of his office. "I did go for a walk, but I didn't go shopping afterward. I spent my day following someone."

"Following? Do you mean someone was leading the way? Or you were following someone without their knowledge?"

"Without their knowledge."

He nods, keeping his face expressionless—something we are both trained to do. Lately it's been the only face I wear, since expressions display our feelings, and I don't seem to have any.

"All right. And who was it that you followed today?"

"A dead woman's husband."

Dr. Alexander's mask slips and his eyebrows widen. His pen spins in his fingers, presses to the notepad, and he scribbles before looking up. "Tell me more."

I look away for a long time, staring out the window at the swaying trees. I don't make eye contact when I finally speak. "His name is Gabriel Wright. He's the husband of the woman that was killed, the father of the child killed."

Dr. Alexander quietly absorbs what I've said. I feel his eyes trained on my face, but I can't look at him. Not yet, anyway.

"Was today the first time you followed Mr. Wright?"

I shake my head. "Second."

"When was the first time?"

"Yesterday."

"And why did you follow him?"

I shrug. "I have no idea. I saw him yesterday at a coffee shop. It was a surprise, definitely not something I'd planned. He looked . . . happy. I followed him. I think maybe I followed him again today to see if it was just a fluke, if I'd caught him during a singular moment where he'd just learned some good news, perhaps. I was curious if after that he'd slip back into a miserable existence."

"And was he? Miserable, I mean. During the rest of the time you followed him?"

I shake my head again. "He seemed . . . normal. But that's not possible."

"Why not?"

"How could he be? How could he be happy after all that he lost? Some days I wake up in a cold sweat, with the image the newspaper ran the morning after the accident haunting me. A tarp covering a tiny little body. A stuffed Hello Kitty on the ground a foot away. What must he wake up to every day? Losing an innocent child and the love of his life? He proposed to her in the middle of a performance of *A Midsummer Night's Dream*."

Dr. Alexander scribbles more notes on his pad. "If we could, I'd like to back things up a bit. I've read your case file that the medical board sent over. But it doesn't go into any detail about the family of the victims. You knew the Wright family before the accident?"

"No. We'd never met."

"Then how do you know how Mr. Wright proposed?"

I look up and meet the doctor's eyes for the first time. "Google. Gabriel Wright teaches at Columbia. He's an English professor specializing in Shakespeare. The way he proposed is noted in his bio. He refers to her as his Juliet. I sat under a tree while he taught his classes earlier today and read everything that came up in a search. That's how I passed the time while I waited."

Dr. Alexander's eyes dart back and forth between mine. "If you've never met, how did you know who Mr. Wright was when you ran into him yesterday?"

"I've seen him before. The night of the accident, I was in the hall at the hospital when the doctor told him his wife and child had died. He crumpled to the floor, sobbing. The memory of his face isn't something I could ever forget. Though last night when I followed him home, I also checked the names on the mailboxes inside the lobby of his building just to be sure. It was him."

"Okay. So yesterday you saw Mr. Wright by chance and recognized him. You followed him because you were curious after seeing him smile. Is that correct?"

"Yes."

"And what about today? How did you come to follow him again?"

"I went back to his apartment early this morning and waited for him to come out."

"How early?"

"Does that matter?"

"No." Dr. Alexander smiles. "It's not important if you don't remember. But if you can recall, I'd like to know. That is, if you're comfortable sharing."

I take a deep breath in and blow it out. "I left my house at four a.m. and stopped for some coffee. It was probably about four thirty when I arrived at his building to wait."

He scribbles some more on his notepad. "So yesterday you followed him because you had witnessed Mr. Wright showing signs of happiness. You wanted to know if that was something fleeting or not, and you seemed to have gotten that answer. What did you hope to learn when you followed him today?"

"I'm not sure." I shake my head. "I guess I just can't believe he's really moved on. So I went back to look for cracks in the mask he wears."

"There isn't a specific timeline on healing. I'm sure you know that from your own patients. Coping with loss is a unique experience for every person. We all grieve differently."

"I know that, but . . ."

Dr. Alexander waits for me to continue, but I don't. I can't argue with what he's said because he's right. In theory, at least. It's what the textbooks all say. Every person heals on their own timeline. Yet I know in my heart of hearts that Gabriel Wright can't have moved on. Part of the process of healing from a tragedy is acceptance, and acceptance requires forgiveness. But some things in life are just unforgivable. Dr. Alexander can't understand that, even though he thinks he does. You need to live it to truly understand it. And I don't have the energy for that type of argument today.

So I force a smile. "You're right. We're all different."

"Do you think you've gotten whatever compelled you to follow him out of your system?"

I shrug. "Probably."

But a person who doesn't plan to follow someone anymore doesn't stop and buy a dark hoodie and baseball cap right before going to meet their therapist. They probably also don't pick up a set of mini binoculars.

"Dr. McCall?"

I hear him call my name but I'm staring out the window again, mesmerized by the sway of the trees. They're so peaceful to watch. My office is too high up for trees.

He smiles warmly when I eventually shift my gaze to him. There's no sign of judgment on his face. "Is it okay if I call you Meredith, rather than Dr. McCall?"

"Of course."

"Great." He nods. "Anyway, Meredith, I think if you're still curious about Mr. Wright, we should discuss that here, rather than you following him again. Aside from the obvious, that stalking someone is illegal and you're already in trouble with the medical board, I think you're playing with fire by becoming emotionally invested in the happiness of the survivor of your husband's victims."

"Gabriel Wright is not only one of my husband's victims."

Dr. Alexander's brows puckered. "Who is he, then?"

"He's the husband of *my* victims, too."

CHAPTER 4
Then

"Hey, Irina." I took my usual seat, two rows behind the Plexiglas barrier, and unraveled the scarf hugging my neck while I searched the ice for Connor. When I saw him skating in one piece, I breathed a little easier.

My friend looked over and squinted. "You okay?"

"Yeah. I've just had one of those weird feelings all morning. Not to sound dramatic, but it's almost like a sense of impending doom. I forgot about it by midday when I got busy with patients. But then it came back on the way to the arena." I sank back from the edge of my seat. "It's silly. I know."

"It's not silly. I get that impending-doom feeling all the time."

"You do?"

Irina grinned. "Yeah, it's usually about ten minutes before my two-year-old twins wake up."

I laughed. "Now, *that* makes sense."

"You're never late," she said. "Did you get stuck on the A train? They've been having track-switch trouble all week. I got caught for over an hour this morning."

My gaze followed Connor as he zigged and zagged, skates cutting into the ice. "No. My train was fine. My last patient was new and went long."

"Don't you have one of those timers? Like in the movies?"

"I have a clock, but if someone is upset and struggling, I can't kick them out. So I don't always stick to the hour allotted."

Irina rubbed her seven-months-pregnant belly. "Shit. I would. Hell, I'd kick this one out if I had the chance. The struggle is real to not pee my pants these days."

I laughed, and it felt good. Everything was *fine*. The game would end, we'd have a round of drinks, and I'd fall asleep next to my husband after celebratory sex. Yes, even after a game, he had plenty of energy. I smiled wider at the thought.

"Speaking of struggling," she added. "Misery loves company. When are you and Connor going to take the leap and start popping out little ice skaters?"

I hesitated, my smile falling away. Sharing personal information is something I'm careful to avoid doing all day long. But Irina was a friend, not a patient. She and I had sat next to each other for the last four hockey seasons. Her husband was Ivan Lenkov, one of Connor's teammates and closest friends, and Irina and Ivan had recently moved into an apartment in our building. Our lives were busy, hers with a growing family and mine with my practice, but we tried to make time for dinner at least once a month and watched all of the away games we weren't able to go to together.

"I actually went off the pill last month." I bit down on my bottom lip. "I'm excited. But nervous, too."

"Oh wow. Well, if Connor's sperm are as athletic as the rest of him, you're probably already pregnant with triplets."

I chuckled. "Don't even joke. Juggling one with our schedules seems challenging enough."

The roar of the crowd dragged our attention back to the ice. Connor was skating shoulder to shoulder with a defensive player, the puck under his stick's control with one hand while the other fended off the opponent. It always amazed me how many things these guys could do at once, all while balancing on a three-millimeter-thick blade. Connor sailed down the ice as if it were as easy as walking. I supposed to him, it was.

Seconds later, the buzzer sounded for intermission. Connor skated off the ice, following his teammates, but glanced back my way. I couldn't see his face, but I was certain he winked. Warmth spread through me, and I waved.

"You two . . ." Irina rolled her eyes. I hadn't realized she was watching me. "Still making googly eyes at each other."

I kept it to myself that my husband, the man I'd been with for almost a decade now, had also sent me flowers for no reason today. Deep purple and cream hydrangeas. My favorite.

I stood. "You want to go up to the Suite for the break?" *The Suite* was short for the Wives' Room, a place where only the wives of players or serious girlfriends invited in by a wife were allowed. It wasn't really my thing. But Irina liked it. Lately, more for the free food than the company. And there was wine in it for me.

Irina hooked her arm with mine. "Lead the way to the pigs in blankets, girl."

Eighteen minutes later, we were back in our spots. The opposing team had taken the lead, and we gripped the edges of our seats, necks craning, hoping the Steel would score again.

We didn't have to wait long. The other team got hit for a penalty, and Connor's team retook control of the game. With the score suddenly tied and their team up a man, the quieted crowd roared back to life. Irina and I jumped up. My heart was in my throat as Connor got the puck. He skated down the center, sharp edges of his blades spraying ice with every leg change. When he reached the net, he swung his stick back.

A defenseman came out of nowhere, slamming Connor from the left, hard enough to rocket him into the air.

"Connor!" His name tore itself from my throat.

The world went into slow motion.

Connor flew into the air.

Another defenseman came in from the right.

Connor flailed, trying to brace himself for the fall.

But gravity waited for no one.

He hit the ice. Hard.

One leg stretched forward and the other splayed back, bending in a way no leg was meant to bend.

My husband screamed, his wail reverberating through the arena.

The crowd went silent.

For a second, I couldn't breathe. Then I bolted down to the ice.

I might've been a psychiatrist, a far cry from an emergency room doctor. But I had gone to medical school. And I knew enough to realize we were headed straight for the hospital.

CHAPTER 5
Now

After a week, I know his schedule. I rise early and start walking the streets of Manhattan as they wake up around me. But I don't rush. I meander. I know I have time before Gabriel leaves his building.

Coffee at the stand on the corner. Perusing the news as I wait for a bagel. Watching the ever-changing leaves turn from yellow to orange to red, a little each day. I chew a thick pumpernickel bagel smeared with cream cheese and lox and think of Dr. Alexander, his advice to stop stalking Gabriel. I don't see it as stalking. Not really. I have no ill intentions. I just need to *know* . . .

I swallow what's in my mouth and pause, envisioning it: Gabriel's face, lit up with happiness.

I need to know it's real.

I fold the rest of the bagel into its paper and toss it in the nearest trash can. The rest of my coffee goes with it, making a satisfying clunk as they hit the bottom. A bookstore is two doors down, and with a quick glance at my watch—Gabriel won't be by for another twenty minutes—I duck inside. The store has just opened, and two employees murmur behind the counter as they sort books. I brush by them to the self-help section.

Build the Life You Want.

Secrets to a Happy Marriage.

Life Sucks. Get Used to It.

I could've written the last one . . .

My eyes catch on a stand near the checkout section. It's half empty, but what remains are spiral-bound journals with bright splashes of color. Rainbows and sunrises and the sort.

I reach out and pick one up. Scrawled across the front is *It's never too late to start writing a new chapter.* I stare at it, slipping back into the before world, when I got to see my own patients. When I'd ask them to pick out a journal and write in it every day as part of their therapy. Dr. Alexander assigned no such task, but a little self-assigned homework never hurts. I look to the register, where the two employees are chitchatting away, paying no attention to the patrons. I make a rash decision and tuck the journal into my purse. My heart starts to pound, a frantic whoosh of blood filling my ears. I've never stolen anything in my life. And I'm certain I have a few hundred dollars in my wallet, not to mention two or three credit cards. I have no idea why the hell I do it, but I feel like I'm going to jump out of my skin with every step I take toward the door. Once I'm outside, I keep walking, power walking almost, until I get to the end of the block, turn right, and duck into the doorway of a store that isn't open yet. Then I can't help it. I smile. It feels exhilarating.

It takes a few minutes for my heartbeat to slow. A glance at my watch tells me it's time. So I head to my post, stop one on my daily Gabriel Wright tour. He comes out right on time as usual.

It's easy enough to not be seen as I follow. The morning rush of people headed to work, to the gym, to the subway, is my camouflage. He strides down the sidewalk, hands tucked into leather gloves and holding nothing, headed north. I let him pass, wait five seconds, then follow.

Within a couple of minutes, I know where he's heading—the same place he went yesterday. Instead of continuing on to Columbia, he takes a left, then another. This time, I stop across the street and press my phone to my face, turning partially away. He enters the redbrick building lined with dozens of little windows that is Manhattan Mini Storage and disappears through the glass door. The same light flicks on as yesterday. This time I count—twelve tiny windows down from the entrance. I haven't gone as far as to follow him inside yet. I'm too afraid he'll see me. Though I am curious what he's doing in there. Plenty of New Yorkers have storage lockers. With minuscule apartments, it's often a necessity. But yesterday he came with nothing and left with nothing. Was he sorting through boxes? Organizing things? Looking for something in particular? I suppose whatever it was, he didn't find it. Maybe that's why he's back again.

A breeze picks up, whipping my hair around my face. I reach for it, tie it at the nape of my neck, and hazard a glance at the sky. It's been cloudy all morning, but those clouds have darkened. With the high buildings all around me, it's claustrophobia-inducing—like the sky might actually fall on me, and there's no escape. But then, soon enough, Gabriel emerges and my blood starts pumping—the same as when I slipped that journal into my purse and walked out of the bookstore a thief. He's again empty-handed, again headed uptown toward Columbia—and I hurry to not lose him.

His classes are the same on Tuesdays and Thursdays, so after he enters his building, I know I've got two hours before he'll emerge and take a lunch break. I find a bench and sit, withdrawing the journal I stole, feeling in my purse for a pen. Around me, students walk to class, clutching satchels or shouldering backpacks. Few seem dressed warmly enough for the brisk autumn day.

I suddenly feel eyes on me, a steady gaze, and I look up, searching for its source. But there's only a passel of students, a group of sorority girls, all bottle-blond, all wearing matching sweatshirts—no one in particular is watching. Probably I'm imagining it. It makes sense that I feel paranoid, considering what I've done at the bookstore, and that I'm sitting around waiting for a man to come out who doesn't know I've been following him. I search around me once more, but it's just college students crisscrossing campus.

I push the thought aside and write about the past week. About seeing

Gabriel in the coffee shop and following him. About wondering how long he can go on pretending to be happy. About the twelfth window in Manhattan Mini Storage, and Columbia University, the sprawling campus in the middle of jam-packed upper Manhattan.

When Gabriel skips down the stairs, presumably headed to lunch, something is different. I notice it right away—the lightness of his step, the lean of his body, the tautness around his eyes. He's not just headed to the cafeteria to grab a sandwich. He's going *somewhere* to do *something*.

And I want to know what.

Five minutes later, he opens the door to an Italian café on the edge of campus, and I can't help myself—I duck in after him. My skin chills, forming goose bumps with the knowledge of the risk I'm taking. It's darker in here, low lighting and fake plants in the corners. Square tables with red-checkered tablecloths. Booths and tables, and a woman at the front who's got ten years on me.

"Any table's fine, hon." She waits with a menu in hand. I scan the dark room, trying to catch sight of him. Then I realize I've passed over him twice, because he's already seated, back to me, in a booth in the rear corner. Directly across from a woman.

"Here is fine, thanks." I take the nearest table, a little two-seater in the middle of the restaurant. Not exactly unobtrusive, but he can't see me. As long as I keep my head down, even if he leaves first, he'll never know I was here.

"Need time to look at the menu?" She sets it in front of me.

I look down at it. "I'll take the caprese salad. And a glass of pinot, please."

She disappears. Seconds later, a glass of wine is at my fingertips. The glass sweats, it's so cold, and I take a tiny sip, watching the back booth. Gabriel's hands are gesturing—tanned skin, creased with whatever hobby exposes them to frequent sun—and across from him sits a petite woman with blond hair tied back in a ponytail. Young. Pretty in a girl-next-door kind of way. Her gaze is focused on him very seriously.

It's probably a meeting with a fellow professor. Maybe she's new—that explains the skin young enough to not have met wrinkles yet. Or she could be a family friend. Perhaps even a business meeting of some sort, given the way she's watching him so intently. A lawyer or an accountant or—

He does it again.

He throws his head back, deep laughter coming from his gut, and she smiles, clearly pleased with herself for garnering such a reaction.

I take a long sip of the wine and let its sweet, tart flavor roll over my tongue.

He's so good at pretending.

I wish I was better at it. I've just barely gained back the ability to eat, to do something other than force myself through the motions. I'd love to actually enjoy food again, order an appetizer and dessert rather than a single dish I know I won't even make a dent in. Then again, I don't deserve to enjoy anything after what I did. What I *didn't* do. I exhale forcefully, then startle when a hand is suddenly right in front of me.

"Oh, my apologies. I thought you saw me." The waitress. Setting down my salad. "Can I get you anything else?"

I shake my head. "No. Thank you."

I ignore the salad, pull out my new notebook, and scribble more notes. Maybe if I search through them later, I'll find a pattern. I'll recognize *something*, some semblance of a hint that will allow me to see the truth underneath the mask he wears.

Eventually, I pick at the salad. I study the spread of the oil and balsamic, eat a piece of cheese, nibble on a tomato. At least I'm getting my veggies. Kind of. But all the while, I'm listening—catching bits and pieces of their conversation, though not enough to make sense of it. Something about a mutual friend, I think. A problem at her work, which may also be teaching. And then he says, "Storage unit," and my ears perk up. I look over, but the blonde notices me staring their way. So I flash a vague smile and force my gaze to move elsewhere, like I'm just a diner alone admiring the restaurant and fellow diners.

I'm more careful after that, not wanting to meet the eyes of the woman a second time. Then a couple takes a table between mine and theirs. The new couple's talking drowns out any chance I have of more eavesdropping. Except for when I hear the woman's energetic laugh come from the booth in the corner. I chance a quick peek. It's a fraction-of-a-second look, yet I come away with a new revelation.

Maybe she's a girlfriend.

My mind catches on that idea. Maybe he and his wife were about to get divorced. Maybe he really is *happy* because she's dead—

But no. Even if he had been ecstatic to be rid of her, he also lost his little girl.

His beautiful little Rose.

Even I had to click away when the picture came up on Google. The sweet, innocent face that would never grow old, too much for anyone to bear. Except maybe a monster. Which Gabriel Wright wasn't. I saw the devastation on his face that night. His world had shattered into a million pieces. He's *pretending* to be happy. He's just mastered the art of camouflaging his feelings. His misery is lurking under the disguise he wears. Soon I'll see it.

Sitting here alone, pushing salad pieces around my plate with a fork to make it look like I've eaten more than I have, I realize it's the first time I've been in a restaurant since—well, *you.* We spent three hundred bucks on dinner and barely uttered two words to each other that night.

Emotion swells in me. I set cash on the table and gather my things, leaving before they do, before Gabriel can lay eyes on me. And before I start sobbing, gaining the unwanted attention of everyone around me. Because I feel it coming. Feel the emotions whirling around like a tornado building strength, ready to touch down where it's least expected.

I don't bother waiting for them to come out. I know where he lives, where he works, and the one place he seems to frequent in between—that storage unit that holds God knows what. Instead, I walk east, ignoring the cold sprinkle of rain from the sky. A subway station appears, and I descend beneath the city, hopping on the first train I see. I ride for what feels like too many stops, then climb the stairs back to the street.

The Financial District.

I guess I did ride pretty far downtown. I start walking, no particular destination in mind. But when I see the street sign for Maiden Lane, I remember that's where the Office of Professional Misconduct is. I still have the paper Dr. Alexander signed in my purse, so I might as well make something about today productive.

The sign on the front door is imposing, the letters larger than necessary. *Professional Misconduct.* It's the adult version of how I felt going anywhere near the principal's office as a child. Still, I take a deep breath and walk in.

"Hi. I need to submit a paper for a case. It came with a return envelope, but I was in the neighborhood, so I figured I'd drop it by."

"Sure," the clerk says. "Do you have the case number?"

I nod. "It's on the top of the paper."

She takes the form and scans it. "Oh. That's funny. I was just working on this file earlier today. I had a FOIA request on it."

My brows pinch. "A FOIA request?"

She nods. "Someone requested a copy of the entire case file under the Freedom of Information Act."

"Who?"

The clerk's face changes. She purses her lips like she's caught herself speaking out of turn. "Sorry. I shouldn't have mentioned it."

"But who would request a copy of my file?"

She shrugs. "Could be anyone. Cases that result in charges are a matter of public record."

"Was it someone from the media?" No one has bothered with me since the story about Connor fizzled from the headlines. It has been months now.

"You'd have to fill out the form online to get that information." She shakes her head. "I'm sorry if I upset you."

I sigh. "Okay. Thank you. Do I need to do anything else to file that paper?"

"Nope. I'll take care of it."

"Thank you."

I step back out onto the street, feeling even more glum than I did when I came in. My shoulders hunch and my feet feel heavy, like my shoes are made of concrete, but I go back to walking. Because what else do I have to do? I walk a few miles, not really paying attention to where I'm going, until I reach a dead end. Iron gates practically smack me in the face. *A cemetery.* Seems an appropriate enough place to end my day. So I keep walking, find the entrance, crunch the browning grass beneath my feet with every step, and start reading gravestones as I pass.

Philip Morrow. 1931–1976. Beloved father, husband, and son.

Matilda Holtz. 1876–1945. Too well loved to ever be forgotten.

Julia Einhard. 1954–1960. Our angel in heaven.

I swallow a lump in my throat and taste salt. *Julia was only six.*

Gabriel's daughter will never get to turn six.

I close my eyes. What am I doing? I don't belong here. And I'm suddenly exhausted. So I turn to leave the cemetery. A small brick hut sits at the exit, and I pause, thinking of them . . .

Gabriel's wife.

His daughter.

"Excuse me," I call through the window.

An attendant turns away from a form she's filling out and peers over her glasses at me. "Can I help you?"

"Yes. Is there . . ." I hesitate. Maybe it's too much. Maybe it's not my business. But I haven't been so good at staying within the boundaries of *healthy* thus far, so why start now? "Is there a way to find out if someone's buried here? I recently lost some friends, but I'm not sure if they were buried here or somewhere else. I'd like to bring flowers." The lie streams out of my mouth easily.

"Of course. What are their names?"

"The last name is Wright. Ellen and Rose. They would have been buried last year."

"Hmmm . . ." She types into the computer. "No Wright interred here since about five years ago."

"Oh. Okay." Disappointment hits. It would've hurt to see their graves. I got off too easy today.

"Sorry, dear. Good luck finding them. Often seeing someone's final resting place can bring us peace."

I nod my thanks and turn away. Unfortunately, there is no peace for me.

CHAPTER 6
Then

His knuckles were white again.

Gripping a chair. Gripping the refrigerator door. Gripping his crutches. It didn't matter. For the last four weeks, ever since his injury, Connor had held everything in a tight fist. I'd mentioned it once, but it only upset him. He'd yelled that *cripples* had to hold on tight, so they didn't fall. But he wasn't even standing now. He was sitting in the penalty box, behind the Plexiglas barrier, watching his team practice while white-knuckling the hockey stick lying across his lap.

He was angry and tense, scared he would never get back on the ice. I understood that. But the constant state of stress wasn't healthy for his recovery. So I tried to ease the pressure without calling attention to the fact that it existed at all.

"Hey." I took the seat next to him and pried his fingers from the hockey stick. Bringing his hand to my mouth, I forced it open and kissed his palm. "How has your day been?"

Connor frowned and motioned to the ice. "Franklin is getting better and better. The kid is faster than me and more agile, too."

Brimley Franklin was filling in as center, the position my husband played. At twenty-three, he was hungry for playing time and eager to make a name for himself. I weaved my fingers with Connor's. "He doesn't hold a candle to you."

"Don't patronize me." He wrenched his hand from mine and pushed to his feet. "Let's get out of here. I need to get my bag from the locker room and then stop at the pain management clinic before we go home. I forgot something there yesterday."

"Oh. Okay."

He stormed off before I'd even finished speaking. The team doctor walked over while I stood outside the locker room, waiting for Connor.

"Hey, Meredith. How are you doing?"

"I'm good. How are you, Dr. Gallo?"

"Tomorrow's the big day, right? Fitz starts PT?"

I nodded. "It is. I'm really excited. It's been a tough month. Connor isn't so great at sitting around. He can't see the progress happening with internal healing. I'm hoping the physical therapy shows him there's a light at the end of the tunnel."

He patted my shoulder. "Don't worry. He'll get there. Anxious is normal. He wouldn't be the player he was if he wasn't chomping at the bit."

I nodded. But it wasn't the anxiousness I was worried about. It was the anger. Last night Connor had thrown a glass at the wall when I'd questioned whether he needed to attend every practice and every away game. The question had been innocent. I wasn't sure of the rules or what he was contractually obligated to do. Yet he had turned red and the veins in his neck bulged.

My husband and I had been together for a long time. I'd witnessed his every shade of pissed off over the years, but it had never been directed at me. Something about his anger lately was different. Though I didn't dare mention that to Dr. Gallo. I didn't mention it to anyone.

During the car ride to the pain management clinic, Connor and I made small talk. I told him I'd gotten two new patients today, referrals from others I'd treated. But that seemed to upset him, too.

"What are you going to do with all these patients when you have a baby?"

Considering you had to *actually have sex* to get pregnant, something my husband had lost interest in since his injury, I didn't think it was a pressing issue.

"We spoke about this. I'll hire someone."

"I don't want a nanny watching our kid all the time."

I glanced at him and back to the road. "I meant I would hire someone at my practice. Another psychiatrist. A part-timer, maybe."

Connor's jaw flexed. "Must be nice to have the future look so bright."

I wasn't taking the bait. He could find something to fight about in anything I said or did lately. Instead, I reached over and rested my hand over the balled fist that sat on his lap. "My future looks bright because it's with *you*."

He ignored my comment and pointed up ahead to the clinic. "There isn't an open spot. Just double-park and put the flashers on. I'll run in."

Once I'd stopped, I opened my car door so I could go around and help Connor out.

He shook his head and motioned to the door. "Close it. I don't need help. I won't be long."

As soon as he went inside, the spot directly in front of the building opened up. So I parallel parked at the curb to make it easier for traffic to pass. When I'd finished, a cell started to ring, but it wasn't mine. Connor had left his phone in the cupholder. *Elite Physical Therapy* flashed on the screen, so I answered.

"Hello?"

"Hi. May I speak to Mr. Fitzgerald, please?"

"Umm . . . He's not available at the moment. This is his wife, Meredith. Is there something I can help you with?"

"Maybe. This is Elite Physical Therapy. Mr. Fitzgerald has an appointment tomorrow at nine. We were hoping we could push that back to eleven. One of our therapists had an emergency and is going to be out for a few days, so we're trying juggle all of our appointments."

I looked over at the door to the clinic. No sign of Connor yet. "Can you hang on for two minutes? I want to double-check with him. He also has practice, and I know he doesn't like to miss. It'll just be a moment or two."

"Of course. No problem."

I got out of the car and went inside the clinic. Connor wasn't in the lobby, so I walked up to the front desk. The woman was on the phone but covered the receiver. "I'm on hold. Can I help you?"

"Yes. My husband is somewhere in here, Connor Fitzgerald. He just walked in." I held up his cell phone. "He has a phone call that's important. Can you possibly let him know?"

"Can I see some identification, please?"

"Sure."

I dug into my purse and showed the woman my driver's license.

"Sorry," she said. "He's a pretty big deal, so I wanted to make sure you weren't a fan."

I smiled. "I *am* a fan. His biggest one."

The woman thumbed toward the door behind her. "I'm on hold with an insurance company that's impossible to reach. Mr. Fitzgerald went in the back to speak to the PA. It's the last door on the right, if you don't mind going back yourself. We were just closing up, so there's no one else back there."

"Thank you."

The long hallway had a half-dozen doors, all closed. Light streamed onto the floor from the last room at the end. As I approached, Connor's voice came through a doorway, loud and angry.

"Give me a break. I'm six foot four and two hundred and forty-five pounds. I don't take the same dose as most of your patients."

"It's not the dose I'm concerned with," a man replied. "It's how long you've been on them. You should be weaned off by now, or at least tapering. You shouldn't have as much pain after four weeks of healing. And if you do, we need to consider that something else might be wrong."

I stopped a few feet from the door, holding my breath to listen in.

"Well, I do. *So give me the fucking script.* I have PT starting tomorrow, and I need to be able to work my knee."

A loud sigh. "This is the last time, Connor. I mean it."

My heart quickened. Apparently, I wasn't the only one concerned my husband was eating oxycodone like they were Tic Tacs.

I waited a minute before approaching the door. When I popped my head in, Connor scowled. "Why are you in here?"

"You have a call from the physical therapy place. It sounded important." I handed him his phone.

Back at home, he disappeared into the shower while I made dinner. When he came out, the chicken was in the oven cooking, and I was in the living room straightening up.

Connor looked around, eyes narrowed. "Where's my bag?"

Unlike most players, my husband didn't leave his hockey equipment in the locker room after practices. He schlepped a big bag back and forth every day. During the season, it pretty much sat next to our front door whenever he was home. But when we'd walked in earlier, his crutch had caught on the bag's shoulder strap and almost caused him to trip.

"I put it in the closet."

"Why?"

"It got tangled in your crutches when we came in. I figured you wouldn't be using it for a while, so why not put it away?"

He hobbled over to the closet on his crutches and ripped the door open. Pulling the bag out, he flung it at the front door. It hit with a loud bang.

"It belongs there."

I held up my hands. "Fine. I was only trying to help."

"I don't need any fucking help," he grumbled and turned, disappearing into our bedroom, slamming the door hard enough that our walls shook.

Once again, I did my best to ignore it, despite the pang of frustration in my gut. Deep down I knew he wasn't really angry at me, though I was getting tired of it being directed my way. When dinner was ready, I set the table and put food out. Connor appeared after I was already seated and eating by myself.

He held on to the back of the chair across from me and hung his head. "I'm sorry. I shouldn't have jumped down your throat."

I ripped off a piece of bread and swirled it in the sauce on my plate. "You've been doing that a lot lately, Connor."

He raked a hand through his hair. "I know. I'm an asshole. I just feel so useless, and I don't know what I'll do if I can't play again. It makes me feel all this rage inside. But I shouldn't be taking it out on you. It's not an excuse for treating you badly. I'm really sorry, babe. You've been amazing through this. I'll do better. I promise."

I nodded. "I'm concerned about you, Connor. Mood swings and anger are side effects of opioid abuse."

A beat of silence.

Then it was like a switch flipped. His face twisted with anger. "Opioid abuse? My mood is not a side effect of the damn painkillers, *Doctor*. It's a side effect of my career being over at twenty-fucking-nine. Of course I'm goddamn angry." Connor shook his head. "I can't expect you to understand, not when your career is taking off so fast you have to hire someone to have a damn baby."

"That's not fair."

He moved toward the door on his crutches. "Yeah, right, my comment is what's not fair."

I stood. "Connor, wait. Don't run away. Let's talk."

"Why, so you can psychoanalyze me like I'm a patient? No, thanks." He ripped open the front door and hopped through. "Don't wait up. One of us has to work in the morning."

I sighed as the door slammed shut. *So much for his promise to do better.*

CHAPTER 7 *Now*

nother month alone. My new normal, as my therapist calls it.

I'm coping, I guess. But coping well? Well enough to fool Dr. Alexander. At least I think I am. But my new normal has its routine. The early morning walk for coffee. The wait for Gabriel, because despite what I told Dr. Alexander, I can't help following him. Gabriel goes to the storage unit nearly every day. And today, like every other day lately, I walk past, turn right at the little alleyway a few buildings down, and sip my coffee, scribbling in my notebook, contemplating Gabriel's secret to happiness.

After twenty minutes at the storage place, he'll head to work, and I'll take off on my newest pursuit—finding his family. Finding where their bodies are buried. I've been to ten cemeteries in the past month. Sometimes I ask an attendant and get a quick no. Other times I wander for hours, seeking out the shiny, new granite headstones, spots where the grass hasn't yet filled in as much. I could go online; there are databases of burial locations now. But I don't, and I'm not even sure why. Instead, I walk through fields of the dead, reading gravestone after gravestone until I'm sure I've examined them all. It's oddly soothing, being among the dead. Often it feels like I belong there with them, yet I'm somehow trapped in the world of the living.

I check my watch, then take one last drag of coffee in the alley. He's late today. He never takes this long at the storage stop. Twenty minutes, no more, no less, and it's been forty now. While I wait, I take out my notebook. I've already jotted down all of my normal stuff:

Walked down 23rd Street at 9 a.m.

Regular coffee stand. Same order as yesterday. Small coffee, corn muffin.

No cigarettes again today.

Did he stop smoking? Maybe the ones I saw him buy were for someone else?

Stopped at storage unit.

I flip the page and begin writing things I need from the grocery store. My appetite has come back. I suppose it should've a long time ago with the miles of walking every day.

Cheese.

Cucumbers.

Almonds.

I'm not exactly eating well-balanced meals, but at least I'm no longer living off coffee and wine, though there's still a good amount of both in my diet.

Another watch check—forty-five minutes now. Maybe I missed him? Maybe I checked my phone, read that text from my brother as Gabriel strolled by. Or maybe for once he went straight home. But it's not a holiday or between semesters. He has class today.

I sigh. *Ten more minutes.* I'll wait ten more minutes, then go on my way. I found a new cemetery to check, one with plots still available for purchase—maybe that's why I haven't found his family yet. Because they hadn't expected to die. Didn't have a place nearby to be buried. Or maybe he had them cremated?

Though something about cremating a child seems wrong. I can't be sure I've ever heard of such a thing. I chew the end of my pen and flip the notebook pages back to some of my early research notes.

Ellen and Rose Wright. Their names are underlined twice. Ellen had been a teacher, too, but at the local high school—English. Something they shared in common. She also coached the girls' soccer team in spring. A graduate of the University of Virginia, but originally from Rhode Island. The single picture of Rose the papers had printed was taken alongside her mother as they volunteered at a soup kitchen on Thanksgiving. Of course. *Of course* they were good people.

I snap the notebook shut and tuck it away. Grab my coffee cup off the ground, though it's coated in alley sludge now, brown muck dripping from the bottom. It's time to go. I must've missed him, or he went a different route, or perhaps he headed home. Pulling my purse up to my shoulder, I stride toward the sidewalk and take a left, back toward the subway.

I don't even see him before it happens.

A head-on collision—not unlike *you* and his wife and child—and there's no time to react. No time to stop it. I bounce off his body, lose my footing, and then I'm falling—

"Whoa, careful." A strong arm grips my elbow. My descent toward the cold concrete halts, and I look up with dread and anticipation filling my body in equal parts. Our eyes meet, and I can't stop blinking.

Gabriel Wright's lips curl in curious interest. "Are you all right?"

"No. I mean—I mean, yes." I still can't stop blinking. But at least my self-protection mechanism kicks in, and I turn my head toward the ground, shielding my face. "Excuse me. I didn't see you—"

"What were you doing in the alley?" His voice comes out bright, teasing. I have the self-awareness to feel heat rising to my cheeks, to follow his glance down the dark alleyway between two brick buildings, to see it as he must—dirty and dank and probably full of rats. My hideout for weeks now, and it never quite occurred to me to consider these aspects. I was so focused on him. And now, well, here he is.

"I'm late—but are you okay?" he asks when I don't respond. His concern sounds genuine.

"I'm fine. Thank you."

Just as fast as it happened, he's gone. I tremble with nervous energy until he disappears around the next corner. I squeeze my eyes shut—I know the route he'll take. Where he'll cross the street, where he'll stop for a quick coffee if he needs another caffeine fix. The building he'll walk inside, the exact room he lectures in. My heart pounds in my chest, and I force myself to take a few deep breaths.

Inhale.

Exhale.

Slow.

Steady.

He didn't recognize me.

Of course he wouldn't. The only opportunity he'd have had to see me was the hospital that day. And a random woman was the least of his worries when his whole family was dead. I've always been careful as I follow him. Never once has he caught sight of me. But now, after literally colliding with him, he will remember me.

A chill runs up my spine. While this must have felt like a random run-in with a complete stranger to him, it was anything but. After all, I know he orders salad frequently for lunch, probably quit smoking, and is missing the bottom button on his lightweight coat. And I know the faces of the three women he frequently grabs lunch or an intimate dinner with—

Shit.

I'm still shaking. My body hums with the need to run down the block, catch up to him, but I can't. He's seen me. This needs to stop. Here and now. I can't follow him anymore. I can't search for his wife's and child's graves, sit outside under the big oak at Columbia, wait for him to return home every evening. What I can do . . . is go home. So I turn on my heel and walk back the way I came, all plans abandoned. Half a block later, the hair on my arms registers the sound before I do. *Footsteps.* I whirl, expecting to see Gabriel behind me, expecting him to be running after me, realizing who I am. Who *you* are.

But no one's there. It must have been the echo of my own footsteps. Though I could've sworn otherwise. I search the sidewalk one last time. Unless he ducked down another alley, it's all in my head—like "The Tell-Tale Heart," except the stalker hears her imaginary stalker.

I go home. Straight home, don't even stop for a salad or a bagel or another coffee. I'm too freaked-out to eat. I need to hide. But when I arrive, I realize I've lost my apartment key. Not *my* key, actually. *My husband's.* My heart sinks. The one on the keychain I had made. The one I gave you the night we decided to start a family. The one that reminds me of hope and dreams and the man you were . . . before. I've been using it ever since . . . Thankfully, I still have mine on my office key ring, which is somewhere at the bottom of my purse. A useless set of keys I still carry. At least they have purpose today. So I dig them out, my hand still shaking.

Inside, I tuck myself into the spare bed—I haven't slept in our room alone yet. It still smells of Connor. I lie on top of the covers, staring at the ceiling for hours, until an alarm on my phone alerts me to the fact that if I don't get moving, I'll miss my appointment with Dr. Alexander this evening.

And then he'll have to report that to the medical board.

And then I'll never get out of this mess.

Though maybe I don't care. I don't need money. Our apartment is paid off, and I can shoplift for food and the necessities. Imagine that? No, actually, I can't. Maybe I would teach if I lost my license for good. I could work at Columbia. Dye my hair platinum blond—Gabriel seems to have a penchant for that look. Then we could grab lunch and laugh together over salads.

Lord, I'm losing it.

It's the awareness that I have to pee that eventually gets me up. And while I'm standing, I might as well put shoes on. Wash my face. Draw my coat over my shoulders. It's literally a forced, step-by-step process to get myself back out of the house when it's time to leave for my appointment. I take the train two stops, count the stairs up from the subway while climbing them, weave through the maze of people. I'm exhausted, mentally and physically, by the time I arrive. Too much thinking, too much stressing, causes potentially toxic by-products to build up in the prefrontal cortex. I've explained it to patients with paranoia a hundred times. Though I'm not the doctor today.

"Meredith, a pleasure, as always. Come in, come in." Dr. Alexander's typical greeting. But his usual polite smile wilts as he lays eyes on me. His brow furrows. "What's going on today? You seem . . ." He searches for a word that won't offend me.

I never judge a patient's appearance or make assumptions about their mental state of being. Better they tell me those things. But he's misstepped, and I let him struggle through it.

"A little off?" he finally finishes.

"I am." And because I have nothing left to lose, I am honest with him for the first time since our initial session. "I've been following Gabriel still. I lied to you." I tell him about the storage unit Gabriel goes to every day. The intimate meals with women. My quest to find the graves of his family. Gabriel's smiles, his laughter, the collision at the alley today.

"I just have to see it," I say.

"See what?"

"The hurt. The pain. I know it's under there somewhere. Under his smile."

Dr. Alexander's eyes roam my face. "You don't believe it's possible for him to be happy? That he could have healed. Like we've talked about."

"How could he be healed? And what's in the storage unit? Why would anyone go to a storage unit every day? You can't house live animals in them. So why?" I finish my sentence and have to take a moment to catch my breath.

"Meredith, I would like to consider why this matters. He is not your concern. What he does with his time is not your concern. So why does it matter why he goes there or what's inside?"

I open my mouth, rapidly formulating a response. "*Because . . .*" But even in my own head it sounds weak, though I say it anyway. "I have to know. I need to know."

"Know what?"

I sigh, exasperated. "*I don't know.*"

He waits, gives me time to think, add to my response. When I don't, he shifts in his seat. "Humor me for a moment. What if Mr. Wright *is* happy and has moved on with his life? How would that make you feel?"

"I would be thrilled for him, of course. But he can't possibly—"

Dr. Alexander holds up a hand. "One moment, please. Let's see this through. If Mr. Wright could move on, wouldn't that help *you* move on?"

"I suppose . . ."

"Do you feel like you deserve to move on, Meredith?"

Of course not. How could I? But I see what he's trying to get at. He thinks I'm refusing to accept that Gabriel is happy as some sort of self-punishment.

After a long bout of silence, he smiles. "I'm going to answer my own question here. You *do* deserve to be happy, and I think this is a topic we need to discuss more in the future. For now, perhaps we can consider the consequences of your actions for a moment. How did it feel to almost get caught today?"

"It scared the living hell out of me. But also . . ." There had been something else, too. He hadn't recognized me, and I was glad for that, but some part of me had been disappointed. I don't tell Dr. Alexander that. "It felt like the high you get from gambling," I finally say. "Like it could go either way."

"Hmm . . ."

That was the wrong answer. Not what a mentally stable person would say. I know that. But it's the truth.

"I'm concerned that without more going on in your life, you're designing risky games to play. Sure, it's not drinking or drug use, but it's no less dangerous. Do you want to get caught, Meredith? Get in more trouble than you already are?"

"Of course not."

"Are you sure?"

I keep my eyes trained down. That's not what I'm doing, is it? I don't want to get caught, do I? Thoughts swirl inside my head. None of them makes sense. I have more questions than answers. But I don't want to ask Dr. Alexander any of them.

Eventually, he shifts in his seat. "Meredith?"

Our eyes meet. "Yes?"

He tilts his head. "You said you've been looking for Gabriel's family's graves?"

I nod.

"Why?"

I look away, shaking my head. "I'm not sure."

"I have to imagine it would be very upsetting to run across them. To read the short number of years a young child lived from her headstone?"

My eyes well up even thinking about it. "Of course."

"Is that the reason, Meredith? You're looking to punish yourself more? I'm not a magician. I don't know what is going on in your head without you sharing with me. But I'm concerned that your actions are very self-destructive."

Tears streak down my cheeks. Dr. Alexander picks up a box of Kleenex and leans forward.

I pluck a few tissues out and wipe my face with a sniffle. "Thank you."

After a long bout of silence, Dr. Alexander clears his throat. "Do you have a daily routine?"

"Um, yes. I mean . . . sort of."

"Tell me about it. What do you do each morning?"

I blow out a breath and tell him how I start my day. My schedule that revolves around Gabriel.

"Okay, tomorrow, instead of following him, I want you to come here. I want you to sit in my lobby and write in your journal. Do that every day for the next week. Get your head out of the current pattern."

I nod and take a deep breath. "Okay." I can do that. I can get my coffee and come *here* instead. It will be better than following Gabriel. Than risking discovery. Risking losing even more than I already have. "I joined a gym," I say, as though that will somehow redeem me.

"Good. Come here and journal. Go there and use a treadmill to do the mileage you've been walking while following him. Let's break the cycle, create a new routine."

I meet his eyes and force a smile. Try to look confident, and as though this has given me hope. But I still can't shake it. The need to see it. The need to see Gabriel Wright's pain. Which I caused.

CHAPTER 8 *Then*

"I believe these are yours." A bag skidded across the kitchen table, stopping right in front of me.

One glance at the folded-up printout stapled to the front of the white packaging and I didn't need to ask why my husband was snarling. *Birth control.*

I closed my eyes.

Connor had gotten back last night from traveling with his team for a game in Cincinnati. I'd been waiting for the right moment to talk to him about my going back on the pill. Unfortunately, it never came.

I met his icy glare. "I'm sorry. I should've spoken to you about it before now. I just thought—"

Connor interrupted. "That your husband is damaged goods? Not father material?"

"No, that's not it at all." I stood and walked around the table. When I attempted to put my hands on his chest, he took two steps back, out of reach.

"Sure it's not."

"You already have so much pressure. It doesn't seem like it's the right time to add to that with a pregnancy and a newborn baby."

"It's nice of you to decide that for us."

I frowned. "You're right. I'm sorry. I should have had a discussion with you before renewing my prescription. It's just that I got my period last night, and there's only a short window of time to start a new pack, so I called." I was in the wrong here, so I should have stopped at that—an apology and explanation. But something occurred to me, and the question tumbled from my mouth before I could stop it. "Why were you at the pharmacy that you picked up my pills anyway?"

Connor's jaw clenched. "The physical therapist prescribed me a cream for the swelling in my knee. I told you I stopped taking the pain meds last month."

"I'm sorry. I didn't mean to imply . . ."

"Yeah, right." He shook his head and tore his jacket off the back of the chair, storming toward the front door. "Enjoy your pills."

"Where are you going?"

"Anywhere but here."

Even though I'd watched him rip open the door and yank it shut behind him, I jumped when it slammed. I was so on edge these days. My heart constantly raced, and I felt permanently off-kilter. The only time I relaxed was when I was at work and could immerse myself in other people's problems.

I stared at the closed door for a long time, not that I expected Connor to come back. He wouldn't. I'd just given him a new excuse to spend hours at the bar getting drunk. At least today he had a legitimate reason to be upset. Lately, he just picked a fight about anything when I got home from work and then disappeared for hours, coming home smelling like a brewery. Sometimes if I was still awake when he returned, I pretended to be sleeping. The alcohol made him emotional, and he'd come back upset and apologize. Then he'd want to have makeup sex. But his overindulgence often had *another* effect—the inability to maintain an erection. Which made him angry all over again. It had become a vicious circle I wanted to avoid.

I had a hollow feeling in my stomach as I thought about what my marriage had become in just a few short months. My loving, thoughtful husband had become someone I didn't recognize. Things kept getting worse by the day. Could he really fault me for not wanting to get pregnant right now? Sure, we were a team, and I should have spoken to him. But in the end, it was my decision what to do with my body. Not to mention, I would essentially be raising a child by myself if things kept going the way they'd been. I couldn't leave a child with a drunk man who had anger issues. I might've been wrong to not discuss things with him, but he was responsible for creating the environment that made me feel like I couldn't.

Rather than wallowing any more, I rinsed my coffee mug and decided to take a shower. Maybe I'd take a walk if Connor didn't come back soon. Head to my favorite bookstore. Pick up an overpriced latte, too. Halfway down the hall to the bathroom, I was stopped by a knock at the door.

Maybe Connor forgot his keys?

Maybe he's come back to talk, rather than drown his sorrows?

Maybe there's hope for us after all . . .

But when I opened the door, my face fell.

"Nice to see you, too," Irina chided. "Jeez. You two are a matching set."

My brows knitted. "Who two?"

"You and Connor." She thumbed over her shoulder. "I just saw him in the lobby. I said hello, but he didn't even hear me. It looked like someone had kicked his dog, and he was on the hunt to find them."

Only it wasn't his dog that had been kicked. It was him. And I'd been the punter.

I sighed. "We had a fight."

Irina rubbed her stomach and shrugged. She was due any day now. "Eh. It happens. I got mad at Ivan last night because he didn't warn me the tiramisu he brought home tasted sour. I should add that I took it out of the garbage to taste it. I can pick a fight about anything these days."

I chuckled and stepped aside. "Come in. I think you're just what I need right now."

She held up a finger. "Not so fast. Do you have Nutella?"

"I think so. Connor loves it on toast."

"All right. I'll grace you with my presence, then."

Irina and I went into the kitchen. I found the Nutella in a cabinet and pulled a loaf of bread from the drawer.

"No bread necessary." Irina waved me off. "Just a spoon, please."

I smiled. "Sure."

She scooped out a heaping spoonful and spoke with her mouth full. "So what's going on with you and Mr. Cranky Pants?"

I sighed. "I did something stupid."

She shrugged. "So? He's a man. I'm sure he does stupid shit all the time. It's much cheaper when we mess up. If Ivan gets in trouble, I get jewelry. If I screw up, he gets a blowie. Just toss a pillow on the floor for your knees, and say you're sorry into the microphone."

If only it were that easy. I shook my head. "We're really struggling lately. It feels like Connor is angry all the time."

"Of course he is. He's terrified that he's never going to get to play again. Hockey is all these guys have known since they were three years old. Remember when Ivan had to have surgery a few years ago? He took a stick to the neck six months before our wedding."

"He had spinal profusion, right?"

She nodded. "We fought so much that I called off the wedding twice. I never let on to anyone how bad things got."

"Really?"

She shoveled another spoonful of Nutella into her mouth. "Their self-hood is so wrapped up in playing that they go through a sort of identity crisis. I remember I suggested we postpone the wedding so he could focus on recovery. Ivan thought I was postponing because I might not want to marry him anymore since there was a chance he'd never play again. Anything I said or did was turned into me not wanting to be with him. I couldn't make him believe otherwise, because he didn't believe in himself anymore."

That sounded *very familiar*.

"But things got better, obviously?"

Irina nodded. "It took a while. Ivan went to a very dark place for a few months. I wasn't sure we'd make it. But things got better with time. I'd like to say it was something I said or did that made it better. But he had to find it within himself." She reached across the table and patted my hand. "Connor will find his way. And you two will once again be the couple that makes everyone else question whether they're really happy in their own relationship. Trust me. He'll figure it out."

I wanted to believe she was right. But something in my gut told me there was more to Connor's problems than an identity crisis and some self-doubt.

The next afternoon, I had an hour break between patients, so I went out to get some fresh air and pick up lunch.

"They didn't have rye bread." I fished my assistant Sarah's sandwich out of the brown paper bag and set it on her desk. "So I got you multigrain instead."

"Thanks." She smiled and motioned toward my office door. "You have someone waiting for you."

"Mrs. Trenka is this early?"

"Nope. A certain hot hockey player is waiting." She picked up her earbuds and pushed one into her ear with a wink. "I'll be listening to music while I eat. *Very loudly.* So I won't hear a thing."

Good, then you won't hear us arguing. Connor and I hadn't spoken since last night, when he'd come home drunk and belligerent, still upset about the birth control. He'd been passed out on the couch when I left for work this morning.

The smell of fresh flowers hit me as soon as I opened my office door. But the visual was the real gut punch. Connor was sitting at my desk, his hands wrapped around the largest bouquet of hydrangeas I'd ever seen. He stood, and my heart squeezed. My beautiful man looked beautifully broken, sadness and pain etched into deep lines that hadn't been there only a few months ago.

We'd both said hurtful things last night, but none of that was important at the moment. I went to him, cupping his cheeks in my hands and wanting to do anything to take away his pain. Tears welled in my eyes. "I'm so sorry."

"I'm sorry, too."

"I should've never made the decision to go back on the pill without discussing it with you."

He shook his head. "You were right to do it. I'm not in any condition to be a father. I'm a fucking mess, Mer."

"No, you're not. You just need to believe in yourself. I know in my heart you're going to get back on the ice, but even if you don't, we'll figure it out. Together."

Connor looked down for a long time. When he met my eyes again, he swallowed. "You were right. The painkillers were making things worse. I didn't stop taking them when I said I did a few weeks ago. But I'm done now. I had a few left, and I dumped them down the sink this morning. I'm also going to ease up on the drinking."

Tears streamed down my face. "You're getting stronger every day. You need to believe in yourself, Connor. You can do this. I know you can."

He nodded. "*We* can do this. We'll do it together."

Relief flooded me as I threw my arms around his neck, hugging him as tightly as I could. We stayed that way for a long time. After we finally let go, we shared my lunch and enjoyed each other's company for the first time in what felt like forever. He left only because my next patient arrived.

The rest of the afternoon, everything seemed a little lighter, a little brighter. After two months of dreading going home, I was actually looking forward to finishing up and seeing my husband after my last patient of the day left.

"Anything we need to talk about?" I pulled on my coat and spoke to Sarah in the waiting room.

She smiled. "Someone is in a rush tonight."

"Connor is making me dinner."

"Enjoy. I'm just going to finish up this letter to an insurance company and then I'm right behind you."

"Good. Enjoy your night, Sarah."

"Oh, wait. Did you leave the prescription for Mr. Mankin? He's going down to Florida to take care of his mom for a month because she's having some surgery. He needs a paper script to fill down there when he runs out in a few weeks. Dumb insurance won't let him fill it this early. Not sure if you saw my note in your messages. He called earlier to say he would pick it up first thing tomorrow."

"Shoot. Yes, I did see the note. But I totally forgot. Thanks for the reminder. Let me write it now in case he comes in before I get here." I set my purse on Sarah's desk and went back into my office to grab my prescription pad. But when I opened my top right drawer, the place where I always kept it, it wasn't there. I pushed around some papers. Not finding it, I checked the other drawers.

"Sarah?" I yelled. "Have you seen my prescription pad?"

"Last time I saw it, it was in the top right drawer."

I pulled it out farther this time and rummaged through again. No luck.

Sarah walked into my office. "Did you find it?"

"No."

"Maybe you used the last one?"

An ominous feeling washed over me as I remembered my husband sitting within arm's reach just hours earlier. "Umm . . . Yeah, that must be it."

CHAPTER 9 *Now*

T he second day of the new year. *Happy New Year!* signs replace the glittering glow of Christmas lights and menorahs in windows. I pass a gym whose windows proclaim *New Year, New You!*

For once, they're right.

It's been a good month. I'm getting outside every day. Working out at the gym. I think I even see the beginning of toned muscles when I look in the mirror—who would have thought? Not me. But with my headphones in, the pulsing music pushing me, I've focused entirely on myself for once.

I pull at the mittens my brother gave me for Christmas—I stayed with him and his family, his two darling little girls. It's true they reminded me of another little girl I'd never met. It wasn't easy. His cheery family reminded me of all the dreams I used to have, of all the things Gabriel Wright lost. But I wrote about it and walked on the treadmill and somehow got it out of my head. And I was happy for my brother. Holidays haven't always been easy for the two of us, with losing our parents to different illnesses when we were in our early twenties. All in all, I think I did pretty well. I've fought off the desire to return to an old path and wait until Gabriel strode along it. I'm in a better place now.

A few blocks later, I realize I'm close to my office, so I decide to walk by. It's the first time I've even attempted it since I'd carried my boxes out the door months ago. In fact, I've avoided the block completely until now. But soon my suspension will be up, thirty-seven days and counting, and I'll be returning to work, returning to my practice. One step closer to normalcy.

I turn right at the corner, see my building up ahead. My heart pounds as I step closer, but it's a good feeling this time. Excitement, more than anxiety. A fresh start, not dreading the past. At least until I get to building number 988 and see my face plastered on the bus stop out front.

My heart thuds to a halt.

What the hell?

A close-up picture of my face is taped to the glass bus stop covering. Words are typed underneath, but my jittery eyes are so freaked-out it takes a solid minute for me to be able to focus enough to read them.

DRUG DEALERS AREN'T ALWAYS STREET THUGS

Dr. Meredith McCall prescribes drugs to known abusers.

Support Bill S0178 mandating permanent suspension for
doctors who deal drugs.

Underneath is a logo of two fists with *MAAD New York—Mothers Against Abusive Doctors*.

My eyes dart around the street. It feels like everyone is staring—like they know what I've done. I expect to see people angry, people pointing. But I'm the only one paying the sign any attention. I reach forward and rip it from the glass, leaving only remnants of the white page taped at all four corners. Then I take off running.

I run and run, until my lungs burn and my legs feel so shaky that I start to worry I'll fall. Collapsing onto the stairs of a random brownstone, I lean over, head between my knees, and suck air.

"Are you okay?" a woman stops and asks.

I nod.

She smiles. "I tell everyone I'm fine, too. Just remember, whatever it is will eventually pass."

I doubt it. There are some things in life we don't deserve to run away from.

———————————

The following week, Dr. Alexander crosses an ankle over his knee. "Happy new year."

"Thanks. It's my birthday, too."

"Oh? Well, happy birthday." He adjusts his tie. "Any plans?"

"I . . ." I pause. I was going to make something up to make him feel comfortable. A habit of mine now. I do it for my brother often. Tell him I'm meeting a friend for lunch or going to a museum or—or something. But I don't need to soothe my therapist's worries. Plus, I've been better since I started being honest with him. "No, not really. Actually, I'm feeling really lonely right now."

"Tell me more."

I settle into the couch and cross my legs, staring at an abstract painting on his wall. "Well, I mean, I have my brother, but he's got a whole life. A wife and kids and a job. And he lives in Connecticut, so he's close, but not too close. I don't have a ton of friends. The ones I had in college, I lost touch with during the demanding years of medical school. After that, I was a busy resident, and, well . . . I wrapped a lot of my life around Connor. My friends were his teammates' wives or people we spent time with as a couple. And with everything that happened, most of them faded away. Or maybe I couldn't face them. I don't know anymore. I was pretty close with Irina, the wife of Connor's best friend on his team. But she has three kids under five and she couldn't . . ." I struggle for the right words. I'm also not sure it's all Irina's fault we haven't spoken. "We just drifted apart," I finish. "I do talk to a couple of ladies at the gym in the yoga class I started last month, but it's so hard as an adult—making that leap from casual hellos to 'Want to grab a coffee?'"

Dr. Alexander nods his understanding but doesn't speak.

I do the same thing when I want a patient to continue. Silence is often more effective than words. People feel the need to fill empty space.

"And I'm lonely at home, too." I take a shuddering breath and force the words out. "I've thought about dating. I've been alone almost two years . . . That's long enough, right?"

Dr. Alexander splays his hands wide. "Only you can decide how long is long enough, Meredith."

A half laugh escapes me. "That's what I tell my patients, too." I chew my lip and contemplate. Of course, there are apps for that—for dating. Maybe I'll try one. It seems relatively anonymous. The sort of thing you can try out, then delete and pretend never happened. But my words remind me of something else coming up. "I get to start practicing again next month. I can't believe it's already been almost a year."

"How are you feeling about that?"

"Good. I think. I mean, I'll have to build my practice back up. Dr. Gerald Rodgers—maybe you've heard of him?—came out of retirement to cover me. He's wonderful, but he's in his seventies and has a different style than I do. Between him taking over and the headlines, almost half my patients left. So I'm a little worried about that, but I'll just have to put in the time to rebuild. God knows I have nothing but time these days. And then there's the worry about more signs or . . . worse."

His brows dip. "Signs?"

"There's a group, sort of like Mothers Against Drunk Driving, but they go after doctors who abuse their prescription-writing privileges. I walked by my office last week and found a flyer taped up on the bus stop with my face on it. And a while back, someone requested a copy of my file from the Office of Professional Misconduct. They can do that under the Freedom of Information Act, apparently. I'd originally thought it might be someone from the media trying to write a story. But now I think it might've been them."

Dr. Alexander blinks a few times. "I'm sorry to hear that."

I shrug. "It's my own fault."

"Still. That couldn't have been easy."

"No, it wasn't. But I'm not going to let it derail me. I was in a good place before that. I ripped down the flyer I found. Though I have gone by the building every day since then to see if another one is up. Luckily, more haven't appeared."

Dr. Alexander smiles. "I won't focus on it, then. Talk to me about how you're feeling about returning to practice. Do you think you're ready?"

"Yes." And I do. Absolutely. But I've changed, and the way I see my patients has changed. I tell him as much, adding, "I'll be a different psychiatrist after what I've been through."

"Our life experiences can be invaluable in being empathetic to our patients."

I nod, but my mind is elsewhere—back on the fact that my practice is barely staying afloat. My shoulders hunch. I worked so hard to build it, to not only make it successful but get to the point where it was thriving.

Again, thoughts of meeting someone seep in. Could I start over? Try my hand at dating? I swallow the lump in my throat.

Dr. Alexander peppers me with more questions—about day-to-day life, about my journaling, about my goals for this coming year. Eventually, he says, "Looks like our time is nearly up. Is there anything else you'd like to discuss?"

I shake my head, only half paying attention. The other half is still thinking about the dating apps. Would it be possible to love someone like I loved Connor? The Connor I married and was planning to have a family with, not the Connor who destroyed a family.

"Has your new routine changed lately?"

The question brings me back to reality. He's asking if I've followed Gabriel again. Which I haven't. I've been good. It's been a month now. Not that temptation hasn't reared its ugly head. I still wonder. Think of him almost daily. The fact that he's *happy* . . .

"No, it's pretty much stayed the same." I force a smile. "I figure, if it's not broken . . ." I trail off. "But it will be good to get back to work soon."

"Excellent." Dr. Alexander nods and writes more in his pad.

I leave a few minutes later, wandering out onto the streets listlessly. I didn't bring gym clothes, so I can't go there to keep myself busy. The stores are in the midst of their *after*-Christmas sales, and I stare into a cute shop window, considering going in. But I don't need anything. It would just be a way to pass time. So I head home. Near the entrance of my building, my gaze catches on a couple kissing; they're locked in each other's embrace. The man's hands cup her cheeks; hers are tangled in his dark hair. *Passion.*

I feel a tug of envy inside me as I ride the elevator up to my apartment. But when I arrive at my door and find it slightly ajar, a very different feeling takes over: *Fear.* I freeze, physically paralyzed as my mind races through a million different scenarios.

A man with a mask has a knife.

A patient—one I treated at the psychiatric hospital years ago—has gotten out. He blames me for being institutionalized and wants revenge.

A burglar.

Worse, a rapist.

I lost my key not too long ago. What if someone picked it up and followed me home?

I should run, flee as fast as I can. Get a police officer to come back with me.

But I can't move. I literally *can't move.* My breaths come in shallow spurts, and my head feels like I'm spinning, yet my legs are paralyzed.

So I do the only thing I can and listen. I hold my breath, waiting to hear footsteps or a crash, maybe the sound of my couch pillows being split open by a knife-wielding deranged person. But the only thing I hear is the rush of blood swooshing through my own ears.

Eventually, I can't take it anymore. I lean in and push the door open, enough to see inside. It's dark, though I always leave the hallway light on and it's enough to make out that no one is there, and nothing appears out of place. So I swallow and lean my head over the threshold.

"Hello? Is someone here?"

Silence.

I yell louder the second time. *"Hello? Is someone here?"*

A noise makes me jump, sends my heart shooting up to my throat. But it's only my neighbor unlocking his door.

"Meredith? Is everything okay?" Mr. Hank has to be eighty, but he feels like Superman coming to rescue me at the moment.

I let out a big breath. "My door was unlocked when I came home just now. I'm afraid someone could be inside."

He disappears briefly and comes back with a baseball bat. "You wait in my apartment. I'll take a look."

"Oh, I can't let you do that."

"I insist." He steps into the hallway and gestures to his open door. "Now, come inside."

"I'd feel better if I went in with you."

He shrugs. "Okay, but stay a few feet behind me. Because if I swing, I don't want to hit you in the head with the bat."

I nodded. "I will. Thank you."

Mr. Hank lifts the bat to his shoulder and tiptoes into my apartment. We both look around the living room and kitchen before venturing down the hall. All of the doors are closed, which is how I normally leave things. Mr. Hank opens each one, taking his time to check the closets while I look under the beds. After all the rooms are cleared, he lowers the bat from his shoulder.

"Sometimes my key turns in the lock," he says. "But it doesn't catch the bolt. So I think it's locked, but it isn't. I have to jiggle the handle to check."

"I haven't had that problem."

"Maybe you were just in a hurry, then, and forgot to lock it. It happens."

My head has been in the clouds lately. So I suppose either is possible. Yet I don't feel entirely settled just because no one was inside. I nod and smile anyway. "That must be it. Thank you so much for checking things out for me."

"No problem. Anytime. You just knock if you ever need anything."

"I really appreciate that. Thanks again, Mr. Hank."

After he's gone, I do another sweep through the apartment. My office is the last room I look in. Nothing seems out of place at first, but as I'm pulling the door shut, I notice my desk drawer isn't closed all the way. So I go over and open it, shuffle through the items inside, take a mental inventory. Nothing seems to be missing. At least that I can remember.

At the doorway, I take one more glance back into the room, at my desk, before flicking the light switch and pulling the door closed. Then I head straight to the refrigerator. Wine is definitely needed to unknot the ball of tension at the back of my neck. I drink the first glass while still standing with the refrigerator door open and staring at the lock on the front door.

I try to replay leaving this morning. While I got dressed, I had the TV on, listening to the news. The weatherman said there was a chance of rain. I had on taupe open-toed shoes and briefly considered changing to closed flats so my feet wouldn't get wet. But then I looked out the window and there wasn't a cloud in the blue sky, so I didn't change. After that, I flicked off the television, set the remote on my nightstand, and went into the kitchen to grab my purse from the chair. The round table in the entryway has a colorful Murano glass bowl sitting in the middle—Connor and I bought it on our honeymoon in Italy. It's where I toss my keys as soon as I walk in every day. I remember scooping them out and swallowing down the ache I felt in my chest when I saw the new keychain I'd bought to replace the one I lost. Outside my apartment, the hallway had been dark. The overhead lightbulb has been out for at least a week. But most importantly, I remember pulling the door shut and lifting my hand with the key.

I locked the door.

I gulp back the rest of my wine.

Could I be remembering locking the door another day?

I don't think so. The only time my mind seemed to be clear lately was in the morning, and the memory played out in my head like a video with no break.

I remember turning the key.

I remember the clank.

Which means . . .

I swallow. *I need more wine, that's what it means.*

So I refill my glass and finally shut the refrigerator door. This pour is so full to the brim that I have to slurp a mouthful in order to not spill any when I walk. After I sip half an inch, I carry the glass with me to the door. My keys are in the bowl like always. I set my wine down and scoop them out like I remember I did this morning. My heart pounds as I turn the handle and the door creaks open. I peek my head out—left first, then right. But the damn light is still out in the hallway, and I'm too afraid to go back out there now. So I slam the door shut and lock it, leaning my head against the cold metal until my breathing returns to normal.

Not surprisingly, I finish off my second glass of wine faster than the first, chugging it back like it's medicine I need for my health. I suppose maybe it is lately, my mental health anyway. I really need to relax, so I force myself to go sit in the living room and flick on the TV. But I take a seat on the far left of the couch, opposite from my normal spot. It gives me a clear view of the front door, allowing me to keep my eyes on the knob—waiting for someone to try and turn it again.

By my third glass of wine, I start flipping through the channels. *Jeopardy!* is on, so I occupy myself by playing along as I sip. Eventually, my shoulders loosen and I stop obsessing over the door. I even convince my tipsy self that what Mr. Hank said is right. One day bleeds into the next. I leave my apartment on autopilot. I'm remembering the lock-clanking sound from *another* day. After I get up to pour a fourth glass of wine, I return to sit in my usual spot. I can't see the door anymore, and I don't care. I slump into the cushions and lift my feet to the coffee table. My mind wanders now—back to what I talked about with Dr. Alexander earlier. How lonely I've been lately. If I had someone in my life, maybe they'd have been with me tonight when I came home, and I wouldn't have had to rely on my eighty-year-old neighbor for protection.

I top off my glass once more, push the cork back into the nearly empty bottle of merlot, and head to the bedroom with my wine in hand. I'm physically tired, but my mind is still too stimulated from the events of the evening to wind down. So I pick up my phone, flip through the apps, then go to the app store and search *dating*. My finger hovers over the first one that pops up, considering. I rub my legs together, realizing I haven't shaved them in at least a week. The bristly roughness leaves me annoyed—Jesus, how could I date when I'm such a mess? And what would come of it? One glance around the room shows remnants of my marriage. Our wedding picture is still on the dresser.

Connor's hockey bag, which I finally moved out of the entrance, still falls out of the closet every other time I open the door. I don't even know why I still have all the reminders—yes, I loved my husband, but I hate him more now. Hate what he did to the Wright family, what he did to us. A few weeks back, Dr. Alexander had asked if I still kept memories of my marriage around. When I admitted to having a few, and told him how often I'd contemplated getting rid of them, he delved into why I hadn't gone through with it yet and suggested perhaps I was punishing myself with the constant reminders. At the time, I didn't think that was it, but as I sit here staring now, it certainly causes me pain to see them. Maybe the good doctor wasn't that far off base after all.

An alert on my phone buzzes—just a CNN update, but it brings me back to the app store.

The dating app.

I stop thinking about it and press download. Hold my breath while the circle slowly fills, then open it. I tap through, creating a skeleton of a profile. I just want to do a search. Just want to know what it feels like to look at another man's profile. Test the waters, know if it's even something I should waste time considering. But it wants a photo of me. I'm not sure I'm ready to go that far, put myself fully out there. Though it won't let me continue without uploading something. So I scroll through my old photos and find a photo Irina took while we were at a game in Canada what seems like a lifetime ago. It's snowing out, the wind is blowing my hair so it covers almost my entire face, everything except a giant, painted-red smile. I look happy. Which is of course now a lie. But nonetheless, I upload it since I'm fairly certain no would recognize it as me.

I set up search parameters—between the ages of thirty and forty. Male. It defaults to living within a mile of me, and I hesitate—why would it do that unless it's just a hookup app? But I leave it as is and skip past the stuff that doesn't matter to me—color of eyes, hair, ethnicity—and then suddenly a list of men pops up. Images, with basic stats attached. My chest squeezes as I scroll through them. I stop, look up at our wedding photo one more time.

But it's been twenty-two months, nearly two full years.

I scrub my face with my free hand and realize I'm trembling. God, why is this so hard?

I scroll again, and again. Hit the NEXT tab for more profiles. Just trying to normalize this in my head—get used to the idea of considering seeing someone. I open the profile of a moderately handsome man, ignoring the fact he actually looks a little like *you,* and swipe through his photos until I come across one that makes my jaw drop—a photo of him and a blonde who probably models in her spare time. *Looking for a third*, it reads. They're wrapped up together, her ass practically hanging out of a shiny silver skirt. I swipe back as fast as I can. I'm not *opposed* to that sort of thing for others, just—just not what I'm looking for.

I take a steadying breath and scroll again, inspecting a few profiles more closely. I even hit the heart button once or twice, saving them so I can come back later. Or maybe it tells the man I've done it and puts the ball in his court? I'm not sure. I just know this is how everyone is doing it these days. Meeting people.

I finish my wine, rise long enough to apply a foaming facial cleansing mask, and to pour yet another full glass. An hour goes by, then two, maybe more, and I roll my wrists, getting the stiffness out of them. My eyelids droop with exhaustion. I've looked at hundreds of men, but none of them seems quite right. None of them I want to meet.

A heavy sigh works its way through my body.

I stare at our wedding photo again.

God, I love you so much.

God, I hate you so much.

My heart feels like it's being strangled again. Or maybe it hasn't stopped feeling that way since the night my phone rang. The night *you* ruined our life. But that's it. *I'm done.* I stumble to my feet and walk over to the photo, taking one last long look, before placing it face down.

There. That's something. Baby steps . . .

CHAPTER 10
Then

I t's never good news when the phone rings at two in the morning.

I fumbled for my cell in the dark. "Hello?"

"Is this Mrs. Fitzgerald?"

My heart skipped a beat. "Yes?"

"This is Dr. Bruner at NewYork-Presbyterian Hospital."

I twisted to look at the other side of the bed. Connor's side. It was still empty. He hadn't come home after our fight last night. I somehow already knew that, yet I stared at the empty spot where he should be. "What's happened?"

"Mrs. Fitzgerald, I'm very sorry to tell you this, but there's been an accident. Your husband, Connor, was in a car accident."

I swallowed. "Is he okay?"

The doctor stayed quiet for a few heartbeats too long. "It's very serious. You should come to the hospital immediately."

I don't remember hanging up. Or getting dressed. Or hailing a cab. Did I even say goodbye to the doctor? I must've lifted my arm to get the attention of the taxi driver. But I couldn't for the life of me recall the simple motion. It's like there was a gap in time after speaking to the doctor and now suddenly we were pulling up under an overhang at the hospital.

EMERGENCY

Big, red block letters. All caps.

An ambulance waited off to one side; two men in uniforms leaned against it drinking coffee. One laughed at something the other said. Business as usual. For them.

We pulled up at the wide sliding doors, and I rushed to get out of the cab.

"Hey, lady!" I already had the door open and one foot out on the pavement when the driver yelled. "You gotta pay for the damn ride."

I shook my head. "Oh. Sorry. Of course." I dug into my purse and grabbed two twenties without looking at the meter, handing them to the driver. "Thank you."

Inside, I rushed to the reception window. A woman sat behind Plexiglas, talking on her cell phone. I was certain she saw me, yet she kept her eyes trained down as she smiled and laughed, continuing her conversation.

I bent down to the small opening made for passing papers back and forth and spoke through it. "Excuse me?"

She frowned and spoke into her cell. "I'll call you back, Bebe."

I couldn't even wait for her to hang up. "Someone called me. A doctor. My husband was in an accident. He was brought here."

"Name?"

"Connor Fitzgerald."

She gestured to the chairs behind me. "Have a seat, and I'll check in with the doctors."

But I couldn't sit. So I paced. Counting the number of times I went back and forth to keep my mind focused on something other than *"It's very serious. You should come to the hospital immediately."*

Thirty-two.

Thirty-three.

Thirty-four.

Finally, someone opened the door a few feet from the reception window. The woman looked right at me. "Mrs. Fitzgerald?"

I rushed over. "Yes."

"Come with me, please."

I took a deep breath and followed. The treatment area was a wide square, with glass, podlike examination rooms lining all four walls. Patients lay in beds, and doctors and nurses sat around chatting at the center nurses' station. This was supposed to be an emergency room, but no one was moving like anything was urgent. When we got to the last room on the left, the woman held her hand out.

I expected to see my husband lying in a bed. But instead there were three men standing, a doctor in a white coat and two men in gray suits. The gurney next to them caught my attention. The entire top half was a deep red, stained with so much blood.

The doctor followed my line of sight and pulled a blanket up to cover it. Though I could still see the red through the threadbare linens. He extended a hand. "Mrs. Fitzgerald?"

"Yes."

"I'm Dr. Bruner. We spoke a little while ago on the phone."

I nodded. At least I think I did. "Where's Connor?"

He exchanged a quick glance with the two men and pointed to a chair. "Why don't you have a seat?"

"I don't want to sit. Where's my husband?"

One of the two men in suits extended his hand. "Mrs. Fitzgerald, I'm Detective Green. Your husband was in a very serious accident. I arrived at the scene when Mr. Fitzgerald was being extricated from the vehicle."

Extricated? My nerves couldn't take it anymore. "Can someone please tell me where Connor is?"

The doctor stepped forward. He reached out and took my hand. "Mr. Fitzgerald sustained very serious head injuries in the accident. He was unresponsive when brought in by ambulance. I'm very sorry to tell you that we were unable to revive him. Your husband died, Mrs. Fitzgerald."

The room started to spin. "What?"

The doctor put his hand on my back. "Is there anyone we can call for you?"

"Call?"

He nodded. "To be with you. You shouldn't be alone right now."

Nausea rose from my gut. My hand went to my stomach. "I need to sit down."

The shorter of the two detectives grabbed the chair next to him. Metal legs skidded across linoleum as he pulled it over to me.

"Can I get you some water?" The doctor guided me to sit. "I'll grab you some." He nodded at the men in suits before stepping out and sliding the glass door closed behind him.

I looked down at my hands, rubbing my thumb over the tip of each finger.

I couldn't feel it. Couldn't feel the tips of my fingers.

I watched my thumb touch each one, but there was no sensation at all.

Was this even real?

Maybe I'm dreaming.

Why aren't I crying?

A doctor just told me my husband is dead. I should be crying. Hysterical. Gasping for air.

I looked up at the two men who watched me in silence.

"Am I dreaming?" I held up my right hand and showed them how my thumb touched all of my other fingertips. "I don't feel this."

Detective Green crouched down in front of me. "You're likely in shock, Mrs. Fitzgerald. It happens."

But I was a psychiatrist. Wouldn't I know if I was in shock?

Maybe.

Maybe not.

The detective cleared his throat. "Do you feel well enough to answer a few questions, Mrs. Fitzgerald?"

I shook my head. "What happened?"

"The accident, you mean?"

I nodded.

"We're still trying to piece that together. But it appears Mr. Fitzgerald was speeding and ran a red light. He struck two pedestrians, lost control of the car, and crashed head-on into a nearby building."

My eyes widened, my stomach dropping. "He struck two pedestrians?"

The detective's face was somber as he nodded. "I'm afraid so."

"Are they okay?"

Detective Green looked up at the other man before shaking his head. "No, unfortunately they're not. Can you tell us anything about this evening? Where Mr. Fitzgerald was coming from at the time of the accident?"

I shook my head. "I don't know. We had a fight earlier. He left."

"What time was that?"

"I'm not sure. It was just getting dark. I looked out the window of our apartment to see which way he was walking. The sun was going down. I remember the sky was orange."

"So probably about five thirty or six, then?"

I shrugged. "Maybe."

"Did Mr. Fitzgerald have a history of drinking?"

"He was drunk?"

"We're not sure. It will take a bit of time before toxicology reports come back. But an eyewitness reported his car was swerving before the accident. What about drugs? Did Mr. Fitzgerald have a history of drug use?"

"Drugs? No. He's a professional athlete." I immediately thought of illegal drugs—heroin, cocaine, the type of stuff addicts used. But then it hit me that not all drugs that impaired a person's ability to drive needed to be bought on the street. Some people went to a pharmacist to feed their addiction.

I covered my mouth and stood. "I need a bathroom. I'm going to be sick."

The detective yelled for a nurse, and the next thing I knew, I was standing in front of a sink and someone shoved a pink, kidney-shaped plastic bowl into my hands. The woman was kind enough to hold my hair back while I emptied the contents of my stomach. After, I splashed water on my face, and she walked me back to the glass enclosure. The police were no longer there. Instead, they were on the other side of the nurses' station, along with

Dr. Bruner. The three of them ushered a bearded man into an identical glass pod, and the doctor slid the door closed. He looked up and our eyes caught for a moment from across the room, before he turned to face the man.

The nurse who had helped me in the bathroom stood in the doorway of the treatment room. "I have to go check on a patient," she said. "Are you going to be okay?"

I motioned to where Dr. Bruner stood. "Is that the family of the other people who were in the accident?"

The nurse's face fell. "The little girl was only five."

Tears streamed down my face for the first time. It was awful to watch, yet I couldn't tear my gaze away.

The doctor motioned to a seat.

The man shook his head.

A now-familiar scene that had probably happened a thousand times here.

A regular occurrence.

Normal, even.

But not to us. Not to the families destroyed.

Detective Green shook the man's hand.

Dr. Bruner rested a hand on the man's shoulder and bowed his head while he spoke.

The man's eyes widened in horror.

He collapsed, falling to his knees.

Sobbing.

Shaking.

A loud wail echoed through the glass.

Shattering the man.

And shattering me.

CHAPTER 11
Then

"The Lord is gracious and righteous; our God is full of compassion."

I stared at the priest, hanging on to the words of Psalm 116, even though he'd moved on to swinging a chain with an ornate censer around the casket, blessing it with incense.

The Lord is gracious and righteous? The little girl was only five years old.

Full of compassion? For whom, exactly? For my husband? Who doesn't deserve it?

I should've fought Connor's mother harder to not have this big funeral service. It was disrespectful to the family he'd devastated. I wasn't even sure why so many people showed up—teammates, coaches, friends, family—after the news broke last night with the final toxicology reports. My husband had been driving under the influence. I figured his friends would scatter like ants to footsteps, but no such luck. The church was full. Every last row, and some standing.

I just wanted to be alone.

To cry.

To scream.

To bounce back and forth between hating *you* for what *you'd* done and hating myself for not finding a way to stop *you.*

I knew *you* were in a bad place.

I knew.

This happened on my watch.

The mass finally ended. The graveside ceremony that followed was a blur. More crying. More useless words from a priest about how great God is. After it was over, the best I could do was put one foot in front of the other and walk to one of the waiting limousines. My brother, Jake, followed me.

He spoke to the driver standing outside the car as I climbed in. "Do me a favor? There's enough room in the other two cars to fit everyone else. Stand in front of this door and tell people the car is full. My sister needs a break." He extended his hand, and I knew without a shadow of a doubt there was a bill tucked into his palm. That was my brother—tip big and make it happen. He'd inherited the move from our father. *Our father.* Thinking of him made my heart heavy. It was the first time in my life I was glad both my parents were gone. They didn't have to be publicly disgraced by what my husband had done. What *I* could've stopped.

Jake climbed inside the car and pulled the door closed behind him.

He unbuttoned his suit jacket as he took the seat across from me. "You looked like you were about done."

I smiled sadly. "I was done before I left the house this morning."

"I sat in that church today trying to think of something to say to you to make you feel better, but the only thing I could think of was that Aunt Francine looked really surprised to see me."

"Why would she be surprised to see you?"

Jake used his fingers to pull both his eyebrows into Spock-like arches. "What *the fuck* did she do to her face?"

I covered my mouth and laughed for the first time in days. "Oh my. She does look like that. Bad Botox injections, I guess."

Jake smiled and pointed at my face. "There she is. My little Merry Berry. I knew she was under there somewhere."

Only my brother could make me smile at a time like this. Though it didn't last long. Heaviness seeped right back in. I sighed and shook my head. "I feel like I'm in a bad dream. And I just want to wake up already."

"I can't even imagine. You two were so happy. Once, when the four of us went out to dinner, Raylene yelled at me when we got home. She was mad because I didn't look at her the way Connor looked at you."

I frowned. "Things hadn't been so great the last few months."

"Really? You could've fooled me."

Apparently, I'd been fooling everyone, *myself* included.

Jake leaned forward and took my hand. "Come stay with us. Raylene already made up the guest room. We don't even have to go back to your place for the stupid reception dinner. We can just tell the driver to take us straight to Connecticut."

"I wish I could. But Connor's whole family is coming over, and half his team will probably show up. I can't not be there."

"How about tomorrow? I can drive into work instead of taking the train and scoop you up after?"

"I think I want to be home for a few days alone. I think I need that time to myself."

Jake frowned but nodded. "Maybe over the weekend, then?"

"Sure. Maybe."

"Now isn't the time, but we also need to discuss some business. So even if you blow me off about coming to stay in Connecticut, which I have a feeling you will, we need to at least get together for lunch soon."

I hesitated, my mind tripping over itself, working through the haze of the grief to try to understand what he meant. "What kind of business do we need to talk about?"

"I think we should do some planning, in case you're sued by the family."

I clutched my throat, which suddenly felt tight. "I haven't even thought about a lawsuit."

"And you don't need to. That's what I'm here for."

My brother was a trust and estate lawyer at a big firm in Manhattan, but at the moment, that provided little comfort.

"When we probate the estate, there may be some assets we can shield from judgment, depending on how things are titled," he said. "So we should go over how your assets are held and all of the details of Connor's pension and life insurance."

I shook my head. "I can't think about any of that now."

"We'll see if you feel up to it in a few days. If not, we'll have you sign some documents so I can handle it all on your behalf. I want to help, Mer." He squeezed my hand and waited until I lifted my eyes to meet his. "I don't know how to make you feel better, to take away the pain you're going through. So let me at least take care of these things for you."

I took a deep breath and nodded. "Okay. Thank you."

The ride back to my apartment was quick. Since the limousines all left the cemetery at the same time, I didn't get even a moment to myself when we arrived at my building. Connor's parents and an aunt and uncle were already waiting out front, as was the catering van from the place where his mother had ordered all the food.

Over the next two hours, dozens of people came and went. One generic condolence rolled into another, and every time someone expressed how sorry they were for my loss, I felt like screaming that they should be sorry for the Wright family, not mine. Thankfully, the wine kept me from doing that. But when Connor's mother started telling stories of how her son had volunteered at a soup kitchen in college, I was grateful the door buzzed again because I had reached my limit on how much I could take.

I opened the door to find two men who looked familiar, but I couldn't place their faces. That had happened a lot today, especially since I didn't know many of the operational people from the team, and several had come by.

"Dr. McCall?"

"Yes?"

The taller of the men pointed to himself. "I'm Detective Green." He motioned to the other man. "And this is Detective Owens. We met at the hospital, the night of the accident."

Oh God. How could I have not placed the faces? These men were with me at the worst moment of my life. "Oh, right. Hello. Thank you for coming by." I thumbed behind me. "Would you . . . like to come in? We have plenty of food."

Detective Green glanced over my shoulder into my packed apartment before waving me off. "No, thank you. We're sorry to bother you when you have a house full of company, but we have some questions that really need to be answered." He nodded toward the hall. "Maybe you could come outside and talk to us for a few moments, so we have some privacy? We won't take too long."

"Umm . . . sure." I stepped into the hall and pulled the door closed behind me. Folding my arms across my chest, I nodded. "What can I help you with?"

Detective Green pulled a small notebook and pen from the inside pocket of his suit jacket. "We have some questions about Connor's injury. The one he sustained on the ice a few months back."

"Okay . . ."

"It happened on February first, is that correct?"

"Yes."

"And how was his recovery going?"

"Slow, but as expected. Connor had started physical therapy about three weeks before . . ." It felt like I got sucker punched in the gut, and I had to take a moment. "Before the accident."

"And prior to physical therapy? He was seeing a Dr. Martin at the West Side Pain Management Clinic, is that correct?"

I blinked a few times. Detective Green had said he had questions, but why was he asking them if he already knew the answers? It caught me off guard and gave me an uneasy feeling. "Yes, he went there for about four weeks after his surgery."

"Was Mr. Fitzgerald drinking the night of the accident? When he was with you, I mean?"

I shook my head. "He hadn't had anything to drink before he left here."

"And you had an argument of some sort that evening?"

My brows furrowed. "How did you know that?"

"You mentioned it at the hospital, on the night of the accident."

"Oh." I forced a smile. "Sorry. The last few days have pretty much been a blur."

"That's understandable." He nodded. "Can I ask what the argument was about?"

My eyes welled up, remembering the trivial thing that had set off a series of events that would ruin so many lives. "Garbage. I gave him a hard time because when I got home from work, the garbage in the kitchen was overflowing."

He nodded again. "Getting back to the pain clinic, Dr. Martin prescribed your husband a painkiller, is that right?"

"Yes. Oxycodone."

"And when did Dr. Martin stop prescribing those?"

"I'm not sure of the exact date. But Connor filled the last bottle the day before he started physical therapy."

Detective Green pointed at me with his pen. "And that's when you started writing the prescriptions for your husband? After Dr. Martin stopped writing them?"

My heart skipped a beat. "What? I didn't write Connor any prescriptions."

"You didn't write Mr. Fitzgerald any prescriptions for oxycodone?"

"Of course not." My throat threatened to seal up around my words. "Never."

The detectives looked at each other.

"Maybe there's a mistake in the information we were given," Detective Owens said. It was the first time he'd spoken.

I looked between the two men, trying to make sense of it. "There must be."

"Dr. McCall, one more thing," Detective Green said. "When I go to the doctor, they don't give me a paper prescription anymore. They send it in electronically. So why do doctors even have the old-school script pads these days?"

"For when a patient travels out of state. Each state utilizes their own electronic system. It's mandatory to use New York's system, except in certain exceptions like when a script is filled in another state."

"And your husband still traveled with his team after his injuries, correct?"

"Yes."

"So your paper scripts being filled when he was out of town for a game, those wouldn't be tracked too easily, then?"

"I would imagine not, but again, I didn't write Connor any prescriptions."

Detective Green closed his little notebook. "We'll look into it. Thank you for your time, Dr. McCall. Again, we're sorry to have taken you away from your company."

Back inside the apartment, I went straight to our home office. Connor and I shared it, but he hardly ever used it except for the occasional call with his agent. My heart pounded as I took a seat and looked down at the drawer where I kept my spare prescription pads. There was only one left at home since I'd taken one to the office to write Mr. Mankin's prescription when I *ran out* there. Part of me didn't want to open the drawer. Didn't want to find out. Though deep down I already knew, didn't I?

Squeezing my eyes shut, I reached for the handle.

What was it that the priest had said today?

"The Lord is gracious and righteous; our God is full of compassion."

Please, God, I could use a morsel of that compassion right now. Let it be there. Let me have this one thing.

I took a deep breath and opened the drawer.

My pounding heart came to an abrupt halt.

Empty.

CHAPTER 12
Now

*N*othing is right.

I rearrange a series of pots holding succulents on the windowsill. Lift the blinds so the cheery outside sun can come in. When I turn back, I see *you*, waiting for me on my desk—the same desk you helped me move in here, three hundred pounds of solid walnut. The image is so real, I feel like it can't possibly be my imagination. You smile back at me, all teeth and squinty eyes and the scar on your eyebrow from when the puck—I blink and then you're gone. Just like that. I shake my head and force myself back to cleaning.

My heels click across the room. I snap up a framed photo. Add it to the growing pile of things that have to go. My breath comes in fast, ragged bursts, but I only have seven minutes before my first patient in a year comes into this room and sits on my teal couch to pour her heart out. It's nerve-racking, but things *will* be right once I'm working again.

They have to be.

Finally, I've removed all signs of *you*—the desk itself the one exception.

Four minutes.

I shove the box in the corner, behind the ficus that somehow survived my absence. Gerry, my temporary replacement, was able to keep it alive.

Unlike my practice.

No, my practice is not dead, just . . . waning. I exhale as the outer door squeaks open and closes with a thud. My assistant Sarah's muffled voice greets my patient—a patient I've, thankfully, treated for years. One of the early ones. One of the handful who've stuck by me.

I sink into my desk chair. Most who remain probably don't know what happened—the patients, I mean. I somehow managed to keep my face out of the papers and off the news. I shielded my face going in and out of my apartment, in and out of the services. It helped that photos of famous hockey players walking into a funeral parlor probably fetched more money than the partially covered face of a woman the media had never noticed before. My name made it into stories, but not the name my patients know me by. I've always practiced using my maiden name, something *you* weren't fond of, but now I'm glad I did. It's been my safety net.

I hear Sarah say something about new insurance and paperwork, and I close my eyes, grateful for a few minutes more. It feels like I've been waiting for this day for months, wearing out the soles of my shoes to pass the time until I could come back and have purpose in my life. But now that it's here, what if I can't do this anymore?

What if, after all that's happened, I'm incapable of making a difference?

I pull out my phone to distract myself, my finger gliding automatically to my email, where a confirmation awaits:

> Your ad has been approved and will run for another fourteen days—

I swipe the email away, disgusted. We're running advertisements for the practice—like I'm a two-bit ambulance chaser—when previously, all my clients came from referrals. I should be grateful that Sarah knows how to do these things for me, instead of bitter about the fact that I must.

"*You'll get back to that,*" she reassured me last week when I came to check in and expressed wariness about using ads. "*But right now you're down forty percent of your patients. You have to do something.*" So I agreed. Now we're placing ads and running discounts for people who pay out of pocket and all kinds of stuff I would have turned my nose up at not too long ago.

But it's about survival.

The practice's and mine.

Someday it will be about more. Someday people will come because they've heard good things.

I open a different icon, eyeing my door—I probably have another minute or two before my patient finishes updating her medical forms. A rush of nerves and excitement sends tingles down my spine when the dating app tells me I have *New Messages.*

Two of them.

One from a man five years my junior with sandy red hair, blue eyes, and a teasing grin. His name is Phil, and while I'm not usually attracted to his particular combination of looks, there's something about his smile—it makes me think there's more to him than meets the eye. It's pure fantasy, of course. We've exchanged flirty comments, and he's suggested grabbing coffee. I'm not planning on saying yes anytime soon. But I type out a quick message, because this is good for me. I'm getting my feet wet. Easing into the idea of companionship in the future. Plus, it feels safe, anonymous almost. I can say anything, mess up, or decide to stop responding without real repercussions, since I didn't use my last name to create my profile and my photo is nothing more than a vague smile.

I tilt my head, chewing the end of a pen, and open the second message. This one is from a man I haven't chatted with yet. Though we must've both hearted each other or he wouldn't be able to send me a message. He's handsome. Dark hair, dark eyes, and a dimpled smile that makes me think he's adventurous. I read through his introduction. The first paragraph is filled with compliments, telling me he loves my smile and all of the things that caught his attention on my profile. It's a good start. The second paragraph dives into details about him—attorney, thirty-eight, lives downtown. But things turn south when he gets to his hobbies. *"I'm a hockey fanatic who played in college but didn't have what it takes to get to the big leagues."*

Delete.

And just like that, the smile is gone from my face and I'm dragged back to thoughts of *you* and whether I'm ready to date yet.

A knock at my door quiets my ruminations. Sarah pokes her head in with a smile.

"Your first patient is here. You have a few more minutes. She's still up-dating some forms."

I take a nervous breath. "Great. Thank you."

She steps inside. "And this package came for you. I'm sorry I opened it. I thought it was paper I ordered from Amazon yesterday."

I haven't ordered anything for the office. Not that I remember, anyway. But lately, my memory hasn't been so sharp. I take the open box. There's a book inside.

You, by Caroline Kepnes. I've heard of it, but haven't read it. "I didn't order this, Sarah."

"Really? I did notice that the address has the wrong suite number. But it has your name on it." She shrugs. "Amazon must've made a mistake. But did you see the show? The book was made into a series."

"No."

She smiled. "It's so good. Creepy as hell, but addicting. It's about a guy who stalks women."

I blink a few times, looking down at the label. My name is definitely there, even if the suite number is wrong. "It's about a stalker?"

"Yeah. You should read it. Just don't do it at night alone. It'll scare the crap out of you. There's gory murders and stuff."

I drop it back in the box abruptly. "Send it back. I don't want to read it."

"Oh. Sure." Sarah forces a smile. "No problem. I'll send Mrs. Amster-dam in as soon as she's done."

"Thanks."

My assistant shuts my office door, and I feel more than a little unsettled. A book about a stalker shows up addressed to me? It's a very strange coinci-dence. Though a guilty conscience will do that to you, connect dots to form a line that isn't really there. How many times have I told that to patients? It's a not-so-subtle reminder that I'm playing a dangerous game.

A few minutes later, there's another knock at the door. This time, Sarah shows my first patient in. I feel panicky, but when Mrs. Amsterdam smiles, I welcome her, telling her I missed her, too, and yes, I'm back for good. Something turns on in my brain after that. Words come from my mouth, and my hand sketches notes across a pad. She tells me about her husband and her dog and her daughter-in-law. It's like riding a bicycle, and I've hopped right on, started pedaling along like nothing ever changed.

Even though everything *has* changed.

Soon enough, the soft buzzer that keeps time on the table next to me goes off. I check my watch, certain an hour hasn't really passed. Surprisingly, it has. Mrs. Amsterdam and I finish up our conversation and discuss meds—she needs something different for anxiety—then I'm walking her to the door.

"How'd it go?" Sarah greets me with a fresh cup of coffee and a supportive smile. I smile back, wondering if we could be friends. Would that ruin our professional relationship? We are *friendly* . . .

"Good," I say. "I'm relieved the first patient was one I'm familiar with. I think it helped me ease into things."

"I'm glad." She takes something from her back pocket and holds it up, though not offering it to me. "I'm sorry to tell you that this person dropped by."

I peer over at the business card in her hand and notice the logo immediately. *Two fists.* I frown. "Someone from Mothers Against Abusive Doctors came here? Inside the office?"

Sarah nods. "Her name was Mary Ellis. She was kind of scary-looking. Manic with a nervous facial tic and nails bitten down so far she barely had any nail beds. Her hand shook when she held out the business card for me to take."

"What did she want?"

"She asked to talk to you while you were in session with Mrs. Amsterdam. When I said you were busy, she told me about her group and what they stand for. Then she asked if she could make an appointment to speak to you. I told her she could leave a message with me, and if you were interested in speaking to her, we'd call her."

I feel sick. First the book arrives to set me on edge, and now this. "Did she leave a message?"

Sarah nods. "She said to tell you that more than sixteen thousand people died from prescription opioid drug overdoses last year, eleven hundred of them children. I showed her the door and told her this was a private office and she wasn't welcome to stop by ever again. If she did, she'd be trespassing."

While I know Sarah meant well, I'm not sure it was wise to threaten a group that likes to hang my picture around town like a mug shot. It might be smarter to lock up, go back home, and reconsider my career, perhaps something where I'm not expected to be the stable one. Yet I swallow back my fears and nod. "Thank you. I'm sorry you had to deal with that, Sarah."

She shrugs. "Doesn't bother me at all. I'm sorry they're pestering you."

Anxious to change the subject, I force a smile. "So . . . what's the rest of the day look like?"

Her expression brightens. "A full schedule! Just had a last-second add-on, so you have two new patients today." She hurries around the desk, pressing her finger to the schedule where she's written names. "I booked them for ninety minutes, like you asked. Oh, and don't forget, I have to leave by five for Charlie's cello lesson. But . . ." Sarah screws up her face. "Shoot. That means your last new patient won't be here until five fifteen, after I've gone. Tell you what, I'll stay a few after. I'd hate for a stranger to walk in when you're all alone. Maybe he'll come early—they usually do—and I'll sneak out while you're in session."

Sarah's done so much to keep my practice afloat already. "No, you should go. Take Charlie to his lesson. I'll be okay. I'll put the sign out and . . ." I shrug. "It'll be fine."

"Are you sure?"

"I'm sure."

"Well, okay. Let me know if you change your mind."

The outer door creaks with another patient coming in, and I return to my office to finish my notes on Mrs. Amsterdam before my next patient is on the couch. Keeping busy is key. I can't think about the book that just *happened* to arrive today or the group that wants my head. If I allow myself to dwell on things, *I'll* be the one on the couch, curled in a ball, sucking my thumb.

Hours later, the sunlight slanting through the side window changes. That golden glow of late afternoon begins to fade toward early evening. My next-to-last patient waves goodbye, and I take a sip of herbal tea—a replacement for afternoon coffee, at Dr. Alexander's suggestion.

One more appointment. A long one, though, since it's another new patient.

I blow out a breath and reach for my appointment list, skimming down to the bottom until I find the name of the new patient Sarah has added.

But it can't be correct.

Because the name that is handwritten in at the bottom of the typed list is . . .

Gabriel Wright.

I blink down at it and wipe my eyes, as though that will clear away an illusion. But no, the letters are still there, written in black ink, Sarah's familiar bold cursive. My mind short-circuits, goes blank. And that's when I realize what it is—a coincidence. It has to be. It's not actually *him.*

Wright is a common last name. I went to med school with a Bianca Wright and had third grade with a Bobby Wright, before he moved away. New York probably has hundreds of Wrights. This is just one named Gabriel.

Yes, it's definitely a coincidence.

Albeit a shocking one.

But one all the same.

I yank my laptop from my desk drawer. Sarah would have done an intake when she set up the appointment. Basic answers, like date of birth, address, and insurance, are stored in our computer system. That information will set my mind at ease. I type away, logging into the computer, finding the program icon, clicking into that system . . . While I wait for it to open, I fan myself, realizing I've gone hot with anxiety.

It can't be him. It can't be.

I pull up the new patient's chart, navigate to the personal information tab, and feel ice slide down my spine as I read the address that's been entered.

It's no coincidence.

Gabriel Wright, the man I only recently stopped following, has made an appointment. I shake my head—it can't be. It just . . . can't.

But then a knock comes at the door.

A deep voice calls out, "Hello? Anyone home?"

I don't move. I'm paralyzed with fear. I don't even breathe. Long seconds tick by before another knock comes. This time, it's followed by the creak of my door opening . . .

A familiar face peeks through, splitting into a grin.

"Sorry, I didn't see anyone out there. I hope I'm in the right place. I'm here to see Dr. McCall?"

It takes me a second to find my voice. "Y-yes, that's me."

"Excellent." He pushes the door open the rest of the way and stares straight into my eyes. "I'm Gabriel Wright."

CHAPTER 13
Then

I really think this is a bad idea, Meredith. By not putting on any defense, the committee is going to assume you're guilty of negligence. And they'll set the punishment accordingly."

It wasn't the first time I'd heard those words from my attorney's mouth. I knew he meant well. Martin Hastings worked at my brother's firm. He only wanted what he thought was best for me.

"But I *was* negligent, Martin. I should've been more aware of what was going on with my own husband."

"Maybe. But the charges are that you overprescribed by signing *twenty-two* prescriptions for your husband. You didn't sign anything. There's a big difference between not safeguarding a prescription pad located in your private home or office and the committee thinking you signed all those scripts."

I sigh. To the committee there might be a difference, but the end result was the same. People were dead because I buried my head in the sand, refused to see what was really going on with Connor.

"I need this over with, Martin."

He took a deep breath and nodded. "An admission of medical misconduct is grounds to permanently revoke your license. Will you at least let me speak to the committee off the record on your behalf? Explain what really happened? At a minimum, I'd like to try to negotiate the disciplinary action they take."

"Can you do that today, while we're here?" It had been six months since Connor's accident. While I was sure most people dreaded walking into the Department of Health's Office of Professional Misconduct, I'd been marking the days off on my calendar, waiting. I needed to move on. And I couldn't do that until I took responsibility for my actions—or my inactions, in this case.

"Yes. Give me an hour. I'll go in and see what I can do before we start the official hearing."

I hated to wait even one minute more, but following Martin's recommendation on this was the very least I could do. Lord knows I hadn't listened to any of his other advice. I nodded. "Sure. Thank you."

"Great." He pointed to a bench across the hall from the hearing room. "Have a seat. I'll be back as soon as I can."

But I couldn't sit. After Martin disappeared behind the closed door, I paced. Walking back and forth, I rehashed for the hundredth time how I'd gotten here.

Mr. Mankin. My patient who had been preparing for a trip down to Florida to visit his mother and needed a paper prescription to take with him. Only when I'd opened my desk drawer at the office, my prescription pad was gone. On the very afternoon that Connor had been alone in my office.

What had I done about it?

I'd ignored it.

I went home and got one of the other two prescription pads I stored in my home office desk.

Problem solved.

But I should've known.

I should've done something about it.

Not brushed my suspicions under the table.

Connor's anger? Before his injury, he'd never once raised his voice to me the way he did after he started those pills the pain clinic prescribed. He'd also never had trouble sleeping. Or an inability to sit down and relax when he got home.

Side effects of OxyContin abuse: Mood swings. Anger. Difficulty sleeping. Restlessness.

What did I do about it?

Pretended not to see it.

Justified every single outburst. Looked the other way at every other flashing sign so I wouldn't upset Connor.

But deep down I'd known. Hadn't I?

I knew.

I might not be guilty of writing the prescription itself, but I'd buried my head in the sand. I'd failed.

As a wife.

As a doctor.

And so I paced. And paced. And paced. My lawyer had said he'd be out in less than an hour, but it was more like two that passed before the door opened again.

Martin shut the door behind him and blew out two cheeks full of air. "They want a year."

"A year suspension?"

He nodded. "I tried everything. They're not budging."

I let that sink in. A year with no patients. It would be tough. But wasn't I getting off easy compared to the Wright family? One year would likely fly by. I'd be back in my office in no time. But where would they be?

Still dead.

Still buried six feet beneath the ground.

I swallowed. "Okay."

"They also want you to see a therapist during your suspension and for one year after your return to practice. As much as they're holding you accountable, they also recognize that you've been through a lot, that you've experienced a big loss. They want to make sure your mental health is strong enough when you're able to treat patients again."

I nodded. "That's fair."

Martin took a deep breath. "Okay, then. We just need to go in so you can formally accept an admission of professional misconduct and then we'll be on our way. You'll be unable to practice medicine and see patients after today. They'll allow you fourteen days to manage your practice—meaning direct your staff to call patients and cancel appointments or make arrangements for another psychiatrist to cover you during your suspension. After that, you won't be able to have any involvement with your practice whatsoever. I recommend you not have contact with any staff or go into your office for any reason, in order to eliminate any appearance of impropriety. It's best to make a clean break."

"Okay." I nodded.

"I should also warn you that there's a group that could harass you once this becomes public record. It happened to another doctor I represented a few years back. They organized a protest outside his office. They go after doctors who get in trouble for selling scripts or overprescribing. The woman who started it lost her son when he fell asleep at the wheel and drove off the side of the highway. He was addicted to oxycodone. His doctor had written him something like forty prescriptions. This is a very different situation, so they shouldn't give you any trouble. But I thought you should know."

Oh God.

I tugged at the collar of my blouse, feeling suddenly claustrophobic. "Could we go in and get this over with? I really need some fresh air."

"Of course."

Less than fifteen minutes later, I was out on the street. I leaned forward with my hands on my thighs, panting like I'd just run a race.

"You okay?" Martin asked.

I nodded and closed my eyes. "I will be, now that that's behind me."

Martin waited a minute or two quietly. "Are you heading home? Do you want me to hail you a cab?"

I stood upright. "No, thanks. I have another stop to make. I think I'm going to walk."

He rested a hand on my shoulder. "I'm sorry things didn't work out better. But this is only the end of a chapter of your life, Meredith. Not the end of the book."

I thanked him and nodded. But there was still one more thing that needed to happen before I could put this chapter from hell to bed. And I was anxious to address that head-on. Though I didn't share my plans with Martin, because if my brother found out what I was about to do, he'd flip his lid.

Oddly, a half hour later, my cell phone buzzed right as I arrived at my destination. I paused to read the name flashing on the screen. *Jake.* He couldn't possibly know what I was up to, so I guessed Martin had just made it back to the office and filled him in. Still, the timing was uncanny. I waited until it stopped ringing and went to voicemail—not wanting to lie to my brother about where I was or what I was doing—before opening the door and walking up to the front desk of the Seventeenth Precinct.

"Hi. Is Detective Green here?"

The officer gave me a quick once-over. "Name?"

"Meredith Fitzgerald."

"Is he expecting you?"

I shook my head. "No, he's not."

He gestured to a seating area behind me. "Wait there. I'll see if he's available."

A few minutes later, Detective Green walked out from a side door. "Dr. McCall?" He looked behind me. "No lawyer today?"

The only other time I'd been here—or been in any police station, for that matter—was a few days after Connor's funeral. Detective Green had asked me to come in and answer more questions. My brother, Jake, had insisted he go with me.

I shook my head. "No, I don't need one."

He motioned behind him. "Come on back."

I followed him down a long hall, stopping at the same door I'd gone through months ago. He extended a hand for me to walk in first. "Would you like a cup of coffee or something?"

The Unravelling

97

"No, thank you."

"Please have a seat."

Detective Green took the chair across from me. "What can I do for you today, Dr. McCall?"

I went to fold my hands on the table, but they were shaking. Instead, I tucked my fingers under my thighs on the seat. "About a week before the accident, my husband and I had a fight. He showed up at my office with flowers the next day. That same evening, I noticed a prescription pad from my drawer was gone."

Detective Green sat back in his chair and folded his arms across his chest. "Okay . . ."

It was the first time he was hearing the true story. My brother hadn't let me answer most of the questions the detective had back then—citing either the Fifth Amendment or spousal privilege. At the time, I was walking around in a fog and would've jumped off a bridge if Jake had told me to.

"I talked myself into believing I must've used the last page on the pad. But in hindsight, which is finally much clearer to me, I would have remembered pulling off the last one." I paused. "The afternoon of Connor's funeral, after you came by my apartment, I checked the desk in my home office. I'd had another prescription pad there. That one was gone, too."

He nodded. "Anything else?"

"I was telling the truth when I told you I didn't write any prescriptions for OxyContin. But I should have addressed what was going on."

Detective Green rubbed the stubble on his chin. "Why now? What made you come in and tell me all this today, so many months later?"

I looked him straight in the eyes. "I couldn't live a lie anymore. Not even to myself. Today I accepted responsibility with the state medical board, and I'm here to accept the rest."

He pondered my answer for a moment before leaning forward. "I appreciate that. But as part of our investigation, we interviewed your husband's physical therapist and surgeon. They both said Mr. Fitzgerald had significant deterioration in both his knees, from years of overuse and constant injury. So even if you *had* prescribed the painkillers to your husband, it was debatable whether that was outside an acceptable treatment regimen. Plus, it might have been negligent to leave your script pad lying around unlocked, but proving your actions were *criminal* is a much bigger hurdle. It's also my understanding that while it's frowned upon, it's not illegal for physicians to prescribe medications to family members. That's why we never pursued things further with you. In the end, it was your husband who made the decision to take too many pills and drink and drive that night." Detective Green nodded. "And that's on him. Not you."

"But . . . if I had addressed things, maybe the accident would never have happened."

He nodded. "Perhaps. But there's no criminal case."

A few minutes later, Detective Green walked me back out to the lobby. He stopped before opening the front door. "Can I give you some advice, Dr. McCall?"

I nodded.

"You need to find a way to let go of the guilt, or it will eat you alive."

"How do I do that?"

He smiled halfheartedly. "I'm just a dumb cop. You're the doctor. I'm sure you'll figure it out."

CHAPTER 14
Now

y chest tightens, about to burst, as I wait for him to recognize me. The moment when his eyes will go wide and he'll realize who I am—whether that's his family's killer's wife or merely the woman he collided with coming out of an alleyway.

But he smiles pleasantly and sits there on my couch while I gape at him. "Good evening." He nods. "It's nice to meet you."

"Gabriel . . . Wright?" I somehow force my voice into my smooth therapist's tone, hoping that whatever is on my face has transitioned from shock to confidence. I do try to instill confidence in my patients, especially on day one. They come in timid and self-conscious, huddled in on themselves. Though Gabriel doesn't seem to have that issue. His shoulders are relaxed and his dark eyes soak in the room before finally landing back on me. He might as well be waiting for a seat at a local restaurant, not sitting in my office.

Cool. Calm. Confident.

I clear my throat, putter at my desk as my thoughts go haywire. My cell phone sits at the corner, and I reach to put it away in a drawer when it occurs to me—I could fake an emergency.

Pretend to get a call.

Apologize, promise to reschedule.

Have Sarah send him elsewhere, to another therapist, preferably on the other side of town. Then this problem would be gone, and I could go back to focusing on growing my office and *not* following him.

"I'm sorry, do you need a minute? I just walked right in." Gabriel offers an apologetic smile. "I don't mind. I can step out."

"No, no . . . of course not."

Get it together, Meredith.

I manage to land one foot in front of the other and walk to my seat across from him. Staring down at the notepad in front of me, I take a deep breath and motion to the couch. "So, welcome, Mr. Wright. Please, make yourself comfortable."

He sits. "Please, call me Gabriel."

"Of course. Gabriel. How are you doing today?"

I look up and wait for him to respond, realizing I'm holding my breath. But it's more than nerves. I really *want* to know how he's doing. Is he living again? Yes, from the outside it seems he is. I've witnessed him laughing, going out with multiple women, and doing all sorts of things that appear normal. But he can't *feel* normal inside. Not after what I've allowed to happen to his family.

This, perhaps, is the perfect opportunity.

Maybe I'll find out the truth . . .

"I'm okay," he says. "I just . . . think I need to see someone."

I process a moment, trying to sort out how to word my next question. "Might I ask how you found me?" I shake my head. "I mean how you heard about my practice. Were you referred by someone?"

"Yes, I was referred."

"That's wonderful." I force a smile. "And who referred you? I like to thank people when they recommend my office."

"It was Johnson and Johnson."

I squint. "Johnson and Johnson?"

"The maker of Tylenol PM." He flashes a playful smile. "Sorry, I'm just teasing. I saw an ad for your practice, for people who are having trouble sleeping, on the Johnson and Johnson website when I was looking up how long the sleep-aid effect should last for Tylenol PM. I thought it sounded better to say I was referred."

"Oh. Okay." I swallow. "Well, I'm glad you're here. I have a few basic questions I do for intake, and then we can really talk. How does that sound?"

He nods along, and I take him through a basic patient intake—verifying his primary physician, his demographic data, family psychiatric history, medications, and so on. No red flags. No history at all, really, besides the obvious—what *you* did to him. What *we* did to him. Gabriel speaks easily, relaxing back on the couch, talking with his hands. He has good eye contact, and I find myself starting to relax, noticing he's even more handsome up close. Soft fuzz peppers his angular jaw, telling me he hasn't shaved in a couple of days. When he speaks, his whole body grows animated, and his entire face smiles, not just his very full lips. His emotions are on display through his big brown eyes, as though he holds nothing back, and something about that seems almost freeing.

But he can't be free. I know that better than anyone.

"What brings you in today?" I circle back to the moment at hand, waiting, pen poised, to take detailed notes. It's only when I look down and scribble his name at the top—*Gabriel Wright*—that I become aware I didn't pull a patient notebook from my desk. I pulled *my* notebook from my desk. The one that already has pages and pages of notes and observations on *him*. Whatever calm I'd begun to feel disappears, and my hand starts shaking. I grip the notebook as tightly as possible to try to stop it.

"I'm struggling with sleep. I've tried everything—over-the-counter stuff, even got a prescription for Ambien. It does put me to sleep. But I've been on it a while now." He takes a breath. "I don't want to be on a medication forever. I'd rather deal with the root of the problem."

My insides quiver. With dread. With anticipation. I *knew* he couldn't have gotten over what happened. Maybe this is the reason we've crossed paths again. I'm *meant* to help him. Help him move forward, get over his grief.

Grief that I caused.

Something niggles at my brain.

I swallow hard. But how did this happen? There are millions of people in this city—how is it we just happened to be in the same coffee shop at the same time those months ago? And now, for him to sit across from me in my office? Does he really not know who I am?

My eyes come into focus once again, and I realize Gabriel has been silent for too long. He's waiting for me to say something. But what the hell was the last thing he said? Something about sleep. Medication. *Oh! Root cause!*

I clear my throat. "And what is the root of the problem?"

His chest lifts as he takes a deep breath. "Sorry, this is difficult for me to talk about." He looks anywhere but at me, and my gaze follows his to a nearby shelf, books lined up on all topics of psychiatry, mixed with a few coffee table books I swap out in the waiting room. And that's when I notice the piece of *you* I've missed.

Our wedding photo. You, me, arm in arm, white dress and black tux, laughing as though we haven't a care in the world. And we didn't back then. The frame had been on my desk, photo facing away from patient view. But I moved it while I was packing earlier, set it aside to wrap so the glass wouldn't break. Now it's on full display, staring at my patient . . .

Gabriel might not have recognized me, but he certainly would recognize *you*—if not from your days playing hockey, then from the photos that were plastered all over the papers and social media after your "accident."

Shit.

"My wife and child died last year." Gabriel looks down at his hands, loose in his lap. "They were killed by a driver who was under the influence of . . ." He waves a hand. "Whatever the fuck he was under the influence of. Sorry. I didn't mean to curse, I just . . ." He sighs heavily.

I sit in my chair, vibrating with tension. *I have to move that photo.* Have to get rid of the damn thing. But this is important, this moment. Gabriel Wright, sharing his inner thoughts with me. His truths.

Usually I sit quietly, patiently. Silence encourages someone to continue talking, to fill the space. But today I can't.

"I'm very sorry for your loss," I say. "Tell me more. Did your sleeping issues start when they died? And excuse me for a moment, please. I just need to grab a new pen."

I'm on my feet, moving toward the frame. I used to love that photo. It made me smile every time I looked over at it. But now my husband's smiling face no longer looks joyous to me. It's marred with the knowledge of what you did. What *I* allowed you to do. A glass of new pens sits nearby, and I reach for one, simultaneously reaching for *you*—hoping, as blood thrums through my veins, that I can move it before he notices.

A loud slap echoes around the room as the frame smacks face down against the wood of the shelf.

Gabriel immediately stands. "Are you okay? Do you need help?" He takes a step toward me—toward the photo I've just pretended to accidentally knock over.

I wave him off. "Oh no, thank you. It's fine. I'm so sorry to interrupt. Tell me about your family."

He eases back on the couch, uncertain. As though manners dictate that he help me.

I like that about him.

Settling back in my chair, I offer a warm smile. "Please, continue."

It takes a moment, but then he does. Gabriel dives right into the deep end. He tells me things I already know—how his wife and child were mowed down. How they were killed instantly. But he also tells me things that I didn't know, like how his daughter was hearing impaired and wore hearing aids, and his wife came from a wealthy family. I listen, riveted, but when he talks about their funeral, I find myself wondering if he'll mention where they were buried. But he doesn't, and there's no way to ask. I scribble detailed notes, knowing I'll pore over them a million times tonight. I'll try to remember every face he made, every emotion that spilled from his warm eyes. I suddenly wish I recorded my sessions.

I'm also intensely aware that my behavior is anything but professional. That accepting him as a patient—which I've effectively already done by continuing this session—is morally wrong. And yet another thing I could get in trouble for with the medical board. Big trouble. But it's like the universe wants me to right my wrongs.

Or . . . and I can't help returning to this again. Or it's not a coincidence he keeps popping up in my life. I squirm at that thought, at why he might be here besides truly wanting help. Except I started this all by following *him*.

"What do you think?" Gabriel asks.

A pause of silence. I haven't been listening. Too lost in my own thoughts to hear a word he's said in the last minute or two.

"I think . . ." I summon my inner therapist, think of the common phrases I've repeated to my patients over the years. "It's likely you're dealing with something that really digs at your subconscious."

He tilts his head, gazing at me, and I start to panic that I've said the wrong thing, that my response to whatever he's said is inappropriate.

But eventually, he nods. "Yeah, I think you're probably right. My sister thinks I never really dealt with their loss, that it's hitting me now, and that's why I can't sleep."

I consider the smiles, the laughter, the *happiness* I'd witnessed. It was all a facade the entire time.

"That is definitely possible. What do you think?"

"I'm not sure." He rubs at his face with one hand, a gesture that seems almost uncharacteristic for this man who usually seems so collected, so confident. It's like a crack in his shell, and I want to peer into it—to understand what lies beneath so I can help. "I should've been with them that night. But I wasn't. I . . ." A loaded silence follows. Another downcast look, flexing of his hands. I notice the glint of metal on his hand, his ring finger—a wedding ring. One I've never seen him wear before, and I'm certain I've looked. "I have a lot of guilt," he concludes.

At that moment, my timer beeps. I want more than anything to grab it and shut it off and tell him to go on. But that's not what a therapist would do. It's what the twisted part of *me* wants to do, the part that is hardly acting professional. And I need to maintain at least a pretense of professionalism. He is a patient, after all.

"I guess we save the guilt for the next session." Gabriel smiles, and it's real—or at least it seems that way. Though again there's that niggle—*or maybe he's been fooling me this whole time.*

There are just too many maybes.

Maybe he's really not happy.

Maybe he's not okay.

Maybe he really does need professional help.

Maybe we have far more in common than I ever fathomed.

Maybe he knows who I am.

Or . . . *maybe not.*

"Yes, that sounds good. Gabriel, I'm so pleased that you're seeking help. It was a pleasure to meet you today." I stand and usher him to the door. I want to tell him to call immediately and make another appointment—that sooner would be better.

But I control myself.

"Hey, have we . . . " He hesitates in the doorway and turns, studying me with a furrowed brow. "Have we ever met before?"

I respond quickly. *Too* quickly. "No, I don't think so."

My heart races. Though I can't help but feel oddly pleased that something about me is memorable to him.

Gabriel shrugs, steps through the doorway. "Something about you is familiar. I'm sure it will come to me."

After he's gone, I lean my forehead against the door. *God, I hope not.*

CHAPTER 15
Now

My leg bounces up and down.

It's a nervous habit I developed in med school. Test anxiety. But I haven't done it in years. Though my anxiety seems at an all-time high today. Of course, it hasn't even been two years since my husband died, the man I'd thought was the love of my life. My forever. Yet my leg didn't bounce once through the funeral. Nor once during the police questioning. And not when I opened my desk drawer and found another prescription pad missing. Yet while I watch the clock tick down one moment at a time, waiting for my second appointment with my special patient, my leg gets more exercise than it does on the treadmill at the gym. I'm not sure what that says about me as a wife or doctor.

I could still cancel. It's not too late. I *should've* canceled already. Lord knows I thought about it enough this week. I'd even drafted an email to Sarah asking her to refer Gabriel to another therapist. But I couldn't bring myself to hit send. Isn't it the very least I can do to help the man get over his loss? *He needs me.* Sure, it's unprofessional. Probably grounds for losing my medical license. No, *definitely* grounds. If I got caught . . .

I hear the door creak open in the outer office, and my bouncing leg goes still. Gabriel's voice booms as he says something to Sarah, and all the anxiety I've been feeling for a week instantly shifts to something different— exhilaration. The two emotions aren't that different. Both cause the blood to swish loudly in my ears. My palms sweat, and I'm certain I'll jump out of my skin with any sudden noise. But I also feel *alive*. So. Damn. Alive. I imagine it's a lot like jumping out of an airplane—the rush of adrenaline as you lift your arms into the air and let the wind and gravity take you. Only I'm not sure if my parachute works.

I might plunge to the ground at a hundred and twenty miles per hour and splatter like a bug.

Yet as I'm sitting on the edge of the plane, dangling my feet, waiting to lean my weight forward and fall out—*I can't wait* for it to happen.

Knock. Knock.

Sarah opens the door to my office. "Your twelve o'clock is here. I'm going to run out and grab a coffee from the deli down the block. Do you want something?"

"No, thank you." Who can think about food when you're waiting to jump out of an airplane?

She steps in and closes the door behind her. Smiling, she wiggles her eyebrows and whispers, "Your new patient is really sexy. He's not the type I'd normally be attracted to, but there's just something about him."

Yes, there certainly is.

I clear my throat. "Would you send him in on your way out, please?"

"Sure."

A few seconds later, Gabriel knocks twice and pokes his head in with a smile. "Rumor has it you're ready for me?"

My heart has been pounding nonstop over the last week, ever since he walked into my office the first time. But right now it feels like it's bouncing against my rib cage. I'm terrified.

I should cancel right now. Tell him I'm sick. In fact, I might not even need to say the words, because at the moment I feel pretty queasy.

But I rein it in. Because *Gabriel needs me.*

And a part of me needs him. Needs to make him better.

So I put on my finest practiced smile and hold out my hand, motioning to the seating area.

"I am ready for you. Please, have a seat, Mr. Wright."

He smiles again. Actually, it's more of a half smile. One that's lopsided and cocky. And it stirs something in me. Something feminine that hasn't been awake in a long time. *Something outrageously inappropriate.*

"I thought we were past that." He tilts his head. "It's Gabriel, not Mr. Wright, remember?"

Is he flirting? Or is it in my head? I'm not sure, but there's no time to contemplate that now. I nod. "Of course, Gabriel. Sorry. Let me just grab my notepad."

This time I'm careful to pull out a new notebook, not the stalker ledger I inadvertently grabbed last week. I take the seat across from him and cross my legs, smooth out the skirt I'm wearing today.

Gabriel's eyes drop, and I watch his Adam's apple bob up and down as he swallows. Then his gaze meets mine head-on.

"So . . . did you miss me?"

He's teasing, of course. But he has *no idea.*

"How was your week?" I ask.

He takes a deep breath in and lets it out. "Not bad. I had papers to grade, so it kept me busy. By the way, when did the word *anyway* become *anyways,* with an *s*? Every one of my students says, 'So anyways . . .'" He emphasizes the last letter.

I smile. It's genuine, and it helps me relax a bit. Bad grammar is a pet peeve of mine, too. "I think it was around the time they started beginning sentences with *literally. Literally,* I have no idea."

He laughs. It's hearty. Unrestrained. And maybe a little sexy.

"That's right up there in my book with *slay.* Certain words sound like nails on a chalkboard to me. When I tell a student they got an A, and they respond '*Slay,*' I want to drop the grade to a D."

I relax a little more. I could sit here all day and be amused by this man's wit. But we're not two friends having coffee. He's paying me for therapy. So I dig in.

"How did you sleep this week?"

"Not great."

I nod. "When we spoke last time, you said you have a lot of pent-up guilt surrounding your loss. Can we talk about that a little bit? Is the guilt because you were supposed to be with your wife and daughter that day?"

Gabriel's face falls. He looks down into his lap for a long time before speaking again. "My wife and I were having marital problems."

Oh. Wow. I hadn't been expecting that. "I see."

"We fought all the time." He frowns. "Including the night she died. That's why I wasn't with her that evening, and why she was out walking around with our daughter so late at night. The last thing I said to her before she stormed out was 'Go to hell.'"

My heart clenches. How many times has he replayed those last moments over and over in his head? Regret is like an anchor that wraps around the heart and weighs it down, keeping it from sailing free. I certainly understand that feeling. Connor and I had both said some hateful things before he left that last time, too. I understand the weight of guilt on a deeply personal level. I hate Connor for what he did, yet not a day goes by when I don't think to myself, *if I'd only done something when I found that first prescription pad missing, gotten him help instead of burying my head in the sand.*

I'm not sure how I'm supposed to guide this man to get over that guilt, when I can't even get over my own. So I give him the textbook answer and plow through.

"Well, that's obviously a very difficult memory to let go of. But you can't reduce your entire relationship to only the last moments. May I ask what led to the breakdown of your relationship?"

"I found out my wife was cheating on me with a coworker. I'd suspected it for a while, but she wouldn't admit it." Gabriel looks into my eyes. "So I followed her. And caught them in the act."

My eyes widen. *Followed her.*

"I know." He shrugs. "Not my finest moment."

He's mistaken the shock on my face as judgment, when really it's only the thought of him following someone the way I followed him that rattles me. "No, no, no." I wave my hands. "I wasn't thinking you did anything inappropriate. I was thinking it must have been horrible for you to catch them."

"Oh." He nods. "Yeah, it was." His eyes roam my face. "You married?"

"Divorced."

As a rule, I never divulge personal information about my family to a patient. But his question catches me so off guard that the lie tumbles out before I can even consider that the proper answer would be not to answer at all.

"Did he cheat?"

I shake my head. "No."

"How long ago was your divorce?"

I feel like I'm barreling down a bumpy road, but I don't know how to stop it.

"About eighteen months ago."

He nods. "I went on a date a few weeks ago. She invited me back to her place after. I wanted to sleep with her. But I felt guilty. Part of me still feels like I'm married. I think it's probably easier to jump back into things after a divorce. Is it? My wife died about the same time you got divorced. Have you been with anyone yet?"

"No."

Gabriel's eyes drop to my lips for a fraction of a second. It's so quick that I'm already second-guessing whether it even happened. Maybe I imagined it. I don't know. But the one thing I'm certain of is that I need to stop this line of discussion before it gets any worse. I should've never answered his first question, much less whether I've slept with anyone. So I straighten my back and sit taller in my chair, redirecting our conversation to how he felt when he walked in on his wife with another man. We spend a good deal of time there today, and by the time the conversation lulls, I almost feel like he's a routine patient. *Almost.*

"This is good progress," I say. "The first step in getting over guilt is acknowledging it exists."

"I've known it existed for a long time. What's the second step?"

"Forgiveness. Your wife was human. She made a mistake. You need to find a way to forgive her before you can truly move forward."

"How do I do that when she's dead?"

"Sometimes it helps to talk to the person. They don't need to be there for you to say what needs to be said. Perhaps you might write a letter, letting her know how much she's hurt you."

Gabriel rakes a hand through his hair. "Life is really one big circle, isn't it? I used to write Ellen letters when we first started dating."

I smile sadly. "That's sweet. No one writes letters anymore."

"Not unless you count the messages you send on a dating app when you're getting to know someone."

A dating app . . .

Like the one I was chatting on only last night. There I was, sipping a glass of wine and flirting with a random stranger, while Gabriel couldn't sleep. I shouldn't be allowed to smile until this man is truly happy again.

God, how can he *ever* be happy again after what he's lost?

Poor little Rose.

And there goes my heart, racing again. It feels like I'm doing intermittent exercise today. Speed up. Slow down. Wash. Rinse. Repeat. But I need to keep my head screwed on straight to do my job. So I force myself back to our discussion.

"Are you active on one of those? Dating apps, I mean?"

He nods. "I am."

"Meet anyone interesting?"

"I'm getting to know a few people. It's my first time not meeting a woman the old-fashioned way. You know, in a bar after some liquid courage. I felt like a dinosaur when I first joined."

I smile. "So much has changed in the dating world over the last decade."

"How about you?" he asks. "Have you tried online dating since your divorce?"

I open my mouth to answer, to again talk about my personal life, which is completely inappropriate. Luckily my buzzer saves me this time. I can't believe an hour has already gone by. I reach over and turn it off.

Gabriel meets my eyes and smiles. "Guess we pick up with our adventures in dinosaur dating next week? Maybe we can swap stories about the most bizarre people we've talked to?"

"Sure," I say and rise from my chair. Though I'm pretty sure the most bizarre woman he's currently talking to is standing right in front of him.

CHAPTER 16
Now

"So, how's being back to work?" Dr. Alexander settles in across from me. It's the first time I've seen him since I started seeing patients again.

"It's good. I was a little nervous the first day. But it was like riding a bike. If I'm being honest, it's nice to talk about someone else's problems for a while. I'm sort of sick of my own."

He smiles. "I'm sure your patients are glad to have you back, too."

I nod.

Dr. Alexander is quiet. He catches my eyes, then points his gaze down to my lap. Apparently, I'm wringing my hands and don't even know it. I unclench and sigh.

"Is there something you'd like to talk about today?" he asks.

I hadn't decided if I was going to tell him about Gabriel. But now that I'm sitting here, I realize I need the voice of reason. So I take a deep breath and blow it out with a nod.

"I took on some new patients."

He nods. "You mentioned that some of your patients had left in your absence. And your assistant has been running some advertising to rebuild your practice, in anticipation of your return. Are you finding that more stressful than seeing your regulars?"

I look down for a long time. I'm so tempted to tell him that's what is bothering me. That I'm nervous every new patient who walks through my door is going to want to talk about the loss of a loved one. It hasn't happened with any of my regulars yet, but the thought has been in the back of my mind. What if I break down listening about the death of a spouse? It would be so easy to tell him that's my concern. Dr. Alexander would never know the difference. But I want to get better. I want to move on.

"One of my new patients . . ." I trail off and bite down on my bottom lip. It's not easy to say. I'm ashamed. I know that what I'm doing is wrong. Morally and professionally.

When I don't pick up where my sentence left off after a solid minute, Dr. Alexander assumes my hesitation is for reasons other than what they are.

"We can talk about your patients and their problems here," he says. "A lot of therapists go to therapy and discuss things that come up in sessions. It's natural for things we hear to upset us at times in our line of work."

I lift my eyes to meet his. My heart pounds, and it takes everything in me to say the words out loud. They come out in a rush. "One of my new patients . . . is Gabriel."

Dr. Alexander's brows pull tight. "Gabriel, as in the man you were following? The man whose . . ."

I nod.

To his credit, other than a few blinks, he manages to not display judgment. He somehow maintains his even-keel tone, too.

"Tell me how this came about?"

I babble for a few minutes, explaining how shocked I was when he walked in. That it was a complete surprise. Not my doing. How I jumped into therapist mode and took a history, asked the usual questions, because I had no idea how to handle it. How to act.

"So you've only seen him once?"

I swallow and shake my head.

"Okay. Well, I would imagine you were thrown for a loop when he walked in that first time. It sounds like you panicked and handled it to avoid confrontation. But why did you see him the second time? It would have been simple enough to have your assistant call and say your caseload is too heavy or you think he would do better with a different therapist."

I look away, finding the tree outside the window that I've already become acquainted with. After some thought, I shake my head. "At first, I couldn't believe it was a coincidence that he was sitting in my office. I mean, what are the chances that the man that my husband—that we . . ." I take a deep breath. "That Gabriel Wright wandered into my office. There are four thousand psychiatrists in New York State. I looked it up the other day. If forty-three percent of the population of the state lives in the city, it stands to reason that seventeen hundred psychiatrists might be here. And Gabriel walked into *my* practice. On the first day I returned to work? Even if I put the accident aside, this is still a man I followed on a daily basis for quite some time. I even ran into him once."

"It does sound like an awful lot of happenstance. But I take it you've ruled out anything sinister going on, since you said '*At first*, I couldn't believe it was a coincidence.'"

I nod. "He'd have to be a sociopath to deliver such a compelling monologue in therapy. Gabriel Wright is just a broken man seeking help, who happens to have seen one of my advertisements, and my office happens to be not too far from where he lives."

"Why haven't you referred him to someone else?"

"Because I really think I can help him. Isn't it the least I can do when it's partially my fault his life is ruined?"

Dr. Alexander purses his lips. "You're justifying, Meredith. You have to know you've crossed a line with this. Following is one thing, but treating a man you have a serious personal connection with, without him knowing your true identity . . . It's not ethical."

I sigh. "Then I probably shouldn't tell you I also find myself a little attracted to him."

That does it. I have broken the ever-composed Dr. Alexander. He takes off his glasses and pinches the bridge of his nose.

I frown. "I've disappointed you."

He shakes his head. "I'm concerned for you. Both professionally and as a patient." He fits his glasses back onto his nose and leans forward, elbows on knees. "I don't have to tell you that there's a reason the Medical Code of Ethics bars physicians from having certain types of relationships with patients. Patients, especially mental health patients, come to us in very vulnerable states. Having any type of outside relationship that involves emotions can impair your judgment. You're playing with fire, Meredith. And that's just on a professional level. As your doctor, my concerns for what this could do to your own mental health are grave. It must be devastating for you to listen to how this man's life was ruined by the actions of your husband. Why would you subject yourself to this?"

My throat swells tight, like there's only a pinhole for air to travel through. I swallow a few times, attempting to ward off the sharp sting of tears. But it's no use. They spill over and stream down my face.

Dr. Alexander reaches for the tissue box and holds it out to me. "I'm sorry if I was harsh. I'm usually more restrained. But as a colleague, I feel a sense of obligation to remind you of the consequences."

I sniffle and blot my eyes. "There's no apology necessary. You're right. You're absolutely right. And I needed to hear it." I take a minute to compose myself. "You asked why I would subject myself to something that will cause me pain. It's because I deserve it."

Dr. Alexander's face softens. "Let's start there today . . ."

CHAPTER 17
Now

creen time average this week: 4 hours and 16 minutes per day.

"Go away," I mutter, swiping the notification so it disappears. I'm well aware of the ridiculous amount of time I've spent on my phone. And I'm also aware that 90 percent of it has been on this dating app. It's how I've distracted myself since my appointment with Dr. Alexander last week.

For once, though, at least my time is occupied by something other than Gabriel. I've started chatting with someone new. Someone I find interesting, even. That's a good thing. I should embrace that, and I do, typing a message to Robert, whom I swiped right on two days ago. When you swipe right for a guy—and he swipes right for you, too—a heart explodes across the screen, tiny hearts coming down like snowflakes. Then you have the option to message them. To reach out.

In a moment of weakness—or desperation—or maybe it was the three glasses of sauvignon blanc—I'd typed out a message and hit send. He'd typed back immediately. And now we can't stop.

My heart beats faster for a reason other than something to do with Gabriel Wright. My thoughts turn warm and fuzzy when a notification tells me Robert has sent me a new message. For the first time since the last time *you* told me you loved me and really meant it, I feel wanted. Which now, I realize, I've missed.

I tap out another message to Robert—add an emoji, then delete it, because maybe that's old-school? Do people still use emojis?

I haven't texted a man regularly in ages.

"Excuse me, Meredith?" My office door cracks open, Sarah peering through it.

"Yes?" I look up from the phone, fingers pausing.

She's silent, and for a second, I think something's wrong.

"What is it?" I ask.

"Oh, nothing. It's just . . . you're smiling. I haven't seen you smile in a long time."

"I am?" It takes a moment, and I realize I *am*, my mouth is drawn up in a smile—a *freaking smile*. That same warmth lighting my body.

"You look happy." Sarah opens the door wider, takes a half step in. "It's so good to see you like this."

A flush works its way up my face. I tilt my head down at the phone, then smile back up at her. "Promise you won't tell anyone?"

She laughs. "Who would I tell?"

"I don't know." The words come out fast, flustered. "I joined a dating app. I'm talking to someone." I've never sought Sarah's approval before. Never expected it or wanted it. I pay her to do her job, she does it well, and we exchange pleasantries appropriate for the relationship we have. But her face lights up, and I'm relieved.

"Oh, that's wonderful! I love dating apps. That's how I met Matthew. I don't tell people that, usually. They can be so judgmental about meeting people online. But I think everyone does it these days. People just don't like admitting it."

"Oh." I find myself nodding. "It's my first time, but this guy is really interesting."

"Tell me about him." Sarah perches on the edge of the chair closest to my desk, and suddenly I'm back in college, telling my roommate about *you*. Except you're dead, and I'm talking about a guy I've never met—to my assistant, of all people. But this is good. I need to do this, need to move on.

"Well, I don't know much. His name is Robert, and he's a doctor—"

Sarah squeals, and it makes me laugh—*laugh*. I tell her what little I know, warming up to the topic. He's an oncologist and works in a clinic. He likes tea, hates coffee, but I won't hold it against him—and a myriad of other random facts we've managed to share in our dozens of messages.

"So, do you have a date planned?" Sarah asks five minutes later.

The high of talking about Robert, about our messages, leaves me in a single exhale.

"No. Not yet." My gaze travels back to my phone, the screen dark, waiting for my finger to touch the glass and awaken it.

"Do you want to?"

I think about that a long moment, and I'm about to say yes—I'm sure I am—when a buzzer sounds from the outer room and Sarah leaps from the chair.

"Oh, shoot. I have the outer office locked because I was eating lunch. Your twelve o'clock must be here." She's gone in the next moment, and I'm left alone, staring at my phone. Thinking about whether I want to meet Robert—to see the real person behind the messages—or if maybe there's something magical in the *idea* of him. If maybe that's enough for now.

"Rebecca Jordan is here." Sarah stands at the door again, but she looks as though she has a secret this time. "New patient."

"Okay." I tilt my head. "Is something wrong?"

"No." She grins. "I just wanted to say, you should meet him." She winks and disappears.

A second later, a tall, slim woman is ushered in.

"Ms. Jordan?" I rise and cross the room, extending my hand. "Welcome."

She smiles back, and I can't help but notice she's gorgeous—not just run-of-the-mill pretty but stunning. Probably perfectly symmetrical. High cheekbones and a narrow jaw, heart-shaped lips. A faint blush to her cheeks. The sort of face you imagine someone will "discover" someday, and soon you'll see her peeking out of a magazine as the face of some brand. In fact, I'm not so certain I haven't seen her on a page already. There's a vague familiarity to her. Her hair is long and blond and so smooth she surely has had it treated with something. It extends almost to her rear. And though her insurance info shows she's twenty-three, she looks no older than someone in high school.

"Thanks. I'm a little nervous." She tucks a strand of hair behind her ear, looking everywhere but at me—not wanting eye contact, it seems. Hopefully, by the end of the session, I can help her feel comfortable enough to look at me.

"That's normal. I think most of my patients feel nervous when they first come in. Thankfully, by our second session, they're usually pretty relaxed. I think you will be, too." I observe her a moment as she crosses and uncrosses her legs. She tries to decide what to do with her hands before hugging them around her tiny midsection. Rebecca wears joggers and a strappy tank top, so she must have a jacket on the coat hook outside. It's not nearly warm enough to go without. I realize, suddenly, she's struck a chord with me— some maternal instinct to cover her up. To tell her it will all be okay. Usually I'm better at staying objective.

"I have a few questions I ask everyone at their first appointment, and then we can talk about whatever you like. Okay?"

She nods quickly, eyes still anywhere but on mine. I run through my list of questions, taking notes as I go. Minimal family support. She's in college but only part-time. Works at a coffee shop. No real friends, just a roommate she gets along with somewhat. Eventually, I get around to the most important question:

"So, what brings you in today?"

Rebecca goes still, as though bracing herself. "Um . . . It's kind of embarrassing."

"I've heard everything, Rebecca. I'm not here to judge you. I'm here to help you."

She nods slowly and sits a little straighter. "Okay. Well, I kind of have like a bad history with men. Um, my dad was never really around. My room-mate thinks that's why." She flicks her gaze to me—green eyes, flecks of amber in them—as though looking for confirmation that this is why she has this problem.

"Tell me more."

"Okay. I just . . . I always have a boyfriend. And I like that." Her voice speeds up a notch. "I mean, I like being with someone. But my roommate told me—she told me maybe I should take a break. But I don't want to take a break. And then she said that that's not normal. Not *not* seeing someone sometimes. Or at least between . . ." She stops and takes a moment to collect herself, smoothing a hand over her hair. "And when I'm with someone, I want to really *be* with them. I don't understand doing things halfway. Like, what's the point of casual dating if you know you want to be with him? If you're spending all your time together, why would you not just live together? And if you're living together, I mean, isn't that a *sign?* And why do—why do men get scared at that point? I mean, if they ask me to move in with them . . ." Her voice trails off, and I wait, letting her think.

"And then sometimes they just break it off, and that's not okay," she continues. "I mean, if you *love* someone, you don't just break up with them. My last boyfriend, this guy named Collin, he said I should think about if I liked the way my first name sounded with his last name—he said that after two dates. Two dates!" She looks at me now, so wrapped up in her story she's forgotten to hold back. Left the shyness behind. "So I think that means he's serious, and then one day he just texts me that he needs space. So I showed up at his job, which is *perfectly* reasonable, if you ask me. But he got . . ." Another pause. Another deep breath. Her hands lower to the couch cushions at her side, French-tipped nails scraping the fabric. "I mean, he called me crazy. He got a restraining order. I didn't deserve that. He's the one who said I should try out his last name. *He* was the crazy one, not me. He got all afraid of commitment and just . . ." Again, her voice trails off.

I feel my own heart pounding for her.

"But I can't give up on him."

"What do you mean?" I have a dozen questions scribbled down, but I'm not sure where to start. She's not the first patient I've had who's hurting from a broken heart. But something is different here. I want to let her continue talking, continue explaining.

"So, I can't go within a certain distance of him. But . . . but I know we're supposed to be together."

Unease tingles through me. I shift, tilting my head, urging her with silence to go on.

"So I created a fake Instagram account and followed him. And sometimes I—" She stops. "This all stays between us, right?"

"Yes. What you say here is confidential."

"Okay, good." She takes a breath. "I follow him sometimes, too. I know I shouldn't. But what if . . . what if he needs me? Like he went to the bar with his brother last weekend, and I know sometimes they drink too much. I had to make sure he got home safely. And I just want to know where he's going. You know?" She looks at me imploringly, like I'll tell her this is all normal.

But it's not normal.

In fact, her behavior is incredibly abnormal. The sort of thing that may indicate neglect and abuse in childhood. That may point toward undiagnosed PTSD or possibly even borderline personality disorder. Her affect alone is cause for concern—the quiet, shy girl who suddenly became the passionate, fervent young woman looking for approval in front of me.

And worse . . .

My own actions flash through my head. Following Gabriel. Stalking him on social media. Sitting outside his work for hours waiting for him to emerge. Searching for his wife's and child's graves.

Not to mention I'm his goddamned therapist.

How is what I'm doing any different than what Rebecca here is doing?

It's not.

"I even pretended I was someone else and messaged him. Just to see what he'd do. He told me he needed space, that he didn't have time to date. And I wanted to see if that was true or if he was lying to me."

I look up from my notes. Her voice has changed—anguish coming through the frustration.

I think about how when Gabriel told me he was on a dating app, I went home and spent hours swiping, to see if I could find him. Thankfully, I didn't. And I've since found Robert, who fills a void I hadn't realized needed filling. Yet I'd started down the same rabbit hole as Rebecca, hadn't I? It's not the same thing, exactly. Gabriel is not an ex-boyfriend I was stalking.

But maybe what I was doing was even worse. Because technically, I was a therapist stalking her patient.

Rebecca breaks down in tears, reaching for a nearby tissue box. I think about myself, across from Dr. Alexander, admitting truths not so different from Rebecca's.

But I stopped. I *did*. I made a choice, and I stopped, and I'm done now. I need to suggest to Robert that we meet in person for coffee or maybe a drink. I can move on. I *will* move on.

And yet my gaze travels over to the list of patient names on the printed schedule for tomorrow. *Gabriel Wright* is still typed there. I haven't canceled, even though I promised Dr. Alexander I would.

I look up at Rebecca and wonder if I'm qualified to be her therapist— since I'm clearly not doing much better than she is.

CHAPTER 18
Now

Robert: Would you like to have dinner Friday night?

My heart stops. A date. I haven't had one since Connor and I first met. The reality terrifies me, even though I've thought about it. Of course, what did I expect? I'm on a dating app, talking to a man for hours every day. Meeting is the next logical step.

Robert and I have been messaging back and forth since I got home from the office, but I don't respond right away this time. I need wine before I can decide how to reply. So I grab the open bottle of cab from the refrigerator door and pour myself a full glass. I'm still mulling things over fifteen minutes later when my phone buzzes.

Robert: You disappeared on me. Did I scare you
            away?

I smile sadly. He's attentive even when I'm not saying anything. I decide the best course of action is to be truthful. I've been on a roll with honesty lately, ever since Dr. Alexander's office last week.

Meredith: I'm sorry. I'm nervous. I haven't been on a
            date yet.

Robert: I get it. The first one was the hardest for me
            too. I won't push if you're not ready.

My shoulders relax a bit. This is exactly what I like about Robert. We
have so much in common. We're both doctors. Both lost our spouses in our
early thirties—though it's been eight years since his wife passed, and the
circumstances weren't as ominous as mine. Breast cancer.

My phone pings again.

Robert: Would you like to hear about my first date?

I smile.

Meredith: Sure.

Robert: I met a woman through a dating app. I
            thought we really hit it off great. It took me
            three weeks to work up the courage to ask
            her out. I got to the restaurant early. By the
            time she was due to arrive, I was going to
            have to keep my sports jacket on. Pit stains
            from profuse sweating.

I chuckle and sip my wine, watching the dots jump around as he continues to type.

Robert: Anyway, she stood me up. My first date was
            a nondate.

Meredith: OMG. All that stress for nothing.

Robert: Actually, I think it turned out for the best. It
            was like having a dry run. (Well, not so dry
            under the arms.) And the next time I went
            to meet someone, I wasn't so nervous. I'll

tell you what. Say yes to dinner. Get yourself
all dressed nice. I'll stand you up. Then you
can forgive me and we'll really go out. You'll
have your first-date jitters out of the way.

I smile from ear to ear. That happens often when I text with Robert.

Meredith: I don't think it'll work the same *knowing* I'm
going to get stood up. But I appreciate the
offer.

I sip my wine for a while, sucking on my bottom lip and staring down at my phone. This man is handsome. Very handsome, even. Intelligent. Funny. We have a lot in common. I want to move on. No, I *need* to move on. From Connor.

From Gabriel.

So I take a deep breath and bite the bullet.

Meredith: How about drinks instead of dinner?

He types back almost immediately.

Robert: Sold.

My heart races. Did I really just agree to a date? I believe I did.

Robert: I have to run. Evening rounds or I'll never
get home. I'll text you tomorrow so we can
pick a time and place. But you made my day.
Looking forward to meeting you, Meredith.

I sit in shell shock for a while after that. I can't believe I'm going out on a date, after all these years. I thought that part of my life was behind me.

Change in life plans is a common reason people wind up in my office. I think of what I'd tell a patient who was unexpectedly single and getting ready to hurl themselves back into the world of dating. I'd try to get them to acknowledge that their life has taken a new path and accept that we can't rewind time and change things. Then I'd work with them on living in the present. That's always the hardest part. Not dwelling on the loss. Not living in the past.

I finish my glass of wine and decide to follow my own professional advice. I can't move forward while tethered to yesterday. This time, when I pick up my phone, it's not Robert I text. It's Sarah.

> **Meredith:** Hey. I'm sorry to text you so late. But would you please call Mr. Wright first thing in the morning and give him Dr. Pendleton's number? Tell him our schedule is too full, and we think Dr. Pendleton will be a better fit.

> **Sarah:** But we're not full? We're looking for patients.

Sarah is rightly confused.

> **Meredith:** Please just do it, Sarah.

There's a pause before she texts again.

> **Sarah:** Okay, boss. Consider it done.

CHAPTER 19
Now

I'm doing it. I'm really doing it.

"So, what do you do for fun?" Robert pauses, laughs out loud. "Did I really just ask that? What a first-date line. My apologies, let me try again."

I find myself smiling at him, charmed by his ability to laugh, especially at himself.

"Okay, okay. Girl Scout cookies." He raises a thick, dark, inquisitive brow. "First of all, yay or nay?"

I consider. I do have a sweet tooth, though I usually deny it. But this is a first date. I may be out of practice, but I know this much—I'd rather go out with someone who's not afraid to eat a cookie now and again. And so I say, "Yes. Obviously." I take a sip of wine—we ordered a bottle of cab to share and are both two glasses in. I don't know if he's drinking as fast as I am because he's nervous, too, or if he just really likes his wine.

A waiter approaches. "Another bottle?" he asks.

Robert looks up. "Yes, please." No hesitation. He turns a wry grin my way. "Sorry. I'm assuming. Bad habit. Is that okay?"

A flush works its way from my chest to my neck. Our first date is going . . . well. Well-ish. I don't have much to compare it to.

"That sounds great."

"Perfect." He nods. "So. Favorite kind of Girl Scout cookie?"

I almost reply, but the way he stares at me so intently—I like it. I like *him*. We showed up at exactly the same time, which led to that awkward do-we-shake-hands-or-hug scenario (he went for the hug, much to my relief—shaking hands is for business as far as I'm concerned). So I don't answer. Instead, I ask, "Why don't you guess? Am I a Thin Mint type of woman or more of a shortbread? Or the chocolate caramel ones—what are they called?"

He screws up his face in exaggerated concentration. "Hmmm . . . You like red wine, so I'd say something with chocolate. But you don't seem like the Thin Mint kind. So I'll guess Caramel deLites?"

I almost spit out my wine. "You got it right! How did you know?"

Robert takes a long pull from his glass, looking quite pleased with himself. "Well, maybe I just have a feel for these things. Or for you." We share a smile. "Excuse me." He pushes back his chair. "I'll be right back, men's room."

He gives me a wink and walks toward a nearby hallway. Around us, the wine bar buzzes with conversation. It's a Friday night, and it's busy. I watch Robert's tall form as he strides away. He's a catch, no denying it. A doctor. Tall and handsome, with dark hair and large mahogany eyes. I could see myself getting lost in them, someday. Well, maybe. It is a first date. My *first* first date.

The server delivers the wine bottle a moment later, much to my relief. I pour another glass and take a gulp. I'd hoped the alcohol would calm my nerves, and I *am* feeling the wine, but my nerves aren't quite settled. I glance toward the hall, but Robert isn't headed back yet, so I grab my phone and swipe through the news and social media. I almost go to the dating app, but that's definitely poor form, checking it while on a date. I'm not really interested anyway, just need anything to keep myself from thinking too hard.

About the fact that I'm on a date.

About *you* . . . God, I just want to stop thinking about you.

And about *him*, too, of course. Is Robert attractive enough, funny enough, to distract me from both you and Gabriel? Maybe. He is funny. And just self-deprecating enough to take the edge off the MD from Georgetown.

A form draws close to the table, and I look up, smiling, expecting Robert.

But it's not Robert.

It's not the waiter.

It's . . . *holy shit.*

I blink a few times.

"Gabriel? I mean—Mr. Wright?"

He stares down at me. Robert might be handsome, might have eyes I could sink into, but Gabriel's gaze is piercing. Magnetic. And there's something there—some note of . . . *something.* I can't quite sort out what.

"Just Gabriel. Good to see you. What a coincidence, meeting you here."

My mind goes blank with shock. My mouth stumbles to form words, but nothing comes out.

Because it might have been a coincidence that we ran into each other when I was coming out of the alley that day—I was *stalking* him, after all. And it *might* have even been a coincidence that he walked into my practice.

But this is one coincidence too many.

And yet, oddly, I'm not frightened. Not even creeped out. In fact, I'm— shit. I'm a little turned on. His scruff is heavier than usual, his eyes a deeper shade of brown, too. The latter is probably helped by the dark-colored button-up he has on. If Robert made me flush, Gabriel has my breath coming in a nervous pant. And my armpits have gone damp. I cross my legs, because God, I better not be damp *there*, too . . .

He's watching me, a slight frown pulling at his bottom lip. "You okay?" he asks.

I realize I haven't said anything this whole time.

"Oh, just . . . surprised, I guess."

He leans closer and his scent hits me, masculine and spicy, and I want more than anything to reach up, to grab his shirt, and yank him closer. But I can't. *Ever.* It occurs to me that I had Sarah call him. Had her tell him he needed to seek help elsewhere. That maybe this is what's on his mind as he nudges out Robert's chair and sits down beside me—so close our knees touch as he makes himself comfortable.

"I live two blocks over. Sunny's is one of my favorite bars." He smiles, that nice, confident smile.

"Oh, really?" Again, I'm short of words. My head spins. It *is* close to his place. Which, of course, I suppose I knew when I suggested it to Robert. Not that I was *thinking* that, but what if . . . Shoot, what if this wasn't a coincidence, but not because Gabriel was following me but because *I* picked a place close to him? A wine place, no less, and I've witnessed—from following him around often enough—that he likes wine. Maybe it was *me* who unwittingly set us up for this moment.

And I can't lie, I'm not upset about it.

He nods. "Yep. Less than a five-minute walk. You live around here?"

"Not really. It's my first time here," I add, as though that explains it away. "I'm—" I'm about to say *on a date*, but Robert appears at that moment, hesitant, looking back and forth between us as though trying to judge the situation.

"This is Robert." I beckon to him. "Robert, this is . . ." I hesitate, not sure where to draw the line. Technically, Gabriel is a patient. I can't acknowledge that publicly, though. It would be a breach of privacy. "Gabriel," I finish. I don't explain how I know him, and from Robert's expression—bordering on contemptuous; maybe he *does* have a dark side—he clearly suspects Gabriel is another dating-app discovery. My vagueness isn't helping.

"Nice to meet you." He offers a perfunctory nod. "Mind if I grab my seat back?"

Gabriel hasn't said a word, and I look from Robert to him to find his face lacking an expression entirely. Something I've never witnessed, and I've had a fair amount of experience watching Gabriel by now.

"Of course." Gabriel stands stiffly, looking at me one last time. "I'll see you soon." He casts a last look at Robert as if to check for a reaction to that comment.

But Robert just meets his gaze with a tight smile. "Enjoy your evening."

Gabriel takes a step away, then spins on his heel. "Oh, Meredith—" I try to ignore the rush I feel at the sound of my first name on his tongue. I don't think he's ever said it before. "Your office called twice. I didn't get back to them yet. Is everything all right?"

"Oh, I'm . . . I'm not sure. Probably an insurance thing. No big deal."

He studies me, nods slowly. "Okay. Good night."

Robert reclaims his seat. Whatever uneasiness I thought I saw on his face a few minutes ago is gone now. I'm sure Gabriel's mention of my office, and his subsequent inference that our relationship is one of a doctor-patient type, has gone a long way toward smoothing the worry lines that were etched into his forehead. He smiles and launches into his own Girl Scout cookie preference—Trefoils, whatever the hell those are—and I try to focus on him. On those dark eyebrows and the warm eyes that minutes ago had drawn me in and kept my attention. But my focus is entirely on Gabriel, who now sits at a pub table at the other end of the bar with his back to me. Whenever Robert looks away, I steal glances. When he asks the server for a menu, I stare. And when Gabriel looks over his shoulder, meeting my eyes, I know I won't be able to do this for the rest of the night. Not with him sitting there.

"I'm sorry," I say to Robert just as he's about to order an appetizer. "I'm suddenly not feeling well. Would you mind if we continue this another evening?" I summon a smile. "I really have had a wonderful time. I'm just—I feel a headache coming on, and I get migraines. Sometimes wine does that to me. I shouldn't have had that last glass."

He tilts his head, studying me with concern. "Of course, Meredith. Let me pay, and I'll get you a cab."

We do the end-of-date stuff, wrapping up the conversation, promising to text or call soon, and Robert raises a hand to hail a cab as we step out into the cool evening.

"I'm just going to walk," I say. "I don't live far, and the fresh air will do me good."

He frowns. "Can I at least walk you?"

"I don't think I'll be good company. But thank you again. I had a really wonderful time."

"Maybe we can do it again next Wednesday?"

"Let me check my schedule. I'm working late one night next week, but I'm not sure if it's Wednesday or Thursday."

"All right. Please be careful walking."

"I will."

I can't breathe easy until I turn the corner. I slow my pace, but halfway down the block, I hear footsteps behind me. Like someone's following. I glance back, and there's someone there. But the streetlight misses their form, leaving only a tall, dark shadow on the sidewalk. One that's growing closer. My heart pounds, and I'm just about ready to run when a cab trawls by. I reach a hand up and wave for it.

Thankfully, the car pulls to the curb. I shove myself in, and once the door is shut, I turn back and look through the rear window. But whoever it was is already walking the other way, turning a corner. I catch the corner of a long coat. I can't even differentiate whether it's a man or a woman. But Gabriel had a full-length coat when I used to follow him.

Is he following me now?

Questions swirl around in my head like a tornado forming.

Why would he do that?

He walked right up to me in the bar.

Stalkers don't usually hide out in the open.

I should know.

Yet . . . he showed up tonight. Out of the thousands of bars and restaurants, Gabriel Wright walked into the *one* I was at on my date.

Though, I remind myself again, it was *me* who picked the place to meet Robert tonight. Out of the thousands of bars and restaurants in New York City, *I* told my date to meet me at a wine bar two blocks from Gabriel's apartment, when I knew for a fact that the man was a wine drinker.

So maybe the question I should be asking myself isn't *Is Gabriel stalking me?* but rather *Why am I still stalking Gabriel?*

CHAPTER 20
Now

"Hey." Sarah pops her head into my office. "Package for you."

"Oh, thank you. I ordered some new notebooks the other day."

She sets the box on my desk and lingers. "Would you mind if I leave at three today? I need to take my mom to the doctor. Your last appointment will be done by then."

My brows knit. "That's fine. But I didn't think I was done so early today? I thought appointments went until five."

"They did. But you had me fire your four o'clock, remember? Mr. Wright . . ."

A wash of panic rushes over me. "You spoke to him?"

She nods. "I had to call him three times, but I finally reached him this morning."

"How did he take the news?"

"Surprisingly well—no pushback. He was polite and said he understood."

I should be relieved, but some other emotion is there, too. I pause, searching for what it is, and realize I'm disappointed. And worse, distracted enough by my disappointment that it takes me another couple of seconds to appreciate the enormity of what's just happened. It's over. Gabriel is out of my life. Once and for all.

I'm lost in my head for I'm not sure how long, but when my line of sight finally comes back into focus, I find Sarah watching me. She tilts her head.

"Can I ask why you fired Mr. Wright as a patient? He's the *only* new patient you've had me refer out."

"It—I wasn't the right fit for him."

She bites her lip and takes a half step in. "We're friends, aren't we, Meredith? I mean, I know you're my boss and everything. But I like to think of you as a friend, too."

Clearly she's asking for a reason, so I hesitate before answering. "Umm, of course."

"Okay." She laughs. "I can see my even asking that question made you nervous. So I'm not going to pry too much. All I'm going to say is this: I know how by-the-book you are. But I also noticed the way Gabriel Wright looked at you the last few times he was here. And the way you looked at him. So if you *quit it so you can hit it*, I'm all for it. You go, girl. You deserve to be happy, boss." She winks, and I pretend heat isn't crawling up my face. "Your next patient will be here any minute. I'll go grab you your midmorning coffee."

I think my jaw is still hanging open when she closes the door.

The way Gabriel looks at me?

The way I look at Gabriel?

I shut my eyes and take a few deep breaths. If only Sarah knew exactly how *by-the-book I am.*

Luckily, I don't have time to dwell on her observation. I have patients starting soon and need to clear my mind, distract myself from all things Gabriel Wright. So I reach into my drawer for the letter opener and use it to slice open the packing tape in the middle of the box Sarah's left behind. What I find inside is definitely not what I expected. There are no notebooks. Instead, there is . . . a Hello Kitty figurine. At first I assume it's a mistake, a simple shipping error once again. But then my brain connects a bunch of dots I wasn't even aware were there. In psychiatry terms, I suffer a somatic flashback.

The photo in the newspaper the day after the accident.
The pool of red blood on the white concrete sidewalk.

Connor's mangled car off to the side.

The tarp covering a small body.

So, so small.

The Hello Kitty stuffed animal, no more than a foot from the dead little girl.

I clutch my throat. I can't breathe. *I really can't breathe.*

My hands are shaking, yet I somehow reach into the package and pull out the figurine.

The small covered body.

So, so small.

Abruptly, I drop the toy back into the box and pull over the flap in search of a label.

My name is there. And it's my address. But the wrong suite number.

Just like last time.

Sarah knocks and opens the door. "Your appointment is—" Her brows furrow. "Are you okay? You look pale."

"This isn't my package."

"What do you mean?"

"I ordered notebooks. I didn't order this."

She walks to my desk and peeks inside the box. "Oh, I love Hello Kitty. It's made such a resurgence lately."

"It has?"

She nods. "My niece has a big collection. It's kind of cool how long they've been around. I had them as a kid, too. Didn't you?"

I shake my head.

"Do you want me to email Amazon and send it back?"

I blink a few times. "You think it was a mistake?"

"Of course. What else could it be?"

A reminder? A threat? A warning? My mind immediately goes to that group that put up flyers. *Mothers Against Abusive Doctors.* Those people want me to never forget. I once had a patient whose abusive husband beat her to within inches of death. He'd been physically abusing her for years, but that time she finally had him locked up. Somehow he sent her gifts from prison—the same model pot he'd fractured her skull with, the wine bottle he'd smashed and used to slice open her face. It's called an anchoring tool—planting an item intended to paralyze someone with fear.

"Meredith?" Sarah puts a hand on my shoulder. "Are you okay?"

I swallow the lump of fear in my throat and nod. "Yeah. Just tired. That's all."

She doesn't look like she believes me, but at least she takes the box from my office so I don't have to look at it anymore. "I'll give you a few minutes before I bring Mr. Halloran in."

"Thanks."

Though a few minutes won't help. The damage is done. I'm on edge yet again. A Hello Kitty figurine. Not too long ago a book about a stalker. Coincidence? How many is one too many of those? Three? Six? Or do you not figure out the magic number until something really bad happens . . .

I'm still trying to wrap my head around everything when Sarah shows my first patient in. I'm not ready, yet I'm grateful for the interruption. Work has become my fortress, acting as a barrier from my negative thoughts and worries. Session one feels like driving over rough terrain. Session two, a few speed bumps. By the time my last patient arrives, I'm back to smooth sailing.

Henry Milton. He's been with me for years. Depression. And a pathological liar. The latter is a term people throw around to describe someone with a penchant for telling tall tales, but a true pathological liar is very different from a guy who describes his fish as twice its size or weaves stories about conquests that never happened. The average, common liar lies for a reason—to get out of trouble, to avoid embarrassment, to make themselves seem more important than they are. But a pathological liar makes up stories that have no clear benefit to them. It's a compulsion. And it's often difficult to tell if anything they're saying is the truth. They perfect their craft. But with Henry, I can usually recognize his lies by the level of detail and the outlandishness of the story.

"My friend got hit by a car," he begins today. "Prius. They're so quiet.

He was crossing on East Sixty-Fourth against the light. He made it halfway and—" He smacks his hands together. "Splat."

"Oh, that's terrible. Is he okay?"

He shakes his head. "He broke his back. Well, they're not sure if it was broken. Definitely sprained. But he was in a lot of pain. They went in to do exploratory surgery. He's originally from Ohio, so his parents were driving up to be with him. But he died on the table."

"He died during surgery?"

He nods but looks away. Another telltale sign that Henry is lying. I briefly ponder if Dr. Alexander can read me so easily.

"His parents are suing. They think it was the anesthesia. His father's a big-time lawyer, too. He's got commercials on TV. Real channels like Fox, not just local stations. And get this—the guy who was driving the Prius is a pretty famous actor. Well, not too famous. But famous enough that he'll probably have deep pockets for a settlement."

Now I'm certain this story is fabricated. Because he just keeps spinning it, like a spider—all different directions and round and round. If I don't stop him, in ten minutes the story will have morphed into something unrecognizable from where it started.

"Henry . . ." I use a stern but tempered tone. "Did your friend really have an accident?"

He frowns and changes the subject, rather than answer my question.

"I don't think the guy who was subbing for you while you were out liked me."

"Why do you say that?"

He shrugs. Then babbles on with a new story. This one about a woman he's started talking to who I'm not sure is real. I should be paying better attention, but I've been distracted all day. Ever since Sarah broke the news that a certain patient is no longer a patient. Of course, the *mistaken* delivery didn't help matters, either. Lately my life has felt a lot like trudging through mud. More and more things weigh me down as I go, but I have to keep pushing forward.

My buzzer goes off while Henry is in the midst of yet another story. I wait until he finishes and then wrap things up. Sarah pops in as soon as he's gone.

"I'm going to head out in a few. Are you sticking around?"

I nod. "I have some session notes to catch up on."

"I'm going to make myself a green tea for the road. You want one?"

"I'd love that. Thank you."

After she's gone, I stare down at my daily appointment sheet. Gabriel Wright is the only name not crossed off. Deep down I know cutting all ties is the right thing to do. There shouldn't have even been any ties to cut. Yet I feel a heavy sense of loss. And I can't stop myself from wondering a dozen *what-ifs* . . .

What if he wasn't who he was, and he and I had matched on the dating app instead of Robert? It's lunacy to even think about such a thing, yet I can't deny that part of me was attracted to him. Would I be dating him right now? Would I have met him for drinks the other night, instead of Robert? Would I have gone home with Gabriel? Slept with him? There's some sort of chemistry there. Sadly, his two-minute appearance during my date was a stark reminder that I *don't* have that with Robert. No spark. No fire. No pull. Which stinks because Robert is a great guy—the guy *I should've* been dreaming about last night, rather than my patient. Or *ex*-patient now.

I waste another hour sitting at my desk. My mind isn't focused enough to write the session notes I need to get done. So I decide to pack up for the day and take my work home with me. I have my own appointment with Dr. Alexander first, but maybe after that I'll take a bath with some lavender-scented salts to try to clear my mind. A glass of wine while I soak might help, too.

I haven't even touched the green tea Sarah made before she left. It's cold, so I nuke it in the microwave and dump it into my travel mug to take with me. As I get to the door, I'm still in the fog that's surrounded me all day. I'm also balancing an armful of files, my laptop, and my Yeti, and I have to shift it all to one side to dig my office keys from my purse. My nose is down as I swing the door open and walk through—and crash straight into a person.

One by one, the files in my hands start to slip, and I bend forward to catch them. Which causes my tea to tip over. I must not have sealed the lid right, because the plastic pops off and the entire contents of my large travel mug spill, all over the person I've crashed into. It happens in a split second.

"Shoot. I'm so sor—" I freeze when I get a look at the handsome face looking down at me.

Gabriel.

He reaches out to steady me as I wobble. "Are you all right?"

I stare. "I, uh, I didn't see you. What are you doing here?"

"I came to speak to you." He lifts his sopping-wet dress shirt away from his skin. "That's some hot stuff you got there."

I shake my head and snap myself out of it. I've just spilled scalding tea on this man. "I'm so sorry. Let me grab you something."

Gabriel follows me into the office, where I go straight to Sarah's bottom drawer. It's packed with ketchup packets, soy sauce, utensils, and wads of napkins from different takeout places. Grabbing a bunch of the napkins, I nervously blot at Gabriel's shirt. But when I feel the ridges of hard abdomen underneath, I realize I'm being inappropriate and apologize again, handing him the napkins.

He cleans up as best as he can.

"I really am sorry. I'll pay for your dry cleaning."

"That's not necessary."

"I insist." I take the wet napkins from his hands and toss them into the garbage. When I turn back around, the room is quiet, and there's no distraction to focus on anymore. Gabriel waits until our eyes meet to speak.

"Why are you dumping me as a patient?" he asks.

My heart races, and suddenly I feel how warm it is in here. "I, um, I have to apologize about that. We're too busy to take on any more new patients. I should've known that before we started working together."

Gabriel squints. "Too busy?"

I nod and look away. "I think you'll really like Dr. Pendleton. He's a wonderful listener."

His heavy gaze sears into my skin. "What if I pay you double?"

"Oh, no. This isn't about money. It really isn't."

Gabriel is quiet for way too long. I start to question if he can hear my heart smacking against my rib cage. When he does eventually speak, his voice is low—intimate, almost.

"Meredith?"

My eyes jump to meet his. I hate that I like the way my name sounds, rolling off his tongue in that soft tone.

"You're the first woman I've connected with since my wife died." He pauses, then adds quickly, "The first person, I mean."

I swallow.

"The other night after our session, I slept six hours straight. That's a record since . . ." He pauses and lets the unspoken words hang thick in the air. "Do you think maybe you could squeeze me in for a few more weeks at least? Let me get a little further along before I make the switch to someone new? I feel like I'm making real progress, and switching right now would only set me back."

I open my mouth to say no, but the words won't come out. How could I possibly say no to a patient at an important crossroads?

How could I possibly say no to helping the man I had a hand in destroying?

The answer is I can't.

So I take a deep breath and force a smile. "Sure. Of course. Give the office a call tomorrow and Sarah will get you on the calendar."

And just like that, I'm sucked back in again.

CHAPTER 21
Now

A trill of excitement shoots through me as I board the train to Dr. Alexander's.

I'd felt the loss of Gabriel all day. The awareness that I'd never see him again. At least, not unless I returned to my old ways. Which I was determined not to. I would go to work and help people. I'd go to the gym and work out. I'd write in my notebook, and go to my appointments, and be normal. Absolutely normal.

But maybe I knew, deep in my heart, it wouldn't be that easy.

Gabriel stopping by, begging for just a couple more sessions, well, it's like a balm to my soul. All feels right in the world again. Like when you've ended a relationship, then gotten back together, and just briefly, optimism makes you light and happy, like anything is possible. I catch my reflection in the glass as we pull into a station, see a smile tracing over my face. At least, until I notice another face in the glass—*one watching me.*

I turn in a flash, but it's too late—people are already shoving their way out of the train through the open doors. My imagination has been vivid lately. Too vivid. I need a distraction, so I pull out my phone and read Robert's latest message.

> Robert: On for Wednesday? What do
>   you think?

I tuck it away without answering. I don't know. It's hard to pursue much of anything knowing it's headed nowhere. Knowing my head is elsewhere—namely, with Gabriel. I reach in my purse and reapply lip gloss for something to do. Check my work email and watch my fellow travelers as the train comes to a stop. I step off, eyes glued to the back of a man who's clearly headed to exercise somewhere, with a gym bag over one shoulder and a protein shake in his opposite hand. He's tall and broad, with bulging muscles, but not nearly enough layers of clothes to stay warm. Why couldn't I obsess over someone like that? Someone who's not tangled up in what *you* did, someone who's not a patient.

I sigh. Just someone normal would be nice.

Then again, these days I don't feel so normal. Maybe abnormal attracts abnormal, and that's what draws me to Gabriel. Or it could be the shared trauma. Trauma sometimes bonds people, makes them cling to one another.

I arrive at Dr. Alexander's office ten minutes later, take a seat with a cup of tea his new assistant has prepared for me. It's herbal, decaffeinated, which is good—my pulse speeds away without any help, my mind still spinning from Gabriel's appearance. I can't stop replaying the way he begged me to continue seeing him. How he said I'm the only woman he has connected with since his wife died. I take a settling breath, remind myself that what's important is that I *help* him. This can't be about me.

"Dr. Alexander will be with you soon." His assistant pops his head in. "Sorry for the delay. He got tied up next door."

I nod in acknowledgment and reach for my phone, staring at Robert's text again. But nothing's changed, I'm still not sure how to respond. I click on his profile pic and stare, waiting for an answer to come to me. It doesn't, so I close the app and do something I haven't done in a long time. I go to the Columbia University website and navigate over to the faculty page. Scrolling to the English Department, I click on Professor Gabriel Wright. The moment his face appears, my heart starts to race. And I realize I've found my answer. Though not the one I wanted.

"Meredith! Sorry to keep you waiting."

I slide my phone back in my bag, hands trembling. I feel like I've been caught doing something naughty.

"Were you sending a message? You can finish." He waves a hand as he walks to his desk, opening drawers and searching for the right notebook, I imagine.

"I was, but it's okay. Sometimes it's good to make them wait." I try for a smile.

Dr. Alexander's eyebrows lift. "Oh. That makes it sound like it's a man."

"It is." This time, a real smile breaks through.

"Very good." He nods encouragingly, giving me space to go on, but not demanding it.

"I went on a date," I say. "On Friday."

"And now you're smiling at your phone. That's something. How do you feel about it?"

He's obviously referring to the man he thinks I was texting—which should've been Robert, not Gabriel, whom he almost caught me drooling over.

"I'm . . ." I search for honesty. I do want to be truthful with him when I can. Though he won't know our lines are crossed about *which man* I'm speaking of. "I feel glad. Happy."

Dr. Alexander nods and scribbles something. "I'm pleased to hear that. Will you be seeing him again?"

Yes. As soon as possible. As soon as Sarah schedules him.

"I hope so," I say.

"Do you think you're ready for something physical? It's okay if you're not. Lots of people date for a long time before they feel ready."

I switch the man he's asking about in my head this time, consider the thought of kissing Robert. Of touching him. I liked him enough, but no, I would not take him home with me. The bigger question is, why not? Why not let myself feel good, even if just for one night?

The answer comes to me easily enough, but it's not because of *you*. No, it's because there's someone else I'm attracted to, and I've always been a one-man kind of woman.

Gabriel.

I think of his mouth, his eyes. His thick hair. I think about a dream I had just last night, our skin on skin, his hands clasped in mine, his lips on my neck—

"I had a dream about that."

"And?"

My lips part, and for a moment I think he wants details. But of course, he's only asking how I feel about it. What I thought about being physical in my dream. The same thing I'd ask my own patients, because our dreams often reflect some element of our reality.

"It felt good," I say. "So maybe. Perhaps with the right person."

Dr. Alexander nods, satisfied. "And how is work going? You've been back a few weeks now, yes?"

"It's going well." I bite my lip and consider my words. Dr. Alexander tilts his head, looks at me over his glasses, and I know what he's waiting for. "I referred Gabriel somewhere else," I say. Which is true. I *did* have Sarah refer him out.

"Good job. I'm sure that was difficult. How did he take it?"

"He took it well." Technically, it's not a lie. But the pressure builds inside me—the knowledge that I'm doing something that could get me in trouble again. That like my own pathologically lying patient, I'm untruthful to my therapist. But I'm not pathological—these are normal lies. Tiny white ones. And this time, it's for Gabriel's benefit, not mine.

He said I was *helping* him.

"It sounds like you're making real progress, Meredith," Dr. Alexander says.

I settle back into the couch, a serene smile on my face. "I couldn't agree more."

CHAPTER 22
Now

T hank you again for agreeing to see me for a little while longer."

Gabriel's beard is gone. It's the first time I've seen the angular lines of his jaw, the fullness of his lips. I'd liked his scruff. But this—this is a whole different level. He notices me staring, so I have to say something.

"I'm sorry." I smile and motion to my own chin. "You look so different without your beard."

He flashes a crooked smile. "Different good or different bad?"

Considering he's been hiding bone structure that would make a sculptor weep and lips women would pay a small fortune for, I definitely prefer seeing more of him. Yet I go for the objective answer.

"You can pull off either look."

"That's a very safe response. Something like I might give a woman if she asks me which dress looks best."

"Well, I suppose this way, clean-shaven, I can see more of your face. It shows your expressions more, which helps me understand what you're feeling better. So for professional reasons, I'll go with no beard."

"Uh-oh." He smirks. "I'd better grow it back if you're going to be able to see what I'm feeling."

I smile. He's in a playful mood today. Borderline flirty, even. I'm curious why.

I rest my hands on the closed notebook on my lap. "So how have things been since our last session? Anything new going on?"

Gabriel looks down at his feet. "It's a little embarrassing to talk about, but yeah, something has *come up*." He looks at me with a shy smile, reads the confusion on my face, and laughs. "My sex drive has sort of come back."

I swallow past a lump of unexpected jealousy in my throat. "I see. So you've met someone?"

"No, I just meant—well, it's been a long time since I wanted any pleasure." Gabriel lifts his hand and wiggles his fingers. "Even self-pleasure."

Oh. *Oh!*

The jealousy rising through my chest with a burn just seconds earlier is replaced by something different. Something *very, very* different.

This man.

That hand.

I'm thankful I don't blush that easily.

I clear my throat. "Well, sexual deprivation as a form of punishing oneself is pretty common. You've previously expressed that you felt guilt when you went out on a date, that it felt wrong to be with another woman because you still felt married."

"Which is fucked-up." Gabriel shakes his head. "Sorry. Excuse my language. But it's crazy to me that I could feel like that when our sex life had been pretty much nonexistent for a long time."

I shift in my chair and open my notebook. "Let's talk about that. You mentioned your wife had an affair. How long before she passed away did that occur?"

Gabriel scoffs. "Which one are we talking about?"

My heart squeezes. "Oh. I didn't realize there was more than one."

He looks away. "Why do people cheat?"

"That's a very big question, with many answers."

"Tell me some of them. The answers, I mean."

We talk for a long time about the possible reasons people stray—commitment issues, revenge, emotional disconnect, unmet needs, low self-esteem, even simply falling out of love. When our conversation comes to a lull, I fold my hands.

"Do any of the reasons we've discussed feel like they might be the answer you're looking for?"

"More than one, actually." He sighs and smiles sadly. "But can we go back to this sexual-deprivation thing you mentioned? I wouldn't have to do it intentionally for it to happen?"

I shake my head. "No, we do a lot of things to ourselves unconsciously as a form of punishment—self-sabotage, procrastination, alienating ourselves from others. There are many different types of deprivation that can be acts of self-punishment. The harder we discipline ourselves, the more we can ease whatever feelings of guilt we have."

"It's been nearly two years. I'd say my punishment was pretty severe."

I smile and scribble a note on my pad.

"If I'm, you know, taking care of business myself again," he continues, "does that mean my punishment is over? That I won't feel like crap the next time a woman puts it out there that I should stay the night?"

"I don't know that your mind deciding it's time to ease up on your ability to feel pleasure alone is the same thing as your conscience giving you free rein to be with women."

"Has enough time passed, though? How long are you supposed to wait?"

"There isn't a set timeline for these things. Everyone is different. Only you know the answer to when you're ready."

Gabriel seems to think about that for a moment. Then he lifts his eyes to mine. "What about you? How long did it take you to get back in the saddle after your divorce?"

I smile. "I'll have to let you know on that."

Gabriel lets out a hearty laugh. "Well, at least it's nice to know I'm not the only one depraved."

I smile. "Deprived, not depraved."

My eyes drop to his mouth. When the tip of his tongue peeks out and glides along his bottom lip, I feel it everywhere. *Everywhere.*

There's a crackle in the air as my eyes lift and meet his. At least, there is for me. My heart slams against my ribs. My breaths grow shallow and rapid. *Oh God.* Maybe it's just me? But I can't seem to unlock my eyes from his. And then . . .

The buzzer goes off.

I'm not sure if I'm more relieved or more disappointed, but it effectively kills the moment, the one I'm still not sure whether I was alone in feeling.

I clear my throat. "Well, it seems our time is up."

Gabriel's eyes give nothing away. "I guess we pick up where we left off next week?"

Normally, I don't rush a patient out the door, but today I stand to move things along. I need a minute to myself. Maybe an hour. Maybe a day. And definitely a tall glass of cold water. Possibly a shower.

Gabriel is quiet as he makes his way out. He stops and turns back with his hand on the doorknob. "Any dates in the near future at Sunny's?"

"No."

He flashes a smile. "See you next week, Doc."

It's after midnight, and I'm still obsessing over my session with Gabriel today. The attraction. The spark. It's been a long time since my senses came alive like that. Not since *you.* Even all these hours later, the yearning inside me is so overwhelming that I can't seem to relax enough to sleep.

I stare up at the ceiling in the dark. Every time I shut my eyes, I picture the way Gabriel looked today. Piercing eyes, that sexy ghost of a smile playing on his lips, the way his tongue ran along the flesh of his mouth . . .

Sweat breaks out on my forehead as I think about what he would've done if I'd made a move.

Would he have kissed me back?

I imagine Gabriel's lips crushed to mine.

My nails digging into the skin of his back.

Him inside me.

Vi Keeland

Hard.

Deep.

Oh God.

The rational part of me itches to rear its ugly head and berate me for even thinking about a patient this way. And not just any patient, of course. But the irrational part of me is stronger tonight. It wants to be reckless. So I do something I haven't done in a *very* long time. I reach into my nightstand to take out my vibrator.

It hums to life with a sound that immediately sets my body on fire, and I trail it painstakingly slowly along my skin—down my chin, over my collarbone, pulsating on my nipples until I'm trembling. Then still lower and lower until it slips into my panties and I open my legs wide, feeling the build of an orgasm already forming. Like thunder before the storm.

Maybe Gabriel was right after all. We're depraved, not deprived.

CHAPTER 23
Now

I'm tidying the apartment Sunday morning when my phone rings. I pause, mid-pillow-fluff, and look across the room to where the screen is lit up.

I don't get many calls these days.

Well, that's not really true. I do get calls. I just don't answer them. Irina reached out just the other day. She left a message inviting me to lunch. But I can't face her. It's hard to face anyone from that part of my life—*the Connor and Meredith decade*. I'm ashamed. So much of my life feels like a lie now.

But it might be important, might be the after-hours phone service calling about a patient in crisis. I replace the pillow and hurry across the room, feet padding over soft carpet. I'm thinking I should sell the place. Get a new apartment, or maybe a smaller one. Just one that's not so . . . you.

My brother's name crosses the screen, and I swipe to answer.

"Jake," I say. "How are you?" We haven't spoken since . . . I'm not sure when. Christmas? Our communication is mostly in the form of texts or exchanging memes on social media.

"Hey, Mer, how's the weather in the city today?"

I laugh, because he works here and lives a train ride away in Connecticut. His weather is likely within a degree of mine today, yet he always acts like he's across the country.

"Good. Today is a little warmer, finally. How are the girls?"

"Great. They're both doing soccer this spring."

"Good exercise."

"I think they mostly just sprint down the field in a herd after the ball, but you gotta start somewhere."

"Mmhm." I perch on the couch and reach for another pillow to fluff. It's not that I don't like talking to Jake. It's that I can already tell he called for a reason, and he's just being polite, playing catch-up before we dive into whatever it is. His tone gives it away, his forced casualness.

"So what's up?" I ask.

"Well . . ." Jake clears his throat. "I've been working on the life insurance claim for Connor."

"Oh." The blood drains from my face. I can *feel* it, my whole body chilling at his words. I haven't wanted to deal with it, to even think about receiving anything after what he did. So I told Jake he could handle it. I signed a form giving him power of attorney, and I'd forgotten about it.

"It's been a battle. The life insurance company doesn't want to pay out. Neither does the team pension plan. They're saying he died while committing a crime, which is an exclusion from policy benefits."

While committing a crime.

Which crime? Stealing prescription pads? Killing yourself? Killing them? Driving under the influence? It could be so many things. You fucked up so badly. *I* fucked up so badly.

"Of course, it was never determined that Connor actually committed a crime. There were no criminal charges or trial. We never got to put on a defense."

I think of the detective, of my admission to him. *It was my fault.* But he waved me off as if to say *go home, live your life.* As if I could.

"But the good news is we negotiated a seventy-five-percent payout. It's a lot of money, Meredith. This could change things for you."

"Change things?" The words come out like they taste—bitter. "It doesn't change anything, Jake." I'm still alone. My husband is still dead. Gabriel Wright's family is forever lost to him. I rack my brain for what to do. The last thing I should get is a lot of money—I've done nothing to earn it. If anyone committed a crime, it was me. I don't deserve it. And I sure as hell don't want it.

"I don't care about the money."

"Well, it's arriving tomorrow." There's a lapse of silence, Jake probably waiting for me to give in. To say *well, okay, fine.* But the idea of any money being deposited into my account, almost as a reward for my inability to take action, to stop you from doing what you did, to stop three people from dying—it's too much to even consider.

"No. I don't want it."

"Meredith, what do you want me to do? I can't just stop payment. I spent months negotiating this, making sure you got what you're due—"

"You're not listening." I pick up the nearest pillow and squeeze it to my chest. Squeeze anger and frustration into it. "I don't *want* it. You know what? Send it to the family Connor destroyed."

"What?"

"Send it to them. They lost a mother, a daughter. If anyone deserves it, it's them. They should have sued the estate and taken it all anyway. I wish they would have."

"This is money your husband *worked* for. It's his retirement savings, the insurance plan he paid into. It's almost three and a half million dollars—" Jake's words come faster, like I'm a client he can convince.

"No. I'm serious. Send it to the family. Keep my name off it. Put Connor's name on it—only his—say it's from his estate. Okay?"

"Meredith, I know you feel this way now, but what if—"

"Please just do it, Jake. I'm not going to budge. Not ever. And I need to go. Thank you for handling everything for me." I disconnect the call, essentially hanging up on my brother. My head sinks into my hands, and I sit there for I don't know how long—maybe twenty minutes, maybe an hour. My phone buzzes, probably Jake texting because he knows me well enough to realize I won't answer a call. At some point, I'll have to apologize to him. I know he's gone above and beyond, but I need him to respect my wishes on this.

Eventually, I raise my head. The light has changed, late morning shifting to early afternoon. I rise and go to the bedroom, change my clothes, pull on a jacket, grab my notebook, and go outside.

It's time for a walk. A long, meandering walk to clear my head. The sort I used to take, before Dr. Alexander told me to walk on the treadmill. It's better outside now than then. The soft spring breeze rustles through the budding trees. The sidewalk, uneven in places, requires my brain to focus and pulls it away from deeper, darker thoughts. I wander past shop windows, stealing glimpses at all varieties of people.

At some point, I buy a coffee. Later, a croissant. I briefly stumble across my old path, the one I used to follow Gabriel on. But today when I reach the university, I don't stop. I take a turn and keep going. The sun is no longer overhead but on the horizon. Not quite golden hour. But soon. I keep walking. I'll get a cab home. I'm somewhere new now, where buildings become unfamiliar.

Orange streaks across the sky as I come down a hill and find a vast lawn surrounded by a wrought-iron fence. It's a cemetery, one I've never seen or explored.

One I've never searched for their graves.

It's too late for anyone to be in the little building where I might inquire as to whether the Wright family is buried here, so I walk row after row of headstones. It's well-kept, soft, green grass beneath my feet. Fresh flowers planted here and there. Some stones are older, but most are new—from the 2000s.

When my gaze happens across two identical stones, I pause. Not just identical, like husband and wife, but both polished to a sheen. New. As though they were placed at the same time, and that time was not so long ago.

Ellen Wright.

Rose Wright.

I've found them. Air rushes from my lungs as I sink to my knees in front of their names.

Gabriel's family. The grass has grown in over their graves. But the date of death is right. It's a day I'll never forget. I open my mouth as though I'll say something to them—*I'm so sorry* or maybe *He misses you.*

But they don't need to hear that from me. Hot tears trickle down my cheeks. Of course he's been here. Roses placed atop each headstone that are just starting to wilt show that much. He's surely visited and said what he's needed to say to them, probably a hundred times over. They lie here because of *you*. Because of me.

A sob tears its way out of my throat. My hands tremble as I reach out and touch the headstones, wishing I could somehow change this. Make this better.

I stay there a long time. The world grows dark around me. I should be concerned for my safety, but I'm not. It would serve me right to suffer at the hands of someone else. A shadow walking across the graveyard toward me, silhouetted against a single streetlamp, finally makes me move. I take one last look at the graves, noting that the stones say *Beloved Daughter* and *Beloved Mother*, but there is no mention of *wife*—strange—and I'm on my feet.

Across the cemetery is a road, and I walk that way, not looking back until I'm a safe distance. When I stop and glance over my shoulder, the visitor is standing where I was. At Ellen's and Rose's graves. Even in the darkness, I can feel the penetration of their gaze. I wish I could see who they are—or even if they're male or female. Maybe it's the groundskeeper, and they were coming to tell me to clear out now that it's dark.

I wave for a cab, and seconds later, one comes to a stop. Pulse racing, I climb in—but I can't stop myself from looking back again. Chills run up my spine when I find the person still hasn't moved. It feels like they're watching me.

"Where to?" the cabdriver asks.

I give him my address, and the cab pulls away from the curb.

But the dark figure remains in the graveyard . . . watching.

CHAPTER 24
Now

I've counted the days, so it's difficult to pretend I'm not anxious when Gabriel walks in the following week. Yet somehow I manage to maintain my composure. Crossing my legs and settling my notebook on my lap, I offer a tempered smile.

"How was your week?" I ask.

He blows out a breath. "It was tough. I finally wrote that letter you suggested I write to my wife." Gabriel shakes his head. "It was a lot harder than I thought it would be."

I nod. "It's often a cathartic experience, but it also stirs up a lot of emotions to get there. How did you feel while writing it?"

"Angry mostly."

"Because of the cheating?"

He looks me straight in the eyes. "Angry because some selfish bastard decided he was above the law and got behind the wheel and killed my wife."

I swallow and my hands begin to shake. I need to hold something to keep them steady before he notices. So I stand somewhat abruptly and point to my neck. "Excuse me. I'm just going to grab my water. My throat feels scratchy. Allergies."

He nods but stays quiet.

I take my time walking to my desk and make a production out of twisting the cap off a bottle of water, then guzzling half of it down. When I return to my seat, I hold the bottle with two hands to keep them occupied.

"Sorry about that."

"No problem."

He's watching me closely. Does he always watch me this closely? Why does it feel like he can see into my heart and read the black lies? Or am I imagining it?

I take a deep breath and sit up taller. "So, you were talking about the letter. You said you were angry while writing it, but how do you feel now?"

He shrugs. "I'm not sure it will help overnight, but I guess it made me remember the positive things about our marriage. I wasn't sure how to start the letter, so I wrote about the night we met. I sort of crashed her blind date."

"Oh? That sounds interesting. Are you comfortable sharing the story?"

Gabriel looks away. His eyes go out of focus like he's visualizing things. "I was supposed to meet some colleagues at a bistro a few blocks from Columbia. I got there early and was seated at the bar. Ellen walked up and ordered a glass of wine. She was beautiful, so I struck up a conversation. But she politely shot me down. Told me she was there to meet someone—a blind date. I made her laugh, tried to get her to ditch the guy, though she was too kind to stand anyone up. Got her to make a deal, at least. I would keep my eye on her, and if her blind date turned out to be a dud, she'd give me a signal, and I'd rescue her with some sort of excuse. The signal was supposed to be that she would push a lock of her hair behind her ear. Ten minutes into the date, Ellen scratched her nose, so I walked over and pretended to be her cousin. Told her our grandmother was sick, and we had to go to the hospital. She sort of had no choice but to go along with it at that point. When we got outside the bar, she scolded me because she hadn't pushed her hair behind her ear. I lied and told her I'd thought the signal was her scratching her nose. She called me out on being full of shit. We argued. Then I convinced her to have dinner with me."

I smile. "That sounds like the opening of a romance novel, a meet-cute."

"It gets better. Turns out Ellen was a student at Columbia. We were still on summer break. School wasn't due to start until the following week. But when she asked what I taught, and I told her Shakespeare, she called up her schedule on her phone. Sure enough, she was in one of my classes."

"Oh my gosh. So what did you do? Can you date a student as a professor?"

"Technically it's a violation of the code of conduct. But we kept things quiet."

"Wow. Well, I suppose it was fate in some ways."

"We went back to the bistro where we met for Valentine's Day every year, which was also Ellen's birthday. I suggested we go somewhere nicer once, but she said she liked to celebrate the day by remembering her favorite gift—the day we met." Gabriel sighs. "Things were good at the beginning."

"Even though the letter was difficult to write, it seems to have done you a lot of good. You smiled when you just spoke about your wife. It's an important step in the grieving process to be able to talk about the person we lost, remember the good times."

He nods. "I guess. Maybe I'll be less angry when I punch in my PIN from now on. Everything is her birthday—from my ATM code to door codes."

I smile. "What did you do with the letter after you were done? I don't think we talked about it, but some people find burning the letter symbolic of letting go after everything has been said. Others prefer to seal it up and keep it somewhere safe."

"I actually got rid of it already. I brought it to her grave, along with her favorite flowers, and planted them both in the ground."

My brows dip together. "When?"

Gabriel's eyes meet mine. "When did I bury the letter?"

I realize it's a strange question, the specific day of the week isn't relevant to his therapy, so I do my best to cover up. "Yes, I meant did you bury it the same day you wrote it? I'm just wondering if you gave yourself enough time with it."

Of course, there is no time requirement. My curiosity has gotten the best of me, and the question popped out of my mouth before I could think it through.

"I wrote it Friday and went to the cemetery over the weekend," Gabriel says.

My eyes widen, remembering *the person who watched me leave.*

I had been at the cemetery on Sunday, and there were no flowers planted. Just some wilted roses on top of the headstones. The ground was overgrown and hadn't been disturbed. If he'd come earlier in the weekend and planted something, I would have noticed, which I didn't. So he had to have come *after* me.

Was he the person who had watched me leave?

No. No. No. Of course he wasn't. If Gabriel had seen me, he would've said something, asked what the hell I was doing at his family's graves. He certainly wouldn't be sitting here today acting like nothing happened.

Would he?

Jesus Christ. Of course not. Why would he do that?

My paranoia is really getting the best of me today. I suppose that's what happens when you're hiding secrets. You assume everyone else is, too.

I have a difficult time focusing on anything we talk about for the remainder of our session. Luckily Gabriel seems to be in a talkative mood this week, and I can get away with a bunch of *"tell me more about that"* and head nods. For the first time, I'm desperate for his hour to be over. I need to wrap my head around some things we've talked about today. There are only a few minutes left when our conversation comes to a lull. I don't want to dive into another probing topic with so little time left, so I ask what I *think* is a safe question.

"Anything else new and exciting happen over the last week?"

Gabriel frowns. "I almost forgot. I got a check from the estate of the guy who murdered my wife and daughter. Un-freaking-believable. What balls on that family."

I stiffen. "Why does that upset you?"

"My brother tried to get me to sue after the accident. I didn't, because what is money going to do? It can't make up for the loss of lives. It would feel like I was trying to cash in. I don't want that blood money."

My heart races. I'd convinced myself it was the right thing to do, to give Gabriel the money. But maybe I was being selfish, trying to wash *my* hands clean of the blood.

"What about if you used the money for good? You mentioned your daughter had a hearing deficiency and wore hearing aids. Perhaps you could start a foundation to help hearing-impaired children who couldn't otherwise afford devices to assist them?"

He shakes his head. "I don't know. Maybe?"

"Or donate it to a shelter or some charity that is meaningful to you, or perhaps one that was meaningful to your wife."

"I guess."

The buzzer goes off. I've never been so grateful for a session to end. Lord knows how many more times I'd stick my foot in my mouth if we had another ten minutes.

I force my best warm smile while I reach for the timer.

Gabriel rubs his palms on his pants. "Maybe you're right. A foundation isn't a bad idea."

I nod. "Take your time and think about it. I'm sure you can find a lot of good to do with three and a half million dollars."

The moment the words come out of my mouth, everything freezes as I recognize what I've done. *Oh God. I think I might be sick.*

Gabriel squints. "How did you know the check was for three and a half million?"

"Um, you must've mentioned it."

He studies me, his head tilting ever so slightly. "I don't think I did."

I smile. I'm a nervous wreck, so it feels forced. Too big and broad, all teeth and gums. I pray I don't look deranged. "How else would I know?"

He holds my eyes for what seems like forever but is probably not more than ten seconds. Then he smiles. "Yeah. Of course. Same time next week?"

CHAPTER 25
Now

Overthinking is apparently my new thing. Or maybe I'm just now recognizing it in myself. I pace my apartment, reliving my session with Gabriel over and over. And not just what I said—my massive screwup that he obviously noticed—but also the way he looked at me after.

Did he know?

Did I blow it?

Or was it all in my imagination? And everything's fine, and he'll come back like nothing ever happened next week.

Next week.

Shit.

I sink onto the edge of my bed and stare blankly at the wall. I can't do this. I can't keep seeing him. Not when there are so many secrets, when I'm so heavily intertwined with his life and he doesn't even know it. Unless he does. But again, that's all speculation, likely a production of my guilty conscience.

I'm just trying to help.

Right?

I don't even know anymore. I tried to help, and the money only made him upset.

I go to the kitchen and find the wine cooler nearly empty. All that remains is a Riesling, too sweet, too heavy, like honey. But it'll do. I pour a glass and lean against the floor-to-ceiling window that looks out over the city, contemplating it all. I was so glad to still have a view into Gabriel's life. But now that view threatens to expose me.

I swallow more wine, wandering from one room to another. A ghost, haunting my own home. Worse, a ghost who drinks too much. I ignore my phone when it pings with new messages on the dating app, silence an alarm to remind me to send an email for work. My mind is too muddled anyway. I swear the sweet wine goes to my head faster. Eventually, I sit down and catch up with a dozen notifications—a request for a refill through my work email, a message from Sarah reminding me about a last-second schedule change. Three messages wait for me on the dating app, but I'm not sure there's any point.

Another glass of wine.

Leaning back in the recliner you loved so much—the right bend to your knees, you said, to let your sore back relax—I think about a dozen threads that could unravel in a second if Gabriel realized I've followed him, that I have my own personal notebook of his comings and goings, that I've stalked his family's grave site, that I'm *your* wife. Your widow.

Another random thought hits, and I suddenly bolt upright. *What if Jake didn't do as I asked and my name was included with the check he sent?*

I grab my phone, move my fingers along the surface, pressing to go from screen to screen until I reach my destination, until a distant ringing comes through the speaker.

"Hello?" A man's weary voice greets me.

"Jake, I need to ask you something."

"Mer? Are you okay?" He coughs. "Jesus, it's one in the morning. What's wrong?"

I pause hearing how late it is, remembering that I finished most of that bottle of sweet wine on my own. And now I'm calling my brother in the middle of the night, likely waking his wife, his family . . .

"I asked you to make sure my name wasn't on the check. Or any of the paperwork."

Jake doesn't respond. Likely he's confused.

"The check, Jake! For the family Connor killed."

"Jesus, Mer. You woke me up for this? I told you I'd take care of it. Your name wasn't on anything. Everything came from the Estate of Connor Fitzgerald."

"You're sure?" My voice comes out too high, too desperate. Even I can hear it.

"I did what you told me. Now tell me what's going on. What's happened?"

"Sorry. I'm sorry." I want to let the phone fall from my hand. Want to curl up in a ball and sleep and pretend today never happened. Pretend the last two *years* never happened. But Jake will only call back. He might even show up at my door. "I'm okay. I promise. I'm sorry I woke you. I just—I can't sleep. My mind started circling."

"I'm concerned. You don't sound like you can't sleep. You sound frantic."

"I'm fine. Really. I'll text you tomorrow, okay?" I don't wait for him to reply. Instead, I hang up, stare at the phone, and start making a mental to-do list. At the top of it: *Tell Gabriel our time is over.* I agreed to a few more weeks. That's come and gone. I'll do it first thing Monday. I have to.

But for now, I need a distraction. Anything will do. So I go back to my phone, opening one app at a time—the weather app (rain tomorrow), my email (ugh, deal with it Monday), social media (too many happy wives and smiling children; don't they care at all about how it makes people like me feel?), and last, the dating app. Because I have nothing to lose.

The new messages waiting are from men looking for a sugar mama. Men who think posing with cans of beer is attractive. Men who actually mention their ex-wives in their profiles. One red flag after another.

Why can't I meet someone normal?

Then I remember, I have. The doctor. Robert.

I'll need more wine for this. I wander into the kitchen, almost fall on my face stumbling over my own two feet, and arrive at the empty bottle I've consumed. I've forgotten I poured the last drops only ten minutes ago.

I won't feel well tomorrow, but if I already know I won't feel well, why stop?

I find a tiny bottle of prosecco hidden in the back of the fridge and un-twist the top, let the cork pop out, and sip at the bubbles as they spill over and onto my hand. I lean over the sink, keeping the wine from making a sticky mess on the counter.

And I can't help but think of *you*. How you'd stumbled around the kitchen in search of whatever alcohol you could get your hands on near the end.

I push that thought from my mind in favor of downing my bottle of prosecco. After it's empty, I decide it's a good idea to send Robert a text.

> Meredith: Don't you owe me a second date?

I completely ignore the previous messages—the one where I told him I'd check my schedule and get back to him, the several that followed where he checks in, but I never responded. I ghosted him, just like the story he shared with me about his first date back in the dating game.

Seconds tick by, then a minute. Somewhere in there, my eyes focus on the time—1:32 a.m. Jesus. I forgot it was so late. Again. I'm about to toss my phone down, let myself slump over on the couch and pass out.

But it chimes, a new message comes in. I straighten and read it.

> Robert: Is this a ghost?

It takes me a second to get what he means—he's giving me a hard time. For ghosting him. I smile and write back.

> Meredith: Sorry. Work has been busy.

> Robert: I'm surprised to hear from you, to be honest.
> The headache excuse is the oldest one out
> there.

> Meredith: I really did have a headache. Maybe *I* owe
> *you* a second date.

I tap my fingernail against the empty bottle of prosecco, suddenly flush with giddiness. I'm excited to talk to him. Too excited. I force myself to take a deep breath and consider that—consider *why*. If I were my therapist, what would I think?

That I'm lonely, probably.

Maybe that it's good for me to be talking to anyone besides Gabriel.

> Robert: Maybe.

My heart does a funny thing—*maybe*. Like maybe he doesn't want to talk to me. To see me again. But the three dots pop up, indicating he's still typing.

> Robert: It's late. Unless you're in, say, London. In which case it's early. Are you in London?

My chest squeezes with joy. He's teasing me. Flirting.

> Meredith: I wish. Maybe we should go.

> Robert: Sure. Right now?

For a second I imagine it—meeting him at the airport, hopping on the first flight to London. Taking a vacation with a handsome near-stranger. The exhilaration of doing whatever I want in that moment. I could do it. I could. My passport is in the safe. An Uber is five minutes away. I start to type back—Yes, let's do it! But he replies before I can.

> Robert: Ahh, to be young again. To be able to leave at a moment's notice. I'll have to take a rain check on globe-trotting, but maybe international cuisine is the next-best thing? Tomorrow night?

And here I was going to tell Sarah to move my appointments. I was going to do it. Take off, abandon my life on a whim. I was excited about it, too. Or maybe I'm just drunk.

Meredith: Perfect!

———————————

Morning comes late for me, the sun well above the horizon when I open my eyes and find myself staring at the living room ceiling. A throw is half over me, like I dragged it down when I got cold in the middle of the night. My neck aches as I sit up, reminding me I'm not in my twenties anymore. I can't just pass out wherever.

Speaking of passing out. I squint at the nearby coffee table. A big bottle of Riesling. A tiny bottle of prosecco.

Jesus. I must have drunk them by myself, because I sure as hell didn't have company. I search the couch cushions for my phone and check the time—11:08 a.m. It's the day I work late, so my appointments don't start until noon, but I'll have to hurry. I'm already in the shower, voice-messaging Sarah that I'll be a few minutes late, when I see I have a text waiting. I send the message to Sarah and set my phone down to hurry the shower along.

But when I'm out and wrapped in a towel, I have to check it—it might be important.

It's a message from Robert, the guy I went on the date with and ghosted. I clear the fog on the mirror and find myself frowning. It's been weeks. Why would he message now? Isn't it obvious I'm not feeling it?

But then I see his message.

Robert: Looking forward to it!

Looking forward to what?

I nearly drop my phone as I adjust my towel and lean in, scrolling as fast as I can. There are a dozen texts back and forth between us. Texts I have no memory of. I drank a lot, but surely not enough to completely black out, right?

Oh God.

Shit.

And *I* initiated the texts. After midnight.

Another text comes in just then, from Jake.

Jake: Are you okay? I still haven't heard from you.

I study his words, try to figure out what he means. Coming up empty, I check my call log, and sure enough—I called him. We spoke for three minutes and forty-two seconds.

And I have no memory of any of it.

I sit down on the closed toilet seat, trying to recall what I said. What I did. I have no memory of most of last night. What if I did something worse? Like call Gabriel?

My breath catches in my throat as I frantically double-check my call log.

Thank God.

Thank freaking God.

I stare at myself in the mirror. I've worried my brother. Set up a date with a man I have no real interest in. Hell, apparently I was ready to hop on a plane with him to *England*.

And that's when it hits me that I'm a little afraid. Of myself.

And what I'm capable of.

CHAPTER 26
Now

*D*on't be so hard on yourself. Just do your best.

It's advice I've often given to patients, yet I'm not good at listening to myself lately. I stop at the restaurant door and take a deep breath. Yes, I made a date with this man while inebriated. But maybe it's for the best. Maybe this is just what I need—a push to put myself out there. And *really* try this time. *Dinner.* Not just drinks. Date number two.

I open the door and look around. Robert is only a few feet away, but that's not who I'm looking for, is it? *Damn it.* This time I didn't pick the place to meet. Robert did. And yet we're still in Gabriel's neck of the woods.

Robert smiles and walks over. There's an awkward few seconds where neither of us is sure how to greet the other. Kiss? Hug? Both? None? We somehow settle on an inelegant hug, one where we both go for the right side at the same time and then both move to the left in unison.

He laughs and puts both hands on my shoulders. "How about I go left and you go right?"

The acknowledgment of our clumsiness helps break the tension and we hug.

"I'm sorry if I'm a minute or two late," I say.

"No worries. I didn't even notice." He winks. "It was only a minute and thirty-six seconds, by the way. Not that I was worried you'd ghost me."

I smile. He's a nice guy. The right mix of wry humor and wit.

Robert steps behind me to help take off my coat. "They said our table is going to be a few minutes. Would you like to get a drink at the bar while we wait?"

The thought of alcohol after how I felt when I woke up this morning makes me queasy. But we had drinks together last time, and I don't want to admit I'm hungover, which would give away that our date was the result of my drunk texting. So I nod. "Sure, that sounds great."

Robert lets the hostess know where we'll be, and we take seats at the bar. The layout isn't that different from the last place we met, with bistro tables and small booths lining one wall of the bar. I can't help it: I scan each one looking for Gabriel.

"So." Robert turns to face me. "I was surprised to hear from you after you hadn't answered my last few texts."

I look down. "I'm sorry about that. I guess I just lost track of things."

Robert waits until our eyes meet to speak again. "Is that true?"

My gut reaction is to be defensive, say "*of course it is*." But if I want any shot at a relationship with him, lying isn't the way to start things. So I sigh and shake my head. "No, I'm sorry. It's not."

He nods. "Getting back out there after you lose someone can be hard. I get it."

I act like I've just come clean, but is that what I've really just done? Did my ignoring Robert have anything to do with Connor and jumping back into the dating pool? Or was it something—or *someone*—else leaving me too distracted? I'm not sure anymore. I nod, though. "Thank you for being so understanding."

A little while later, the hostess shows us to our table. My seat has a clear view to the door, and I wish it didn't. With my back to the entrance, it would have made watching every person come in and out of the restaurant a lot more difficult. I couldn't have twisted my entire body every two minutes. But this way, I smile and nod, sip my wine, shift my eyes slightly over Robert's shoulder, and glance at the door. He doesn't even notice my incessant checking.

Halfway through the second glass of wine I'd told myself I wasn't going to have, I finally start to relax. My nerves calm and my shoulders lower. I even stop looking at the door as often.

"So what made you go into psychiatry?" Robert asks. "Is that the field you were interested in when you started medical school?"

I shake my head. "I went in thinking I wanted to do cardiology, believe it or not."

"That's a pretty big change. But most of the people I went to med school with were interested in one thing and came out practicing in another area. When I started, I wanted to be a plastic surgeon. Two nose jobs and a breast augmentation and drive my Porsche home by five."

I laugh. "Did you at least wind up with the Porsche?"

"My only car is the subway car." He chuckles. "But during my second year of medical school, my mom was diagnosed with pancreatic cancer. The outlook was grim, and I wound up doing a lot of research, trying to find her clinical trials and stuff. While I was doing it, I realized I was actually interested in the field. She died the day after my graduation. Made me appreciate that life was short, and I was only going into plastics for the money. So I pivoted and went into a field that felt right."

"I'm sorry for your loss. But it sounds like your mom led you to something that brings you happiness, which is a beautiful thing."

"Thanks. I like to think she did." Robert sips his wine and lifts his chin. "So why psychiatry?"

"I like the diversity of it. A cardiologist treats the same thing for most of their career. Of course, new treatments and procedures move medicine forward, which is always exciting. But I liked that mental health patients were all so different, with varied diagnoses. Plus, during my clinical rotations, I asked every resident I worked with if they would recommend their field. Across the board in almost every specialty, only about forty percent said yes for one reason or another. But a hundred percent of the psychiatrists said yes, and usually with a smile."

"I bet you get some interesting patients."

My mind automatically goes to Gabriel. But I tamp down those thoughts and force myself to gaze across the table and not gawk at the door.

Robert and I spend the next hour talking over a delicious meal. Aside from medicine and having lost our spouses, we have other things in common, too. We're both lefties, love psychological thriller movies, prefer cold-weather vacations to warm, and oddly, our grandparents were huge Elvis fans, which turned us into fans, too. After dinner, we stand outside the restaurant.

"So how was it?" Robert asks.

"Dinner? It was delicious."

He smiles. "No, I meant your first dinner date in a decade."

"Oh." I laugh. "I had a really nice time. Thank you."

But then I get a feeling, the kind that prickles the hair on the back of your neck because you're certain someone is watching. My eyes dart around the street until they land on a figure down at the end of the block. It's dark out, so it's hard to see. But there's definitely a person leaning against a building. As soon as I spot them, they pull up a hoodie and turn to face forward. The fabric drapes over the sides of their head so I can't even make out a profile. But when a puff of smoke billows into the crisp air, my eyes widen.

Is that . . . ?

Gabriel bought cigarettes once.

I squint to get a better look, but whoever it is shoves their hands into their pockets, pushes off the building, and starts walking in the other direction.

God, I'm really losing my mind.

Robert turns and looks over his shoulder. "Is everything okay?"

I keep staring, watching the person turn the nearby corner and disappear from sight. "Um, yeah. I'm sorry. I thought I saw someone I knew." I force my attention back to my date, my heart racing wildly. "I'm sorry. You were saying?"

Robert reaches out and takes my hand. He laces our fingers and swings our joined palms playfully. "I was trying to work up the courage to ask you if you'd like to come back to my place and check out my Elvis collection and maybe have a drink. But no matter how many ways I practice saying it in my head, it sounds pretty cheesy." He smiles, and I can tell it's a nervous one. "I'm not ready for the night to end. It would just be a drink, I promise. I get that dating is new to you."

Someone yells from down the block, the direction the person leaning against the building just went. But a few seconds later, two teenagers pop out from that same corner. They're laughing as they jog across the street hand in hand. One of them is wearing a hoodie. Is that who it was? Just a kid? Though the hood is down now, and the color doesn't look as dark as the other one. At least, I think it doesn't. No, I'm wrong. It's probably the same color. My mind is just screwing with me.

Isn't it?

When I finally drag my attention back to my date, he smiles. "What do you say? One glass of wine and one Elvis album and I'll call you an Uber?"

I look over his shoulder again. The street is empty now. Even the teenagers are gone. The stalker I've made up in my head is nowhere to be found. *God, I really need to let this paranoia go.* To let *everything* to do with my past go. And since there's no better way to put the past behind you than to take a step forward, I force a smile. "Sure. I'd like that."

CHAPTER 27
Now

"Rebecca, I'm so glad to see you today." I pull out a pen and a notepad, writing her name at the top. She sits in the same spot on the couch, legs crossed, wearing high heels and a short sundress she had to tuck carefully under her bottom, as though it's July. Once again, she's dressed revealingly—which in and of itself is fine. People can express themselves however they want to. But it's a cool day, overcast, wind rustling through the early spring leaves just budding, and she must be freezing.

"Thanks." She's folded in on herself, shoulders curved. Hands pressed to her knee, Rebecca studies the bookshelf to my right as though it's filled with something besides out-of-date, boring medical texts. Today I've kept my mind on work. Kept focused on my patients, and only occasionally let my mind wander to Gabriel. I've been texting with Robert, flirty texts, full of winking emojis. It feels cozy and warm, and I know that when this session ends, I'll have messages from him.

"How have you been doing since our last session?" I ask.

"Okay."

I tilt my head, leaving silence, hoping she'll go on. Last time it took her a bit to warm up, too. I want to give her the space for that to happen again.

"Anything new?" I finally say when a solid minute has passed. Rebecca is one of my youngest patients—I don't see children or teenagers, so I rarely have patients reluctant to speak with me. Adults come to therapy for help.

Even if it's hard to get to what they really want to say, they naturally fill the silence talking about something.

"I have a new boyfriend." Her eyes shine with the word *boyfriend*. Discomfort flits through me—she's undeniably obsessive. We've barely skimmed the surface of what we can work on together, but the diagnoses tumble through my brain, interwoven like spaghetti. She needs help. Once I would have known exactly what to do, what to say to start her on that journey. Now that flicker of self-doubt rears its ugly head. But I can do this.

"Oh?"

"Yeah. His name is Steve. We met online."

I fight to keep my face neutral. There's nothing wrong with meeting a partner online. Heck, that's how I met Robert. But Rebecca seems to be bouncing from one man to the next. No sooner than the thought crosses my mind, I realize I'm not much better these days. While Robert kissed me, while his hips were pressed against mine, while his hot breath warmed my skin, I was thinking of Gabriel.

I clear my throat. "Steve. Tell me more. What do you like about him?"

My hope is to focus on the traits that will create a positive relationship for her. And to let her share her frustrations, so we can plan how she handles them—hopefully in a more resilient, appropriate way than showing up at Steve's work or stalking him. Especially if poor behaviors were modeled for her growing up, that's likely what she'll turn to now. But maybe we can create a better relationship. Even if she has deeper underlying issues.

The thing about therapy is you can't tell people what to do. You can guide them, but their realizations have to be theirs alone. I'm not planning her life—I'm helping her learn to plan her own life, hopefully in a more adaptive way.

"He's cute. And he plays baseball for St. John's University. I like the way he looks at me. Like I'm special." She stops, nibbles on her fingernail, and glances nervously over at me. Our eyes meet for the briefest moment. "He brought me flowers for our first date. No one's ever done that."

"How sweet of him."

"Yes, he's really sweet." Indecisiveness flashes across her pretty features.

She sucks her bottom lip between her teeth. "I don't know. There's something about him. I really like him."

Something about him.

I can understand that. *Something about Gabriel . . .*

No, no, no. I press the point of my pen to the paper too forcefully, and it scrapes, ripping it.

"Anyway, we decided to be girlfriend and boyfriend. And I wanted to ask you something."

"Go ahead." I lean forward, smiling kindly. She's opening up. Acknowledging to me and to herself that she wants help.

"Is it . . . is it normal to think about someone, like, all the time?" Her eyes widen. "Because, I mean, I think I love him. And I think about him *all* the time. When I wake up, when I'm taking a shower, when I'm in class, even right now. I mean, I'm talking about him, right?" She laughs nervously.

I keep my psychiatrist face on—kind, impartial. A hint of a smile. But inside, Gabriel's name pounds with the beating of my heart. The thought of him. How I almost feel like we've *been together*, the way I imagined it was his hair I ran my fingers through, his mouth I was kissing, his hardness I pressed up against . . .

Even though I know it was Robert.

Is it normal to think about someone all the time?

My gaze darts toward my desk, where my phone is stowed away, ringer off. I know Robert is not Gabriel. I *know* that. And yet I'm using him. Using him as a replacement for my own obsession.

"Early in relationships, we often think of the person a lot," I hear myself say. "It can be euphoric. It's because of the release of dopamine in our brains. Of course, that doesn't make it any less real."

It's a neutral answer. Not telling her she's wrong. Not telling *myself* I'm wrong. Just the facts.

And the fact is, I'm not so different from Rebecca. Although from I am making different choices. I've chosen to step away from my obsession. To leave him in the past. To focus on Robert, even if I did allow myself that one fantasy.

"Well, it's not all perfect. Like, is that even possible?" She rolls her eyes, breaking my inner monologue. Reminding me she's a patient, and she's twenty-three, and I'm supposed to be helping her. This is an opportunity to help her. To guide her.

"Tell me more about that."

"So . . ." She huffs out a breath. "Okay, this is kind of embarrassing, but he won't do, you know, certain things." We make eye contact for half a second and she looks away again. "I got really mad at him last night."

I'm missing something. I'm just not sure what.

"Well, our partners certainly can't be mind readers. Have you spoken to him about it?"

"Yes. Oh yes. Every time."

"Every time . . . ?"

"Every time we have sex." Now she looks at me straight-on, a wild glint in her gaze. "I mean, I just want him to do what one of my exes would. Or do it how he would. I mean, sex is about pleasing *both* people, you know? And if I want it a certain way, he should do that. Right?"

I have to take a moment before I answer. My mind spins out possibilities of what it is she might be asking this new boyfriend, Steve, to do. But before I can ask for clarification, she continues.

"So, the last guy I really liked—the one I thought was *the one*—I mentioned him last time. He was intense. *So* intense." She licks her lips. "He liked everything, and I mean everything. And there was no holding back. I didn't even know I liked it like that . . . like, so *rough*." She exhales shakily, as though even the thought of what she and her ex used to do has her bothered. "He'd shove my face into a pillow until I could, like, barely breathe. And it was . . ." She seems to search for the right word. "I mean, a little scary the first time, but I looked it up. It's called breath-play. And it's a whole thing. And it totally takes it up a level. You know what I mean?" Again, she looks at me for affirmation.

"What do you mean, it 'takes it up a level'?" I lean forward with interest. I've heard of this before. But it's outside my realm of experience. Both in my own sex life and in treating patients. I've never had a client come to me and tell me a partner kept them from breathing—at least, not outside the realm of abuse. Is that what really happened, and she's confusing it with something positive?

"So there are all these studies, and by restricting oxygen, it like, enhances the sexual experience or something." She uses air quotation marks as though quoting an actual study. "He'd shove my face in the pillow when we were doing it doggie-style, or he'd, like, lock his elbow around my neck." She mimics it for me. "But, like, he could do it just right. And the orgasms—like nothing else I've ever experienced. And he just knew how to . . ." Her face pinks. "Pound," she whispers. "I didn't know I liked it like that. But I do. I really do."

This time, I'm silent because I have no words. I copy a few of the things down that's she said—because at some point I'll have to wrap my mind around it. Really understand how this does or doesn't weave into everything else she's dealing with now and has dealt with in the past. Or maybe this is good. Sex can be a place for play, for role-play, for acting out things that are not okay in real life.

"So you want . . ." I swallow, staring at the words I've written. *Pound. Choke. Face smashed in pillow.* It's like I'm sketching out an erotic scene. "You want Steve to do what this ex did?"

"Yes!" She practically explodes off her seat. "And he won't. So I'm not satisfied. And I told him that, which of course pissed him off because it questioned his masculinity or something. He wound up trying it, but he wouldn't actually do it hard enough that I couldn't breathe. Which completely ruins the whole point, and I had to imagine it was my ex, not Steve, to finally get off."

Rebecca goes on and on, but I'm stuck on how she pretended Steve was her ex.

Just like how I'd pretended Robert was Gabriel.

It makes me wonder. What else do I have in common with my patient? Would I like it a little rough, too?

CHAPTER 28
Now

Today is the day.

I hear Gabriel speaking to Sarah in the outer office and my body responds instantly—heartbeat quickens, skin flushes, and my damn nipples look like they're ready to salute. It's an eye-opening reminder of what needs to be done—today will be Gabriel Wright's last session. The insanity has gone on long enough. I started out with good intentions, but somewhere along the line, they've taken a turn.

Sarah knocks twice and pushes the door open to my office without waiting for me to respond. There's a gleam in her eye, and the corners of her smile hold a salacious quirk. I'm clearly not the only one attracted to my patient. "Your two o'clock is here," she singsongs.

I take a deep breath and nod, slipping on my mask of professionalism. "Great. Send him in."

Gabriel steps into my office. Today he offers a curt nod instead of his usual playful-type greeting. Tension lines are etched into his forehead, creases scored between his eyes, and his crow's feet have deepened. He's been squinting or frowning a lot lately.

I extend a hand toward the couch and offer a measured smile, coupled with a practiced greeting. "Hello. It's good to see you."

He takes a seat and still doesn't say anything. Now that we're only a few feet apart, I think I might've mistaken stress lines for worried ones. He looks like his dog got run over by a car. But I don't comment on a patient's appearance.

I cross my legs, one over the other. Gabriel's eyes stay trained down as he drags a hand through his hair.

"How are you doing this week?" I ask.

"Not great." He sighs.

"Oh? I'm sorry to hear that. Tell me what's going on."

"I went on a date. It didn't go well."

Jealousy rises up, thick and fast. It heats my cheeks, and I hope Gabriel doesn't notice. "What happened?"

He stares off out the window. "I took her out to dinner. We had a nice time. She invited me back to her place."

"Okay . . ."

His lips curl. "I couldn't . . . you know."

"You mean physically?"

"Yeah, I mean physically. Do I have to spell it out? Do you need me to say I couldn't get my dick hard?"

I blink a few times. "I'm sorry. I didn't mean to upset you. I wasn't sure if you meant you couldn't go through with it mentally or physically. We've talked a lot about the pent-up guilt you have, so I thought perhaps . . ."

He blows out two cheeks full of air and hangs his head. "I'm sorry. That was rude. I'm just frustrated. And talking about it is embarrassing."

"Okay. I understand. But why don't we back things up a bit? Because while this may have manifested itself as a physical problem, this type of issue often stems from anxiety and stress. Our minds are almost always in control of our bodies. How about you tell me about the woman you went out with? Is she someone you've known for a while or someone you've recently met?"

"Recently met."

"How did you meet?"

"Dating app."

My lips flatten to a grim line. "What does she look like?"

He lifts his head up to face me and squints. "Why does that matter?"

Shit. It doesn't. Other than to feed my morbid curiosity. I can't help but wonder about all the little blondes he flitted around with at different restaurants. It makes me wonder if all those women were dates, too.

Thankfully, I've grown adept at covering my missteps. "Perhaps she resembled your wife and it brought up a lot of mixed emotions."

"I don't think it has anything to do with her." His eyes bounce back and forth between mine for a long time, like he's contemplating something, then come into focus and lock with my gaze. "There's another woman."

It hits like a blow, a gut punch to a soft belly when you're least expecting it.

I swallow. "Go on . . ."

Gabriel rakes a hand through his hair once again. "I'm consumed by her. I can't stop thinking about her. The only time I seem to be able to, you know, get hard is when I think about her."

My heart has been racing since Gabriel walked in, but now it feels like it's trying to batter its way out of my chest. There's not one woman but *two*. "Tell me about the other woman. Is this someone you've gone out with previously?"

He shakes his head. "She's off-limits."

"Is she . . . a student?"

"No." His jaw clenches.

I think back to when I was following him, to the woman at the Italian restaurant. The young blonde with the boisterous laugh. Is it her? Or maybe it's the woman he sometimes walks between buildings with after class? *Another blonde.* That one is older. Is a work colleague off-limits? Maybe she's his chairperson? That would make things sticky . . .

"Have you had these feelings for the other woman for a while?"

He looks away, seeming lost in thought, then meets my eyes. "Why is sex so much better when you have it with someone you shouldn't?"

"I suppose it's the forbidden-fruit effect. It's a thrill to think about being in a sexual or romantic relationship with someone we're not allowed to have. It heightens all of the senses. For some people, though, thoughts of being with someone—even someone as taboo as a priest or your boss's spouse— also provides a sense of safety."

"Or maybe . . ." Gabriel swallows. "Your doctor."

The air ignites, crackling dangerously around us.

I grip the armrest of my chair. "The safety comes in because while you can fantasize about the off-limits person, the reality is that it can't ever happen. If we fantasize about a person who is attainable, it's not as safe, since the reality of it is an actual possibility."

Gabriel leans in, inches closer from his seat. "What if the person who's off-limits isn't really as off-limits as we think? Then does it become dangerous?"

I open my mouth to respond—with what, I have no idea—but nothing comes out. Gabriel's eyes gleam, almost like he's enjoying my squirming. But it can't be that, can it?

He shifts back from the edge of his seat. "Have you ever had forbidden fruit, Dr. McCall? Maybe slept with a patient?"

"What? No, of course not."

"Think about it?"

My mind shuffles through the dozens of times I've thought about it— how I've masturbated to thoughts of Gabriel, how I kissed Robert while imagining it was my very own, off-limits patient—one who is more off-limits than any patient could ever be—how I wanted nothing more than to feel his big hands all over my body.

The corner of Gabriel's lip curls. "You're turning red. You have."

"No. I, I . . . don't think this is an appropriate conversation for us to be having."

Things are spiraling out of control, and I have no idea where the reins are to pull them and stop it. In the middle of my freak-out, there's a knock at my office door. No one ever interrupts a session, but I jump at the opportunity for it now.

"Come in!"

Sarah cracks the door open and pops her head in. "I'm really sorry to interrupt. I just got a call from my son's school. He's got a fever, and I can't reach my mom to pick him up. Is it okay if I run out?"

"Of course. Go."

"Thank you." She looks at Gabriel, who never even bothered turning his head, and makes an apologetic face. "Sorry again to interrupt."

The door closes and my office, which is a decent size for Manhattan, suddenly feels very small. And apparently, I was the only one who allowed Sarah's interruption to cut through the tension. Because Gabriel is staring at me with an intensity that makes me feel like I've touched a live wire.

"Sorry about that," I say. I force a smile, but at best, it comes out troubled.

"Can I tell you about the woman I fantasize about? Some of the things I want to do to her?"

"I don't think—"

"I want to bend her over her desk."

My jaw goes slack.

"Slide into her from behind."

My breathing comes in quick, shallow spurts. I should say something. Stop this conversation. But I can't. I want to hear more. Ride the edge.

My eyes drop to his lips, and I start to feel dizzy. The warm brown of his irises is almost completely gone, pushed out by dark pupils. I imagine what he's just said. Me, folded over my desk, Gabriel's lean body over mine. Harsh thrusts. Maybe hair pulling. Giving in to the feeling of being completely overwhelmed by another human being. *Deep, deep penetration.*

I don't even realize my eyes are fixated on my desk until they're on their way back from it and they meet Gabriel's. His lips curve to a slow, wicked smile.

"I think we should end our session for today." The words come out of my mouth so fast I don't even get a chance to give them any thought before they're spoken.

Gabriel closes his eyes. He swallows and nods. "Okay. I'm sorry."

Without another word, he gets up and walks to the door. I hold my breath as he reaches for the doorknob, pinch my eyes shut—feeling desperate for it to open, even though Sarah isn't on the other side, and there's no one to save me from myself.

I wait and wait, dying for the creak of the door opening and closing to come, but when it does, I panic and jump up.

"No! Don't go!"

Gabriel doesn't move. He stands rigidly still while my heart thunders in my chest. *What am I doing? What the hell am I doing?*

Long seconds tick by. I might not have any clue what I'm getting myself into, but I know the ball is in his court, so I wait for him to speak. When he finally does, he doesn't turn around.

"I think about you all the time," he says. His voice is so strained it sounds like he's in pain.

I swallow. "I think about you, too."

He drops his head and shakes it. "I know it's wrong."

"Me, too," I whisper. "But I don't care anymore."

There's another long stretch of silence. Heaviness fills the air like a room full of secrets waiting to be unveiled. I keep staring at Gabriel's back, waiting . . .

Eventually, he reaches for the doorknob. I shut my eyes, thinking it's over. Unlike me, he's strong enough to walk away. But then . . .

A loud *sch-liff* echoes through the room.

The door lock clanks closed.

He's locked my door!

My eyes flare open.

Gabriel turns, and our eyes meet. He stares at me with an intensity that burns my skin.

He begins to walk. Slowly. Like he's giving me a chance to stop him. But every step makes my pulse quicken. By the time he reaches my desk, I feel like a pot of boiling water and the lid is about to blow off. I don't move. Not an inch. But Gabriel keeps coming, right around the barrier of my desk, until he's so close behind me I can feel the heat of his body, his hot breath tickling my neck.

"I won't do anything you don't want." He nips at my earlobe with his teeth and an electric current races down my body. "All you need to do is tell me to stop."

A few heartbeats pass. I don't turn around. Don't face him. But I step back and press my body to his. I feel his erection digging into my lower back. Yet I still sense a hesitancy. He hasn't touched me, at least not intentionally. I let my head loll back against his chest.

"Touch me," I groan.

Gabriel reaches around and gropes my breast through the silk of my blouse. It's rough and punishing, but it's exactly how I want it. What I deserve.

"Tell me you want me to fuck you, Meredith."

I close my eyes as I pant. Gabriel buries his head in my hair and sucks along my neck. "Tell me," he growls, his lips vibrating against my skin. "Tell me you want me to fuck you."

"I do," I croak. I already know I'll hate myself tomorrow, probably even sooner, but I've never wanted anyone more than I want this man right now.

His hand slips between us. I can feel it travel down to his hard-on, and then there's a sound that makes my eyes roll back into my head. *Zipper teeth coming undone.* It's the most erotic thing I've ever heard in my life. Gabriel goes to turn me around, but I stop him and bend forward, bringing my chest to the top of my desk like he told me he'd imagined.

He bends over me so his mouth is again at my ear. "Do what? I want to hear you say the words."

I can barely speak, my breath too tangled in my throat for words to pass, but somehow I manage to squeak out a whisper. "I want you to hold me down and fuck me hard."

"Good girl . . ."

He stands, but keeps a heavy hand on my back, not allowing me to rise. Then he bunches up my skirt, pulls my panties to one side, and before I can brace for what's about to happen—I'm about to sleep with my patient—no, sleep with the husband of the woman my husband killed—his thick crown is at my opening.

And I'm wet. Dripping. Shamelessly ready and inviting.

Gabriel enters me in one thrust. There is no foreplay. Or maybe that's what we've been doing all these months. I don't know. But he buries himself deep and lets out a thunderous groan. His hips are flush against my ass, and I can feel his body shaking from the inside out. Once he steadies, he gathers my hair into one of his hands and yanks until my neck is fully extended back. Then I do something I've never done before. In the moment, I don't even realize where it's coming from, but I hold my breath. Gabriel plows into me from behind, thrust after thrust, deeper and deeper. I start to feel lightheaded, desperate for air. My body begins to shake as the seconds tick by without oxygen. Just when I think I might pass out, he buries himself and knocks the wind out of my lungs with a rush. My body responds with a surge of dopamine, serotonin, and endorphins that brings an exhilaration I've never felt before. It's an ecstasy I want to last forever. But too soon it ends. Gabriel pulls out, finishing with a roar.

I'm sated, every bone in my body liquefied, but my brain kicks on.

What did I do?

What the hell did I just do?

I'm still in a fog interrogating myself when Gabriel lets go of my hair. He tugs at my skirt, pulling it down to cover my ass once again.

"Meredith . . ." he says softly.

I feel a surge of adrenaline kick in. It hits so fast I feel like I might throw up. My hand clutches my throat. "You need to go."

His breathing seems to grows louder. I need it to stop. Now.

"*Please,*" I say. "*Please* just go."

The room is silent. He must be holding his breath like I am. Thirty long seconds tick by, then suddenly footsteps are crossing the room. No words. No discussion about what has just transpired. Only the jingle of the door handle, the creak of the door opening.

"I'll see you next week, Dr. McCall."

CHAPTER 29
Now

I spend the rest of the week distracted. I almost expect Gabriel to call, to reach out in some way.

We had *sex*.

I had sex.

With someone other than my husband.

You were the only person I'd had sex with in . . . over a decade.

I know sex doesn't mean what it used to, that lots of people have sex all the time and it means nothing more than *sex*. Fun. An activity to do together, no strings attached.

But with Gabriel, there are all sorts of strings. All kinds of fucked-up, twisted knots and complicated ties, because on the list of people I shouldn't have had sex with, he's at the very, very top.

He pulled my hair, and I liked it.

He called me a *good girl*, and I loved it.

Worse, I'd tried to self-asphyxiate to take the high even higher.

Something *a patient* told me she likes.

A very ill young woman.

And I'd been the one to initiate the entire thing. Gabriel had been ready to walk away.

I stopped him.

And told him to fuck me *hard*.

I'd never even done those types of things with my husband.

Not to mention we hadn't used protection. I'm still on the pill, but he didn't know that. Plus, there are other concerns than pregnancy, aren't there? We were reckless.

Yet I smile at that thought. *Reckless.* And I loved every damn minute of it.

I tap my fingers over my coffee mug, still full to the brim. An untouched salad sits on the corner of my desk, compliments of Sarah, who volunteered to go for lunch. But my eyes are glued to the spot where he bent me over, and I liked it.

Loved it.

Spent the next three nights remembering and turning my vibrator on *high*, because there are no low or medium settings when it comes to Gabriel.

I shake my head, try to shake off the thoughts, the imaginings. I should reach out to him. Tell him it was a mistake. Apologize, even, for encouraging it to happen. As his psychiatrist, I'm in a position of power. I could lose my license. Again. Maybe this time for good. It was wildly inappropriate, even if he'd all but told me he wanted me during our session . . .

My mouth goes dry. He wanted *me*.

"Meredith?" Sarah pokes her head in. I jump like I've been caught doing something bad. "Oh, I'm sorry to startle you. Are you all right? You look a little pale."

That's better than beet red.

"I'm fine, just tired. What's up?"

"I have an updated patient list for the week." She offers the papers to me—three total, one for each day. I flip to Friday, but instead of the five appointments I previously had scheduled, I see only four. And a name is missing. *His* name is missing.

"I thought I was seeing Gabriel Wright on Friday?"

She shrugs. "He called and canceled this morning. Something about going out of town suddenly for work."

"Okay, thanks." Sarah takes her leave, but I'm still staring down at the list. What in the world would Gabriel be called out of town for suddenly? He's a professor. Maybe a conference?

My immediate reaction is a deep emptiness that feels a lot like disappointment. Not the sort of emotion I should feel for a patient. Even Gabriel. And then something else—a flicker of panic.

He doesn't want me.

The sex wasn't good for him.

I fucked it up.

No. No, no, no. I'm his psychiatrist, and what we did was wrong. It would be normal for him to cancel on me. Hell, for him to report me.

If, a couple of years ago, I'd heard of a psychiatrist doing what I've done—and not just the sex but *stalking* him . . .

Oh Lord. I drop my face into my hands on my desk, but even that reminds me of him. Of me bent over, him holding me against the desk as he—

I should burn that skirt. Those panties. I'll never wear them again without thinking of him. Of *us.* Heat flushes over me, and I grab the stack of papers Sarah dropped off, fan myself with them.

Maybe he's avoiding me. Or maybe he's actually busy. But either way, it's better that I don't see him. Better we never let *that* happen again.

When my appointments end just after five, I get on the train and head to my own appointment. When I scheduled it, it was routine—see the therapist every few weeks. Check in. Assure him I am still fit to be practicing.

But today I'm glad for it. Glad I scheduled it weeks in advance, glad I have someone to talk to. Because talk I must. And with seemingly no one in my life, I'll gladly pay Dr. Alexander to listen.

"Dr. McCall, welcome." He gives a general wave of his arm as he frowns down at the notebook in his lap. "Please, sit."

I do, folding my hands in my lap. He's still doing something—maybe scribbling a note from his last patient or preparing for our appointment. I glance around the office, and the thought comes to me, unbidden—has he ever had sex with a patient? In this very room?

Surely not. Surely he is a good therapist.

Unlike me.

"So, how are you doing today?" Dr. Alexander fixes me with his warm, kind smile. Just like he always does. He must have perfected it in front of a mirror. Practiced it day in and day out. Do I smile at my patients like that? Make them feel welcome just by looking at them?

"I'm . . . stressed. Tense." I force a smile that I'm sure shows him exactly how I'm feeling.

"What's going on?"

"Well." I lick my lips, glance down at my hands. "I told you I'm seeing someone."

"Yes." He nods encouragingly.

I hesitate, trying to figure out how to tell him. Or if I should tell him. I mean, I can't tell him about Gabriel, exactly. But I need to tell him, tell *somebody*.

"I had sex," I say. Not a lie. I did have sex. I know he'll assume it's with the man I'm seeing, with Robert. And I'm okay with that. Relief floods me, realizing how I can talk about it.

"And how was that? How did it make you feel?"

The desk. Gabriel's hands on my body. The sharp, wonderful pleasure and pain—

"It was good. At least, I think it was."

"Wonderful."

The word comes from Dr. Alexander's mouth, and I realize it's true. Having sex with Gabriel, being *fucked* by Gabriel—because that is the only appropriate word for what we did—was confusing and unexpected and obviously not *right*, but it was also wonderful.

"So what's stressing you?" he asks.

"Well." I feel my teeth digging into my bottom lip. I exhale slowly. "He's ghosted me."

It's not totally true. It's not a lie, though. Of course, we don't usually call or text or—well, anything. Except appointments, or me stalking him, which I'm not doing anymore.

But God, I'm even calling what I've done stalking now.

"I see. How does that make you feel?"

"Horrible. Like I did something wrong. Like there's something wrong *with* me. Like I'm—I was used." My chest feels lighter at the admission. At the realization. "And angry. So angry."

"Have you communicated with him at all?"

I shake my head. "No."

"So he hasn't reached out?"

"No. Nothing." My hands shake, anxious energy pulsing through me.

"And have you reached out to him?"

That makes me stop. "No. I haven't."

"Is it possible he feels you've ghosted him as well?"

Dr. Alexander's words linger. It's a fair question. If it were Robert, I would reach out. I would text or call or even drop by . . .

But it's not Robert.

It's Gabriel.

And with Gabriel, there are no rules. Because we're not dating. We're not casually having sex.

We're . . . I search for the right word or phrase, but can't think of anything. It's almost like we're playing a game. A game with no rules or boundaries. It's thrilling and panic-inducing. My fingers clutch at the fabric of my slacks, wondering who will make the next move. And what it will be.

"What do you think would happen if you reached out to him?"

"I don't know. I heard . . . I heard he had to go out of town."

"He sounds like a busy man." Dr. Alexander crosses one ankle over the other and studies me.

His words penetrate. He's being a good therapist—suggesting I consider Gabriel's point of view. And he's right. Usually, I'd absolutely agree with him.

Except this is Gabriel.

And with Gabriel, the normal rules don't apply.

CHAPTER 30
Now

Most psychiatrists would never admit it, but there are patients we dread. Mrs. Rensler, who only wants to talk about her daughter's life and how depressed she is that Gracie doesn't make more time for her. Mr. Altman, who, lucky for me, is no longer a patient. He'd been mandated to undergo court-ordered psychiatry after beating his wife and complained that she'd made him do it, with her constant nagging to get a job. But then there are patients we look forward to. Perhaps we see them making progress, or they're just interesting people with unique stories. I have a few of those. But the reason I've been anxiously awaiting my next patient is a very selfish one.

Rebecca Jordan is a looking glass for me lately. Listening to her gives me a dose of reality. Reminds me where things could progress if I keep up my inappropriate behavior. And since I've barely been able to stop myself from going past Gabriel's apartment twice in so many days, I really need the reminder today.

Sarah escorts Rebecca into my office. Today she's dressed even more provocatively than usual—like a schoolgirl with a white button-up blouse tied at the waist, her slim, tan midriff on full display, and a navy and black plaid pleated skirt that is so short I hope she doesn't drop anything. Knee-high white socks and conservative oxford shoes complete the outfit.

I smile. "Hi, Rebecca. How are you?"

She plops herself down on the couch, much like a child. "I'm tired."

"Oh? Are you not sleeping well?"

She shakes her head. "I broke up with my boyfriend."

"Is it because of what we spoke about? You felt you weren't sexually compatible?"

She twirls a golden lock around one finger and shrugs. "I guess. We started fighting a lot, too. I accidentally called him the wrong name during sex once or twice, and it upset him."

"I see. Are you second-guessing your decision to break things off and that's why you're not sleeping well?"

She looks away. "No, I don't care about him. My ex is seeing someone."

"This is a different ex than the one you just broke up with?"

Rebecca nods.

"Okay, and that's what's upsetting you? Interfering with your sleep?"

"Of course it's upsetting me. *We* should still be together. He was the love of my life. And I was his."

"And what happened to end your relationship with him?"

"He was married."

"Oh." I'm not sure what else to say. So I wait until she speaks again.

"He was going to leave his wife for me."

Of course he was. Aren't they all?

"Why didn't he?"

"How should I know!" Her raised voice catches me off guard. I startle and sit back, putting a few more inches between us. I don't usually do that. In my line of work, patients have outbursts. I'm fairly used to it. Today I'm just jumpy. On edge. Because *he* still hasn't made contact. Because *I* haven't been sleeping well, either.

"How long ago did you and your ex break up?"

"I don't know. A while ago." She looks out the window again, then very randomly smiles. "I slept with someone the day before I broke up with him."

"Him? You mean Steve? The man you just broke up with?" I'm getting lost in all of these unnamed men.

Rebecca rolls her eyes. "Who else would it be?"

I'm not about to point out that she's talked about three men in the first five minutes of our session, so it would be reasonable to be confused. Instead, I nod and offer a smile. "Right. Okay. Do you like this other man? The one you slept with before breaking things off with Steve?"

She shrugs. "Not particularly. He was nice, I guess."

Rebecca and I are probably only a little more than a decade apart, yet I feel like it's an entire generation when it comes to sex and dating. I'd never used an app for dating until recently, nor had a one-night stand. Hell, the term *hookup* hadn't even been coined when I started dating Connor—at least, not in my vocabulary.

"So this other man wasn't the reason you broke up with Steve? It was just sex?"

"Steve and I had a fight, so I stopped at a bar on my way home. A guy came over and tried to buy me a drink. I didn't want to waste time if he was like Steve in bed, so I told him I liked it rough and asked if he could do that for me. If he was into that, I said he should keep his wallet in his pocket and come to my place instead."

Oh my. That doesn't sound safe.

"So you went back to your place and he . . . fulfilled your need?"

Rebecca shrugged. "It was better than with Steve. But something was missing. He smacked my ass and pulled my hair and stuff. But I could tell he was just doing it for me. It wasn't really driven by passion, like it was with my ex."

I look over at my desk, the spot of my own passionate encounter. I picture Gabriel behind me, holding me down. Pinning me. Goose bumps prickle my arms. And I realize Rebecca is talking again, yet I haven't heard her.

"Anyway, he texted again. But I don't think I'm going to see him."

"The guy from the bar?"

She nods. "I'll just ghost him."

Ghost him. Like Gabriel seems to have done to me. I shift in my seat and recross my legs. *Let's talk about that a little more . . .*

"May I ask why you would ghost him, rather than telling him you had a nice time but aren't interested in seeing him again?"

"Why should I? It's not like we were dating. He didn't take me out to dinner or bring me flowers. I didn't make a commitment to him. We didn't even talk much. If he doesn't see it for what it is, then he's dumb."

My shoulders slump. I am to Gabriel what the bar guy is to Rebecca—not even worthy of a courtesy text. But Gabriel and I have more than that, don't we? We've been talking for a while. Albeit because I'm his therapist and he's my patient, but we have *something* more than a bar pickup, right?

Or maybe we don't.

Maybe I'm the only one even thinking about it after.

It dawns on me that my patient is counseling *me* now. Worse, I'm asking questions and probing, in search of advice for myself, rather than trying to counsel *her*. Not to mention my patient has compulsion issues. Probably not the best place to procure dating advice for myself. Or sex advice. Because Gabriel and I are *not* dating. And I need to remember that.

I muddle through the rest of the session with Rebecca, doing my best to counsel a woman who is obsessive with men, when I've spent the last week, the last few months, even, with my own obsession.

I'm exhausted when it's over, thrilled she's my last patient of the day. On my way home, I stop at the liquor store and pick up *two* bottles of wine. Not because I plan on drinking both tonight but because the guy behind the counter smiled at me like I was a regular. It's semantics, I know. Buying two at once or going in twice means I drink the same amount of wine, but at least I don't have to become the Norm of *Cheers* at the local liquor store.

At home, I eat a cheese stick and fry up a bag of frozen pierogi, only to eat two and toss the rest in the garbage. I finish off my second glass of wine and draw a hot bath. My third is three-quarters of the way done by the time the tub fills, and I might as well chug the rest back so I can slip into the tub with a nice full glass, right? So that's what I do. I'm feeling pretty good now.

My neck is relaxed, my mind slows down, and I almost feel calm again. Alcohol is a great therapist like that.

Before I climb into the tub, I tie up my hair, light a candle, and call up some soft jazz on my phone. It's nice. Feels serene. So I keep drinking, sink into the warm water, and let it take away all my troubles. But then my cell chimes with an alert. And I'm the type of person who needs to know what I'm missing. Even when I'm about to finish my fourth glass of wine. So I swipe into my phone to see what the alert was for and find a text message from Robert. Robert, who doesn't ghost me. Robert, who takes me to nice dinners and is a gentleman, even when I go home with him, because he knows I'm not ready.

I'm not ready.

It's laughable, really.

I'm not ready for sex with a man who is a great catch, one who kisses me lovingly and seems completely into me. But I'm ready for breath-play and banging a patient on my desk.

I hold my phone in the air, high above my head, and slip down under the water, immersing the hair I tied up and hadn't been planning on getting wet. I count the seconds as I hold my breath. Fifteen. Then thirty. Sixty. When I hit ninety, I feel pressure in my head. Yet I push to a hundred and five. Ten more seconds tick by, and I burst out of the water with a big splash, panting. Water sloshes over the sides of the tub.

The candle goes out.

And now my hair needs to be blow-dried.

Also, my glass is empty again.

So it's time to get out.

I stumble out of the tub, wrap myself in a towel, and look down at the bathroom mat. I've never sat on it. It looks comfy. So I use the wall as my support to slide down to the ground, then grab my phone again.

Maybe Robert is too nice a guy for me.

Maybe I'm built like Rebecca now. Maybe the accident changed me. I need someone a little rough around the edges. Being punished seems fitting.

I can't picture Robert holding me down. Yanking my hair. He's probably gentle and kind in bed. Warm and caring.

With that thought, I call up the dating app. I've avoided it lately. No use finding a third man when I can't figure out what the hell is going on with the two I have. Not that I *have* Gabriel. But whatever.

I scroll for a while, randomly swiping right on any guy who *looks* a little rougher—guys with tattoos, guys with beady eyes. Motorcycle? Perfect! And then I go to the Columbia website to look at Gabriel's picture. He's even more handsome in person. I stare at his smiling face, wondering what he's doing right this minute. But I also remember all the young blondes he's spent time with.

My heart sinks. He's probably having dinner with a hot, young one right now. Wherever he is. I'm not sure if that thought makes me queasy or maybe it's the four glasses of wine on a mostly empty stomach. But I can't sit upright anymore. So I lie down on the nice rug I've never sat on and pull the towel around me.

I'll just shut my eyes for a few minutes. Then I'll get up and go to bed. I need to brush my teeth and plug my phone into the charger, too.

And that's the last thought I remember when I wake up the next morning—with grimy breath, a dead cell phone, an imprint of the nice bathroom rug on the side of my face, and a horrible feeling in the pit of my stomach that something bad is going to happen.

CHAPTER 31
Now

Another week.

Another trip to the liquor store last night, because I've downed both of those bottles. This time, I buy a half dozen, with the excuse, "Might as well—half a dozen means I get a discount!"

Now I'm in my office, staring at my phone, the dating app pulled up. There's a new message from Robert, but I can't bring myself to open it.

"New schedules," Sarah croons, swinging in the door. She's her usual cheerful self, and I smile, try to appear normal for her.

"Thanks." I shuffle the papers, looking for his name. He's coming on Friday, which means I have three days until I see him. Until we either pretend nothing happened or . . . I lick my lips. Repeat our last appointment. Which I can't do. I can't let that happen. I know that, and I've come up with a dozen ways to put him off. To remind him that what we did was wrong. But in my heart of hearts, I know—I *know*—that if he tries to bend me over the desk again, I won't be able to say no.

I find Friday's sheet and skim the names, but my five o'clock has disappeared. I could swear that's when his appointment was. I bite my cheek, ignoring the way my pulse pounds, because surely I'm just mixed up. I spread the sheets out on my desk, scouring them for Gabriel Wright.

But he's not there.

Suddenly, I feel clammy. Flushed. This means it's over. Canceling once is one thing, but twice? It officially means he's avoiding me.

Unless . . .

"Sarah?" I call. When she doesn't respond immediately, I get to my feet and poke my head out the door. "Hey, Gabriel's off the schedule. Again."

She looks up from her phone, where she's tapping out a text. "Oh, yeah, he said he's still stuck out of town. I offered him a virtual session, but I declined."

I frown. His appointments were put in as standing weekly sessions when I took him back on as a patient. "Did he only cancel this week's appointment?"

She tilts her head. "Yes? Why?"

So he hasn't canceled them *all*. Meaning he hasn't ended our relationship entirely. Our doctor-patient relationship, that is. I swallow, staring at Sarah, thoughts racing. It's possible he's really out of town. Maybe he said it was for work, but actually it was a family emergency, and he didn't want to say so.

"Are you okay?" Sarah sets down her phone and starts to get up, as though she'll come over to me.

"Fine." I frown. "Um, we're done for the day, right?"

"Yes. Mr. Wilson was your last patient."

I nod and give her a tight smile, duck back into my office, shut the door. I walk from one end of the room to the other, considering how little I actually know about Gabriel. Sure, I know his day-to-day habits, and that he has a thing for blondes, a dead family.

But maybe he has parents who called for help. Or a brother or sister. Or, hell, maybe he really did have a work thing come up, though I can't imagine what a professor would need to race out of town for.

Or he is simply avoiding me.

I come to a sudden stop, gaze fixed through the window on the outside world, where nature is coming alive, flowers blossoming, trees blooming. And yet I'm here, unchanged.

I have to know.

Which means I need to figure out where Gabriel is.

The path comes back to me easily, though I usually took it during daylight hours. Tonight the sun has long set, and the sky is speckled with a few stars and a sliver of a moon, a rarity with Manhattan's light pollution. I've swapped my heavy winter coat for a lighter jacket and scarf. When I arrive at Gabriel's building, I stare up at it, debating my next move. I know from his patient profile that he lives on the fourth floor. And from here, the fourth floor looks dark, empty. Abandoned. Like whoever lives there is, well, gone.

I stroll from one end of the block to the other, keeping watch on those dark windows, hoping to catch sight of something, anything, that signals Gabriel is within those walls. After five minutes without a sign anyone is home, I pull my phone from my pocket and try something new. On the train ride here, I downloaded an app that lets the user make anonymous calls and send anonymous texts. I pull it up now and type his number in. I hit call.

And then wait.

A couple passes by, on their way to or from dinner, maybe. A homeless man weaves out from an alley, takes one look at me, and staggers off. And finally, the sound of a phone ringing comes from the app. I press it close to my ear, all but holding my breath.

"Hello?" Gabriel's voice comes through the line. I look back at the fourth floor. No flicker of light. No sign someone's rolled out of bed to answer their phone or wandered from one room to the next. "Anyone there?"

I want to shut my eyes and soak in his voice. Soak in the sound of Gabriel. But I can't. I disconnect.

So he didn't lie. He's not home. He must be away, out of town, wherever he's gone. And of course he doesn't owe me any explanation. It's not like we're *together*. I'm embarrassed for myself. What am I thinking? Stalking this man again. Just like Rebecca—Rebecca, who probably needs far more care and therapy than I'm capable of providing her these days.

I try not to think what that says about me.

I turn the corner, headed for somewhere besides home. The last thing I should do right now is go home, where I'll drink another bottle of wine and probably drunk-dial Robert, or worse, Gabriel. If I'm going to do something stupid, I should at least do it anonymously, without repercussions in my real life. Maybe I'll pretend to be someone else. A different kind of doctor, or perhaps not a doctor at all. I could say I'm a schoolteacher, or an accountant, or anything I want. I'll find a nice bar and sweep in like I don't have a care in the world. Like Rebecca did the night before she broke up with Steve. Find a handsome man to buy me drinks and I'll feel young and desirable and—

And I look up. I've been walking, but I haven't found a bar.

I've walked on autopilot, the way I always walked from Gabriel's home. To the storage unit.

I stop and squint through the sparse light of the streetlamp. There's a form crossing the road, away from the storage unit, toward me.

It can't be him—it *can't be.*

But when the man raises his head, brushes his hair back, and looks up, our eyes meet.

It is him.

Gabriel Wright is not out of town.

He's right here, right in front of me. My stomach drops, and if there were time, I'd turn and run. But there's no time. His gaze is locked on mine, and he's headed my way, determination in his eyes.

CHAPTER 32
Now

"D r. McCall?" Gabriel squints as he approaches. But he isn't questioning whether it's me or not, he's asking what the heck I'm doing here. And it's a damn good question. One I should've asked myself before getting caught.

I blink a few times, reaching for the Academy Award–winning performance I'll need to pull this off. "Gabriel? Oh, hello."

He tilts his head, studying me. "What are you doing in this neighborhood? Do you live around here?"

"I, uh, not too far." I point down the block and make up the first thing that comes to mind. "I was just at the cell phone store. My phone seems to be on the fritz."

He holds my eyes. "Which one? The Verizon at the corner?"

I feel like a drowning woman who was just thrown a lifeline. "Yes, that's the one. The Verizon at the corner."

He smiles. Actually, it's more like a grin. "Is it weird to call you Dr. McCall? You know, after our last . . . session."

My cheeks heat. "About that . . ." He's opened the door. I need to say my piece and slam it back closed. Lock it and throw away the key forever. Yet I struggle to find the words to tell him how wildly inappropriate our last session was.

Before my mouth starts moving, Gabriel reaches out and cups my cheek.

He caresses it with his thumb. "I've missed you, *Meredith*." He steps closer and brings his mouth to my ear. "Did you miss me?"

Goose bumps prickle my arms, and every hair on my body jumps for the sky. My mind races with so many thoughts. I should tell him I didn't miss him and what happened between us was a colossal mistake. But that's not the truth, is it? Well, maybe the last part is, but I *did* miss him. And my body's reaction is proof of that. Though . . . something dawns on me, and I force myself to take a step back.

"You canceled your appointment again. I thought you were away?"

Gabriel's hand at my cheek slides to the back of my neck. He wraps his long fingers around and squeezes. Not enough to hurt, but enough that it reminds me how strong he is, how he held my body flush to the desk with one hand while he took me from behind.

"My plans changed. I just landed a little while ago. I was going to call your office first thing in the morning to see if I could get back on your schedule for Friday."

"Oh."

"Your assistant offered me an online session. But after the way we left things last time, I thought you might need some space. I also figured it might be best if, when we did talk, it was in person."

I stare into his eyes, looking for a hint of insincerity. Is he lying? Did he really just get in? Was he ever actually away?

But I can't find anything—not one way or the other.

He smiles. "I answered your question, but you still haven't answered mine, Meredith."

I'm backtracking through our conversation to figure out what question he's talking about when he chuckles. "I asked if you missed me, too."

"Oh," I say again. Apparently I'm a brilliant conversationalist today.

Gabriel bites down on his bottom lip. "Come home with me. I only live a few blocks away."

It's a terrible idea, and I know it. But . . . I would like to see the inside of his apartment. Maybe it will help me figure out this man. Plus, I'm not convinced he was even away. A suitcase next to the door might put my mind at ease that he's been truthful with me.

Before I finish deliberating, he's already nudging me. "Come on. We'll have a glass of wine."

The next thing I know, Gabriel is opening the door to his building. As I walk through the lobby, I scan the rows of mailboxes, the same ones I snuck in to look at months ago to confirm his identity, the first time I saw him from the coffee shop window.

He pushes a button to call the elevator. "Do you like red or white?"

"Either is fine."

"Does white go bad if it's not opened? I think I have a bottle in the fridge. But it's probably at least three months old."

Funny. Mine only lasts about three hours.

I force a smile. "I think it's good for a few years."

My pulse speeds up as the elevator doors slide open and we step inside. I can't believe I'm doing this. *Going into Gabriel Wright's apartment.* I'm crossing a line, but I've crossed so many already, what's one more?

"How was your week?" Gabriel asks.

"Good. And yours?" I pause and then add, "Your trip was unexpected, right? I hope everything is okay."

"It is now." He smiles.

I have ten follow-up questions on the tip of my tongue. Where were you? Who were you with? What happened that wasn't okay but is now? Yet instead, I merely smile back.

"I'm glad."

When we arrive on the fourth floor, Gabriel puts his hand on my back. He steers me out of the elevator car and to the left. Three doors down, he digs keys out of his pocket. "I hope I didn't leave any underwear on the floor. I wasn't expecting company."

Does that mean he's not seeing anyone else, or did he just not invite them over today? It's funny, I have so many good questions, yet none of them leaves my mouth.

Gabriel flicks on the lights. We walk in through a narrow hallway that dumps into a living room. My eyes jump around as fast as my heart beats. I'm looking for clues, but I'm not sure which mystery I'm trying to solve. The first thing I notice is there's no luggage. Not by the door and not in the living room. It takes a few days for mine to move more than a few inches from the threshold of my apartment when I return from a trip. Could he be the type that immediately rolls the suitcase into the bedroom and unpacks? Perhaps his luggage is already emptied and stowed.

The second thing I notice is he has a lot of books. Beautiful, leather-bound, old ones. The kind you find in a collectible store where the owner wears white gloves to touch editions kept behind locked glass. One entire wall is lined with built-in shelving. The middle, longest section sags from the weight of the stacks.

Gabriel walks up behind me as I take it all in and slips my coat from my shoulders. "I guess my secret is out. I'm a bookworm."

I smile. "Your collection is impressive."

He disappears with my coat and returns to stand close behind me once again. We're not touching, but I feel the heat emanating from his body, his hot breath tickling my neck. He wraps his hands around my shoulders, and I jump at his touch.

"Someone's on edge," he says. He's behind me still, but I can hear the smile in his voice.

"This, us, it's . . ." I'm again searching my mental thesaurus for the right word—inappropriate, unethical, immoral, *depraved*. I need to be careful my choice doesn't represent more than my being his doctor.

"Stop overthinking." Gabriel squeezes my shoulders. "We're two consenting adults. Both single."

Both single because of my husband. Because of me.

He leans in and kisses my neck. Soft lips rumble on my skin as he speaks. "Is this okay?"

I swallow and nod.

"I thought about you often this week," he whispers. "Did you think about me?"

Only every waking moment . . .

My breathing grows labored. His touch feels so good, so right, yet I know it's not. When I don't answer, he nips at my neck.

I gasp.

"You like that, don't you?" Again I hear the smile in his voice. "I have not been able to stop thinking about you telling me to hold you down and fuck you hard."

I swallow.

"Did you think about me?" he asks. "Think about what happened at our last session?"

I nod. It might be the only honest thing I've disclosed since he spotted me on the street.

"Good." He kisses over the skin he's nipped at. "Very good, Meredith."

Gabriel snakes one arm around my waist and uses it to pull me flush against him. His body is so hard, so warm. He sucks along my collarbone, and my eyes close, head lolling back shamelessly to give him better access. And then we're moving. Walking. He's guiding me, his body still pressed firmly to mine from behind. We step through a doorway. I see the bed, feel my knees hit the sideboard as we walk straight to it. I yield to the firm hand on my back that presses me forward until my chest is against the mattress.

Gabriel folds over me, his front to my back. He gathers my hands in one of his and stretches my arms up over my head. His teeth nip my earlobe, and I can't help myself. I moan.

"I love that sound." He groans. "I've dreamed about it every night since your office."

His free hand slips between us, under my dress. It reaches between my legs, impatiently yanks my panties to one side, and then his fingers are at my slick opening. "You think it's wrong, yet you're so wet already." Two, maybe three, fingers plunge inside. I'm not even sure, but it makes me gasp. It's rough, no foreplay, just like last time. My eyes roll into the back of my head, and another moan escapes my mouth when he pumps.

"Beautiful," Gabriel grits. His fingers pull almost all the way out and then sink deeper. I don't even catch my breath before he does it again. Then again. And again. I'm on the brink of flying over the edge when he abruptly stops.

He stands. I vaguely hear the sound of a belt opening, zipper being tugged down, and then I feel his wide, silky crown at my opening. Though he doesn't push inside. Instead, he reaches for my hair, wraps it around his fist.

"You want it hard again?"

I want it any way he wants to give it, but hard—*so hard it's punishing*—feels right. So I nod. "Harder."

The hand wrapped in my hair abruptly yanks—so damn hard that I lift off the bed. Gabriel uses his free hand to hoist me up at the waist, prop me up on all fours on the mattress. My scalp burns from how harshly he's still pulling my hair, but he enters me in one deep thrust, and I forget all about the pain. Or maybe the pain adds to my pleasure, heightens all of my other senses, because nothing has ever felt so good. He's buried so deeply inside me, my neck extended back. I'm completely under his control, and my body actually relaxes, gives in to him. I've been a knot of tension since our encounter last week in my office, thinking I needed to tell him I'd made a mistake, that this could never happen again. But it turns out *this* was exactly what I needed.

Gabriel powers into me from behind. It's rough and demanding, but I need it to hurt more. So I push back when he thrusts forward, each drive colliding with a loud smack. It's pummeling and bruising. I'll probably need to sit on a pillow tomorrow and will still feel battered, but I love every second of it. Each plunge is more punishing than the last, boring deeper and deeper. My body climaxes without warning. There are no thoughts in my head—no worry, no sadness, no regret—only unbridled pleasure rimmed with pain that I never want to end. But of course it does. Gabriel roars to his finish and pulls out.

I'm panting. My mind that was so eagerly blank only seconds ago immediately fills with racing thoughts.

Gabriel moves. My blurry eyes follow him around the room until he disappears behind a door. The bathroom, I assume. Then my vision comes into focus, and I see my surroundings for the first time. Things start to flash faster than my racing breaths.

A framed wedding photo.

A woman's bathrobe hanging on the back of a closet door.

A wedding ring on the nightstand.

Polaroids taped to the mirror above the dresser.

Smiling faces.

Kissing.

A beautiful little girl.

My eyes flood with tears.

A beautiful, perfect little girl.

Who is dead.

Dead.

I stand. And then run.

Through the book-lined living room.

Down the narrow hallway.

Out the apartment door.

Somehow I manage to grab my purse and scarf on the way out, but my jacket is a lost cause.

I find a stairwell and keep going.

Down four flights of stairs.

Out onto the street.

I don't stop running for blocks, until I reach a corner and make a sharp turn. Then I lean against a brick building, hands on my knees, trying to catch my breath. I'm not sure how long it takes. It's a while. But eventually my breathing returns to normal. I stand and look around. People are coming and going, like it's any other boring day of the week. No one pays attention to me. It's New York City, after all. An out-of-breath woman appearing slightly crazed is nothing unusual, I suppose. But then I really look around. I'm at the corner where I told Gabriel I'd gone to get my phone fixed. He'd asked if it was the Verizon store. He'd grinned when I said yes.

But there's no Verizon store here . . .

CHAPTER 33
Now

ours later, I'm still wandering the streets, unable to think straight.

I can still feel his hands on me. Feel him inside me. I picture myself gasping with exertion, with raw need and pleasure, and yet . . . and *yet* when I close my eyes, I see her. His wife. And then his child. The photos. The freaking robe.

A shiver snakes up my spine. It's too cold to be outside without a jacket. Behind me, there are footsteps—a figure moving closer. Maybe Gabriel has come looking for me?

Or maybe there's another random person wandering the streets in the middle of the night.

I don't want to deal with either, so I bolt back the way I came. Left instead of right. Right instead of left. And suddenly, I'm in front of the storage unit once again.

No Verizon store. There was no Verizon store. He smiled like he knew that already.

I stop, lean against a building, catch my breath once again. Maybe the Verizon store closed. Maybe it had been there, but now it's gone, and he didn't realize.

Or . . . he knows I was looking for him, wandering about near his apartment.

The thought seizes my insides. What would that even mean? I chew my nail, and my guts twist—God, the sex was exactly what I needed. Rough and punishing. It let me *relax*. It's addictive. I can understand Rebecca's desire for her boyfriend to do it that way. Especially if that's what she's used to. I mean, how could you go back to *normal* after *that*?

Maybe I was too quick to leave. I just got so freaked-out, surrounded by the remnants of his life from before. The life I destroyed. God, I'll have to say *something* to him after all this. No sane woman just runs into the night after having sex with a man. The doctor-patient thing is obviously still a huge problem. Maybe I can spin it that way. Will he see through it?

Wait—does he see me *right now*?

I look left, then right. The street is empty, so I close my eyes. A long exhale brings me back to myself. To the moment. To the cold New York street, the concrete building pressing into my back. I need to go home. Need to shut my door, lock it, and pretend this never happened. I'm an awful, awful person. Tracking the man whose family *you* destroyed. Then letting all this happen . . .

But as soon as I push from the wall to go, I look back up at the storage unit and let myself wonder what he might have hidden in there. What would cause him to go back day after day and spend not five minutes or ten minutes, but thirty minutes, an hour, in its depths?

Once I would have said it was his family's belongings. Maybe he holds his wife's favorite sweater up to his face the way I have yours, inhaling that lingering scent, fearful that one day it will dissipate into nothingness, and she'll be gone the way you're gone. That last trace, vanished.

But I can't think that anymore. Gabriel's apartment is still filled with his wife's things.

I stare at the brick storage unit once again.

I need to know.

Need. Not want.

I don't even understand *why* I need to know. Not even the good Dr. Alexander could tell me that. But it's a craving that comes from deep within my soul. And there's no stopping me from feeding it this time.

Across the street, a man is walking down the block. He holds two boxes in his hands, one on top of the other. He slows as he approaches the storage center, sets the boxes down in front of the door. My eyes widen. *He's going in . . .* Before I know it, before I have a chance to think things through, I'm jogging across the street, and I reach for the door the man just opened with a key card.

"Let me get that for you," I say. He turns and I offer a friendly smile. "My unit's just down the hall."

If I were a man, the guy probably would've thought twice. But I'm no threat to him. At least, that's what he thinks. Luckily, I don't look as unhinged as I feel.

"Thanks a lot." He picks up his boxes and steps inside, walks to the right a few paces, and disappears into a waiting elevator.

All the while, I'm holding my breath, and my heart feels like it's about to burst at any moment. Once he's gone, I blow out a shaky breath and tread to the right, the same direction I've watched Gabriel go many times before.

I count the units as I walk. Finally I'm making good use of the random notes I jotted down all those months ago. At the time, they were nothing more than scattered thoughts—scribbles from a woman on the verge of a breakdown.

Cigarettes.

Small coffee.

Corn muffin.

Twelve.

The last item being the window count from the storage unit entrance, the window where I watched a light flicker on every time he entered.

I arrive at the unit and stand in front of it. It looks no different from the other garage-type doors surrounding me. It's painted blue, and a round lock hangs from its latch.

I stare at it a long moment, replaying a conversation we had not too long ago. We were talking about the letter I'd had him write to his wife. *"Maybe I'll be less angry every time I punch in my PIN from now on,"* he'd said.

"Everything is her birthday—from my ATM code to door codes." And I couldn't forget that he'd said her birthday was Valentine's Day.

I swallow guilt as I reach for the lock and break another rule. Yet again. What's one more?

When it comes to Gabriel, it seems, the rules don't apply. Or rather, I don't mind breaking them. It might almost be worth suffering the consequences, because I just . . . I just *need to know.*

I turn the lock until the numbers line up—0214. There's a satisfying click. And suddenly, the lock is off the latch, heavy in my hand. And everything he's hidden is now available to me.

Mostly, it's boxes. The big, moving-company sort, preprinted checklists on the side so you can take a Sharpie and mark which room the box goes in. None of these is marked, though, like they were packed in a hurry and shoved in here. They're haphazardly placed, too, and the nearest one looks like the slightest breeze might dislodge it and send it toppling over.

It's not what I expected.

What in the world would a grown man do in a storage unit full of boxes?

I unwind my scarf. It's climate controlled. Not warm, but not cool like outside.

Maybe there's something in the boxes. For a moment, I consider closing the rolling door behind me—it's a little weird to be sorting through someone else's things so publicly, especially when, well, I'm breaking the law. What if someone comes in and knows who the unit belongs to? But one glance down the shadowy hall tells me it'll be a hell of a lot creepier to close the door and be trapped in here.

I run my fingers over the nearest box, then stand on tiptoe to pry open the lid, to see what's inside. A flash of pink, purple—I release the box and step backward, the contents a jolt. Toys. Little girls' toys, a jumbled mess within. A Barbie, a stuffed bear, what looks like an undressed American Girl doll, and . . . I exhale. Seeing his daughter's toys isn't what I expected. It makes it all very real. Very terrible.

My hands shake as I take another step back, second-guessing myself. Maybe I don't want to know. Maybe he comes in here to be around her belongings, belongings he couldn't bear to see in his house every day.

But what does he do, *just stand here?*

I swallow emotion, confusion, and force myself forward toward another box. Something small and square-ish gleams on the top of it, a set of keys or a keychain, maybe. But when I get close enough to make out the details, I recognize it.

The air in my lungs leaves in a single whoosh.

I struggle to breathe, to move.

I recognize it because it belonged to *you.* Your jersey. Your number 17. The specialty keychain I had made for you after you won the championship. I gave it to you the night we decided to start a family. And when you died, I took to carrying it around, carrying a piece of you around, a *reminder* . . .

Until one day it disappeared. The day I came out of the alley and crashed into Gabriel. I assumed I'd dropped it.

Apparently I had.

And Gabriel picked it up.

Meaning . . . I try to temper the rising panic threatening to choke me. *Gabriel knows who I am.*

He's known all along.

I drop the keychain back down and grab for the nearest stack of boxes, holding on for dear life.

No. It can't be.

The blood drains from my face, my body, right into my swirling stomach.

But it is. *It absolutely is.* This is the keychain I had made for you, a one-of-a-kind gift I commissioned from an artist. It even has the small mistake—some of the red paint bleeding into the blue. The maker was going to sell them, but they never made it to production because of the accident. *And it's in Gabriel's storage unit.*

I reach for it again, press the familiar smoothness into my palm. It practically burns a hole into it. A part of me is glad to have this—this piece of you from before everything went bad.

But most of me is confused. Terrified. My thoughts won't *move*, won't work, like my brain is frozen. Fight or flight or . . . frozen. I try to breathe. Try to get my body in motion again.

He—*he* has had this keychain all along? I picture him exiting the storage unit less than an hour ago, catching sight of me. Suggesting a nonexistent Verizon store. Playing me. I swallow, look down at the number. It's clear as day it had to be yours. The same team, the same number. Which has to mean he knows who I am. He knows I'm your widow. But why would he want to know the widow of the man who killed his wife and child?

The answer comes to me fast.

This whole time, I've felt as though I'm the one stalking him.

But maybe he's been the one stalking me?

The cloying sensation I recognize as a looming panic attack threatens to drop me to my knees, and suddenly, I have to get out—*out, out, out.* And I don't want *this.* I toss the keychain, and it clanks on the cement floor. Somehow I make it out of the storage unit. But the second I exit the door to the sidewalk, the echo of footsteps fills my ears.

I don't see him pounding down the sidewalk, don't see *anyone,* and it's entirely possible the footsteps are my imagination. Or someone turning down a nearby walkway or alley. But I don't care. I have to get away.

By the time I'm at my apartment, my breaths come in heavy pants. I've been walking regularly, but not running. Not sprinting. I haven't had reason to. I've always disliked running, often using the old line, "I only run if someone's chasing me."

And tonight, literally or figuratively, someone is chasing me.

Gabriel.

I force myself to sit down on the living room couch, to flick on the reading lamp, to try to think rationally. But my lungs squeeze tight, and my mind races with the ramifications. This changes everything. I flash back to those early days, following him from a distance. Watching him duck in and out of the storage unit, then head to campus. Grab lunch with all the different women.

How long has it been since I dropped the keychain?

And why didn't he confront me? *Months and months* have passed.

The night Gabriel walked in on my date with Robert. When he just happened to show up in my office, acting as though he didn't know me. I thought it was coincidence after coincidence. But it wasn't.

And the following—how many times have I thought someone was following me? Oh God, my apartment break-in. *The book on stalking! The Hello Kitty!*

Frantic, I pick up my cell. My hand trembles as I swipe to my contacts and move to my bedroom. My apartment is suddenly very large. Very empty. More than anything, I need a familiar voice. Irina? Can I call her after all this time? We were good friends at one point. I need someone I can trust to share this secret with. Someone I can go to, who will let me sleep in their spare bedroom. Because I can't stay here. Not tonight. Not alone. Irina will have to do.

I scroll down to her name and press call, while simultaneously grabbing the first gym bag I come across and start throwing necessities in—underwear, a change of clothes, shoes. The phone rings and rings before eventually rolling to voicemail.

"Damn it," I mutter. I throw the phone on the bed.

He knows where I live. He knows where I work. He's followed me repeatedly.

I'm not stalking him.

He's stalking me.

And I have no damn clue what his endgame is—mine was originally to help him. Well, maybe not at first. At first I was curious. How was he smiling? Laughing? But I knew it was a facade. He had to be in pain. And I needed to see it. I needed to feel his pain, deserved to suffer with him. And I had, during our sessions. But then I thought I could help. Repent, maybe.

Find a way to help him deal with his grief. But maybe he already had one—seeking revenge. On me.

No, no, no. If he wanted to hurt me, he'd have done that by now, right?

I stand perfectly still, a pair of pants in my hand, gaze unfocused, trying to understand. It's true, isn't it? If his goal was to hurt me—to make me suffer—he could have done that by now. He's had plenty of opportunity. He could have physically harmed me, or gotten my license taken away again. But he didn't.

Which makes me question what his plan *is*, if not to hurt me. What he *wants* from me.

I swallow. Zip up the bag. Snatch my phone and speed-dial Sarah.

Her voice is groggy, but I don't stop to consider the time. I just start barking into the phone. "Hello? Sarah? Cancel all future appointments with Mr. Wright. No. No, I don't want to discuss it. I don't care what you tell him. Just cancel them."

I disconnect and check the peephole at the front door.

No Gabriel.

I ease the door open, hurry down the hall, and burst out of the building. I don't know where I'm headed, but it will be somewhere he can't find me.

CHAPTER 34
Now

*T*ick. *Tick. Tick. Tick.*

I've been in this office for more than five years, but I've never heard the clock ticking before. Someone had to have made it louder. Did Sarah replace the batteries and the mechanics are suddenly firing on all cylinders? I stare at the second hand, watching its stuttering jumps from number to number and wondering if I'm going out of my mind. It's entirely possible I'm in the midst of a nervous breakdown and don't even know it. I think back to my first or second year of medical school, what the thick psychiatry textbook said were the classic symptoms of a break from reality.

Nervousness. If the constant bounce of my leg isn't confirmation enough, then the way I jumped when the hotel clerk said good morning to me today might seal the deal. Yes, I'm still staying at a hotel nearly a week later. One so far uptown I'm practically in the Bronx. The morning Uber ride in traffic takes me nearly forty-five minutes. But I won't take the train because Gabriel might see me.

Loss of appetite. An easy check mark, considering I can't remember the last time I put anything in my body other than copious amounts of coffee and wine.

Withdrawing from family and friends. I suppose I started this one the day after Connor died. I was too ashamed to face people then, even more so now. I mean, what would I tell people who ask what I've been up to? *Oh, not* much. *Just following the husband of the woman my husband killed. Actually, I'm not sure if I'm the stalker or the stalkee, but whatever. We fuck now, too.* My only real communication has been with my brother, Jake, and Sarah. But I haven't returned Jake's last three calls, and lately I've been holed up in my office, avoiding even my assistant.

Insomnia. Sleep? What's that?

Addiction. Self-medicating and alcohol abuse. Addicts smoke crack and drink four-dollar bottles of vodka in plastic bottles. The bottle and a half of wine I consume each night in a fancy glass makes me above that, right?

Paranoia and delusions. Someone really has been following me. No. Really. I swear they have.

Change in routine. Mood swings. Feelings of hopelessness and despair.

Check.

Check.

And a big fat check.

Tick. Tick. Tick. Tick.

Jesus, that fucking clock needs to shut up.

"Sarah!"

She opens the door in a rush. I point to the wall. "Did you change the battery in the clock?"

Sarah glances over at it. Her brows pull tight. "No. Does it need to be changed?"

I shake my head. "No, never mind."

She steps into my office and closes the door behind her. "Is everything okay, Meredith?"

I force a smile. The way it fits awkwardly on my face, I'm certain I look like the Joker. "Of course. Why wouldn't it be?"

Her eyes sweep over me. "Because you called me in the middle of the night the other day, and you've been really quiet lately. And . . . you wore that shirt yesterday."

I look down, and my eyes widen. That can't be. I went to a boutique on my way to the hotel from the office two days ago. I picked up a few blouses, underwear, and a pair of pants. Yesterday after work, I hung up my shirt and then this morning . . .

I took the shirt off the hanger and put it back on.

Oh. My. God.

"It's the same color," I lie. I'm not even sure why. "But a different blouse."

"Oh. Okay."

She doesn't believe me. I can tell.

Sarah's face softens. "I thought maybe you were struggling because of what this week is."

"What this week is?"

She smiles sadly. "Connor's birthday is still listed on the office calendar."

My heart skips a beat. I pick up my phone and check the date. Sure enough, tomorrow is his birthday. He would've been thirty-two. I feel sick. How could I forget my dead husband's birthday?

I swallow the lump of guilt in my throat and nod. "Yeah, it's a tough week."

"Is there anything I can do? Why don't we have dinner tomorrow night? Keep yourself occupied. I can get a sitter."

I force a smile. She means well. "Thank you. But I already have plans with my brother, Jake." A lie. What's one more?

"Oh, good. Well, at least you only have one more appointment today." She pauses before adding, "Since Mr. Wright is no longer on the calendar."

She's baiting me to talk about it. I know she's been curious about what happened with him. How could she not be? I've had her fire him as a patient twice. Yesterday when she told me she'd reached Gabriel and canceled, she tried to pry for more information. But I shut her down.

The door opens in the outer office, allowing me an easy escape from her curiosity this time. Sarah looks over her shoulder, toward the sound of the door closing. "That must be Mrs. Epstein. I'll talk to you later."

Lucky for me, Mrs. Epstein is one of my oldest and easiest patients. She has OCD, and we're working on some of her repetitive behaviors. I'm able to engage easily—for the first time in days. The hour goes by fast, but I'm so tired when she leaves. I think I might actually get some sleep tonight. In fact, I might doze off in the Uber back uptown. I take my purse out of my desk drawer, pull my phone from the charger, and slip on the cheap jacket I picked up to replace the expensive one I'll probably never see again.

I'm standing, ready to go, when there's a knock on the door again. Sarah opens it after two raps. She, too, has her jacket on. "Umm . . . Mr. Wright just walked in."

I'm sure all the blood drains from my face. "I thought you canceled his appointment?"

"I did. He says he just needs to speak to you for a minute. Do you want me to turn him away?"

I consider it. That would take care of the immediate problem. But dealing with Gabriel requires playing chess, thinking two steps ahead. If I have her turn him away, will he wait outside the building? Approach me when I walk out? What if he follows me to my hotel, figures out where I'm staying? No. No. I can't do that. I need to have some control of this game he's obviously playing. So I take a deep breath in and blow it out.

"No, it's fine. I'll see him. You can show him in."

Sarah nods. "Okay. But I'm staying until he's gone."

For once, I don't want privacy with Gabriel. I want to be able to yell for help, if need be. So I nod back. "Thank you."

Sarah disappears and returns a minute later. Gabriel's towering figure is right behind her. I hate that I notice how good he looks, how the scruff on his face highlights his strong jaw, and how his thick, dark eyelashes line his captivating eyes so perfectly. I muster a smile. "Thank you, Sarah."

Gabriel waits until she closes the door to move. Then he strides confidently to the couch and takes a seat. His arms splay wide across the top, like he's relaxed, comfortable even. I am anything but. I keep my distance, standing behind my chair, rather than sitting in it, like I normally would.

"Hello." I nod. "Sarah said you wanted to speak to me for a minute?"

There's a ghost of a grin on his lips. Unless you were specifically looking for it, most people wouldn't notice. But I do.

"Why did you cancel my appointment?"

If he's going to act like everything is fine, so am I. "You can't be my patient anymore, Gabriel. I think you know why."

He rubs his bottom lip with his thumb. "Okay. But if I'm not a patient anymore, there shouldn't be any issues with us seeing each other. Correct?"

"I don't think that's a good idea."

Gabriel's eyes drop down to my hands, where I'm holding the chair. I'm gripping it so hard my knuckles are white. His eyes eventually lift to meet mine.

"Let's go have a drink, talk outside the office. I can see it's causing you stress to discuss things here."

For my sanity, I *need* to know what he's after. What game he's been playing. So even though I know I'm messing with fire, I nod. "Blackstone's is down the block, and it's usually quiet. A restaurant with a small bar."

Gabriel stands. "Lead the way."

Sarah is still at her desk when we walk out of my office. I'd already forgotten about her. "Um, I'm going to walk Mr. Wright out."

A cheeky grin blooms on her face. "Have a good night."

My head is a jumbled mess as we stroll up the block. I'm not going to let on that I know he knows my true identity, so I'll have to stick to my story about violating doctor-patient rules. It's laughable, really. Sleeping with my patient is the least of my concerns at this point.

At the restaurant, Gabriel pulls out a stool for me, like he's a gentleman and this is some kind of a date. It's barely five o'clock, so the bar area is empty, except for us and the bartender. We order two glasses of wine, but I don't touch mine. I need to be of sound mind. Well, as sound as it can be these days.

"So . . ." Gabriel says. He flashes a shy smile, and for the life of me, I would swear it's genuine. "Was it that bad? That you ran out?"

I look down into my wineglass and shake my head. "The doctor-patient trust is sacred. It should never have happened."

"But now you're not my doctor."

I turn and look him in the eyes. "Did you follow me? The other night . . . after?"

"*What?*" Gabriel's eyes narrow. He rears back. He looks offended. "No. Clearly you needed some space. Why would you ask that?"

This man is either the world's best liar or he's telling the truth. But how can that be? Could he have picked up the keychain and not known who it belonged to? If he had found it on the street the day we crashed into each other, why would he have kept it? And everyone knows the colors of the New York hockey team . . .

My thoughts are interrupted by a voice. A familiar female one.

"Meredith?"

I turn to find Irina standing there. Next to her is her husband, Ivan.

My mouth gapes open. "Irina . . ."

She swamps me in a big hug. "I thought that was you."

Ivan nods with a sad smile. "Hey, Mer."

After the greetings, they both look to Gabriel. I have no choice but to introduce him—*to the best friend of the man who killed his wife.* My world just shrank so small I feel like I'm suffocating.

"This is Gabriel." I don't explain who he is or say his last name. The less said the better. "Gabriel, this is Irina and Ivan."

Ivan Lenkov is even more famous than Connor was. Anyone who's watched a New York hockey game would recognize him. But Gabriel doesn't flinch. He stands and offers a hand, and the men shake. "Nice to meet you."

"I've been meaning to call you," Irina says. "Have some lunch. But the third kid put me over the edge. I don't get out too often lately. I didn't even go to half the hockey games this season."

My eyes flash to Gabriel with the mention of hockey. Once again, he seems unfazed. I feel like my head might explode trying to figure this man out. Luckily, another couple walks in—the people Irina and Ivan are meeting for dinner—so I take advantage and say my goodbyes. Irina promises to call. She probably will, but I'll let it go to voicemail and never return her call. Whatever.

Then it's just me and Gabriel again. My heart races, my head is pounding, and . . . I realize I can't do this. I can't play this game anymore. Can't be the cat *or* the mouse. I just want to go home. I think about running, but I've been running for far too long. So I stand and look over at the man next to me.

"This is over, Gabriel."

His face scrunches up. "You're leaving?"

I nod, and then simply walk out the door. This time without looking back.

CHAPTER 35
Now

I used to enjoy the end of the day. Organizing my files, letting my patients pass back through my mind as I remember how I helped them or try to think of what more I could say or do to get them through whatever they're dealing with.

Today, as I sip supposedly calming chamomile tea, my gaze slips toward the window, checking the sidewalk out in front of my practice.

"Any messages?" I call to Sarah. My voice is strong, confident. I'm anything but.

I've had a dozen messages this week. Eight of them were from Gabriel.

And he didn't stop there. He's emailed, too, filling my inbox with:

Meredith, let's talk—

And

Meredith, don't shut me out. Let's be adults here.

Adults. *Adults* implies we're mature. That we can have a normal, sane conversation. But that's not possible. He's lying to me. Probably to himself, too. Because he knows who I am. He knows who *you* were.

I inhale a rattling breath and wrap my cardigan around me more tightly to ward off the chill. It's not cold in the office—it's cold inside me. Cold dread, trying to understand what his long game is. It's all I've thought of these past days.

I thought I was obsessed with him. Now I think he's the one obsessed with me. And that distinction leaves me breathless.

"Sarah?" I call again, because she hasn't answered.

"Sorry, Meredith. I was just taking a message." She hurries in, holding two yellow sheets with notes scrawled across them. "One is Mr. Wright. He said he was returning your call and to put him right through, but you were with a patient." She raises her brows, waiting for me to confirm or deny, or give details. I nod tightly, taking the paper.

"Thank you."

"And this one is from Ms. Nash." She hands over the other note, lingering.

I thank her again and add, "You can head home, Sarah. I appreciate it." Dismissing her. Shutting her out.

She gives me a tight smile and nods, turns to leave. And for a moment, I hope she'll stop. I hope she'll turn around and demand to know what's going on with Gabriel. Probably she thinks we're having some sort of weird affair. Though I don't know in what world a man calls a woman's office and leaves messages with her assistant on nonstop repeat.

I blow out a breath. If it were something a patient was going through, I'd call it stalking.

But can I call it stalking? I mean . . . who stalked first?

I listen to the sound of Sarah preparing to leave—a drawer opening, closing. Her purse, I know, is now over her shoulder. There's the zip of her jacket, followed by the shuffle of footsteps.

I almost stop her. Almost say, "Can I talk to you?" and tell her everything, because I need someone else's take on it. Am I losing my mind? I might be. I just might be. I take a trembling breath and step forward, toward the door that separates the rooms. I know that at least she won't tell anyone. She's my employee.

But as I open my mouth to call to her, she's gone. The front door closes.

And because I'm not yet ready to leave, and because I wouldn't put it past him to show up here, I hurry forward and turn the dead bolt.

Twenty minutes later, I've gathered my belongings. My body is tense, rigid. I wish there was a peephole through my office door. But at least it lets out into a hallway—a hallway where other offices exist in case I need to call for help.

That makes me pause. Do I think Gabriel means me harm?

I can't say yes. But I can't say no, either.

The second I step outside, I swear I feel eyes on me. That creeping, tingling feeling, like someone's about to sneak up behind me. I'd say I'm nearly used to it—I've felt it every day since that night at Gabriel's apartment. And even before that, though I'd chalked it up to being in my head. So it's not new, but you don't get used to feeling like someone's prey. I wore flats today, just in case.

I swallow.

In case I need to be able to run.

I cast a look behind me. The sidewalk is full of people, hurrying home after hours, hand in hand on an early date, mothers grasping children's hands. But no Gabriel. Random eyes slant toward me as I search the crowd. I'm sure they're thinking, *Who's that crazy lady who won't stop looking over her shoulder?*

I recount the diagnostic material for paranoid personality disorder: pervasive, persistent, and enduring mistrust of others—something like that. But that's not me, right? It's not *all* others. It's just him.

I clutch my bag tighter and turn a corner, varying my route. Because that's what I do now.

My phone is in my hand, my fingers sweaty on it. Perhaps I should call Irina. Or Dr. Alexander? Or even call Sarah, tell her I could use her back at the office, or offer to go to her house. No, no, she has a child. I can't have him following me there, of all places.

I turn again, then step into a minimart. I feign browsing magazines, but really, I'm watching the sidewalk. Two men walk by. A young woman. Two kids, hurrying home from school. No Gabriel.

When I step back outside, a magazine in hand—I didn't want to piss off the guy who ran the place after standing there browsing for ten minutes—I recognize where I am. Dr. Alexander's practice is a block away. Which means I've walked several miles, circling my usual route, trying to catch Gabriel on my tail.

Not normal. Not normal at all.

But it is an answer of sorts to my problem.

I hurry toward his office, glancing at the time on my phone—6:10 p.m. Dusk is just starting to settle over the world. But maybe he'll still be there. Maybe he'll let me in, and I can talk, relieve some of this pressure inside me. Maybe he can give me his professional opinion—*"No, Meredith, I think you're totally normal."* I snort out loud. I'm not normal. This isn't normal. I can admit that much to myself.

I catch sight of him a second later. His tall, lanky form skips down the steps of the building, jangling keys in his palm, whistling, not a care in the world—if only that could be me.

"Dr. Alexander," I call. He doesn't hear me and turns to walk the opposite way, the flowering cherry tree above him making it almost picturesque. "Dr. Alexander!" I call, louder this time, pounding down the sidewalk behind him.

This time he turns. His eyes are wide, his stance defensive—like he's being accosted on the street by a patient, which he is.

It makes me take a breath. Remember myself.

What would I think if someone did this to me?

I'd think they were desperate. Which I am.

"I'm sorry to stop you like this," I say. "I just really need to talk. It's an emergency."

Dr. Alexander stares down at me. His mouth opens, and he hesitates. "I'm sorry, Meredith, but I have plans this evening."

"Please. I can—" I dig in my purse. "I can pay in cash. I can talk while we walk. I really need help."

"Meredith, you know as well as I do that we have to have boundaries around our practice." He gives me a grim smile. "But I can refer you to an emergency clinic, or my receptionist is still at his desk. You could call and see if we can work you in for tomorrow morning. I'll come in early, if need be."

I squeeze my eyes shut. I can't wait until tomorrow morning. And there's no way in hell I'll go to an emergency clinic. I can't tell some random stranger what's happening.

When I open my eyes, I pin Dr. Alexander with my gaze, and it just comes out.

"I fucked Gabriel Wright in my office."

Shock, horror, judgment. They spill over his features a second before he returns to his excellent therapist's poker face. His Adam's apple bobs, and he shifts his weight. Finally, he gives a little nod, and a second later, he's gesturing to the staircase, ushering me back toward his office.

CHAPTER 36
Now

"This box came for you." Sarah points to the corner of her desk. I know exactly what's inside. Thank heaven for Amazon Prime and next-day delivery.

"Thank you." I scoop the package into my arms. "Why aren't you shut down and ready to go home yet? Charlie has cello today, right?"

Sarah nods. "I'll leave in a few minutes. But I wanted to talk to you before I go."

Ugh. Here it comes. I've been avoiding anything more than a chat about scheduling with her for the last week. I see the way she's been looking at me—like I'm a few fries short of a Happy Meal. Which isn't too far off base. Though the last few days I've felt like I was doing better. I look down at the box in my hands, remembering its contents. *Maybe not that much better.*

I force a polite smile. "What's up? What do you want to talk about?"

Sarah waits until my eyes meet hers. "Gabriel Wright."

My heart takes off like a runaway train just from the mention of his name. I hold the box in my hand tighter. "What about him?"

She frowns. "He called twice again today."

That's less than last week, at least.

Before I can address it, she continues. "Did something happen between the two of you? Ever since you had me drop him as a patient, you haven't seemed like yourself. And he just keeps calling. I promise I won't judge if something, you know, personal happened."

A week ago I felt desperate to talk about everything going on. I would have vomited every detail if she'd pushed like this. But talking to Dr. Alexander helped, and the last few days have truly felt like I've made progress. I've been looking over my shoulder less, checked out of the hotel I'd been staying in and went back to my apartment, took the subway rather than an Uber once. I even returned my brother's call and answered a text from Irina promising to have lunch soon.

But I don't want to rehash everything that transpired and cause a setback. Plus, it isn't a short story, and I have a patient in fifteen minutes—Rebecca, of all people. Not to mention Sarah needs to get home to her son. So I tell her the truth, but only a very minuscule part of it.

I sigh. "Mr. Wright lost his wife. Talking about it dredged up a lot of painful memories for me. I thought I could handle it, but it hit me harder than I expected."

Sarah's eyes soften. "I'm so sorry, Mer. That must've been tough."

I nod. "It was. But I'm talking to my therapist about it now. So you don't need to worry about me."

"Okay. But I'm here, too. Anytime you need to talk. Day or night. If we're not at the office, you can always call me, you know."

My smile is genuine this time. "Thank you, Sarah. You're a good friend."

She pulls her purse from her drawer and slips on her jacket. "I'm going to stop downstairs at the deli for a coffee. I'm dragging today. Want me to grab you one before I head out?"

"Actually . . ." I look at my watch. "I have almost twenty minutes before my last appointment of the day. So I think I'm going to run downstairs and grab a cup myself. I could use the fresh air, and it's so nice out today."

"Okay. I'll see you in the morning."

"Good night, Sarah. And thank you for checking on me."

After she leaves, I go into my office with the box that came. Slicing the tape seam down the middle with the letter opener, I remove the packing paper and take out the contents.

The Quiet Clock.

The internet said it was a hundred percent noiseless, but I'll be the judge of that . . .

After I insert the batteries, I hold it up to my ear. *Ah, quiet.* Satisfied, I drag a chair over to the offensive clock currently hanging on the wall and climb up to make the switch. The old one in my hands greets me.

Tick. Tick. Tick.

"Oh no you don't," I say aloud. I remove the batteries from the back before I climb down from the chair. And for good measure, after they're out, I hold the batteryless clock to my ear.

Quiet.

I breathe a sigh of relief.

Now for a quick dose of fresh air and some herbal tea, and I'll be feeling good as new.

Or so I think . . .

Until the elevator doors slide open at the lobby level, and I see the man coming through the building's turnstile door.

Gabriel.

I dart over to one side of the elevator and stand against the wall, sucking in my gut so he can't see me. Then I frantically push the close button on the elevator panel—at least thirty times in ten seconds. I don't breathe until the doors slide shut, and I'm still the only one inside. My body shakes as the car travels up to my floor, and the second the doors slide open, I sprint to the safety of my office.

Once I'm inside, I decide that the only thing I can do is pretend I'm not here. So I lock myself in my office and try to catch my breath so I can be quiet. But as I'm gulping for air, I realize I didn't lock the outer door. I hate to go out there, but I don't even want him in the reception area. Before I make a run for it, I press my ear to the door to listen for noise, and just as I do, I hear the door creak open.

My heart beats so fast I actually start to worry I could have a heart attack. "Hello? Dr. McCall? Sarah?"

Shit. It's not Gabriel. It's Rebecca Jordan. My next patient.

I have no idea what to do. Do I let her in? Will having her here be a deterrent for Gabriel? Stop him from doing whatever he came to do because another person will see? Maybe. But then he'll know I'm here, and Rebecca will eventually leave, and I'll have to leave this office sometime. He could wait. And wait.

The handle to the door I'm pressed against jiggles, and I jump. I have to slap my hand over my mouth to keep from screaming. I need to pretend I'm not here, even if it means standing up my patient.

Knock. Knock. Knock.

"Dr. McCall? Are you in there?"

I hold my breath, even under my covered mouth.

Then I hear the outer door creak open again. Is she leaving already? Or is it Gabriel coming in . . .

The question is answered when a man's voice booms from the other room.

"What *the fuck* are you doing here?"

"I—Dr. McCall is my psychiatrist," Rebecca says. She sounds scared. Even though I'm out-of-my-mind terrified, I can't let Gabriel intimidate my patient. My trembling hand goes for the doorknob. But I freeze when I hear what comes next.

"Bullshit, Rebecca!" Gabriel roars. "You're following me again, aren't you?"

CHAPTER 37
Now

I press against the door, barely breathing. *What the hell is going on out there?* My grip tightens on the knob, but I don't dare twist it. Not yet.

After a long moment, Gabriel adds, *"Answer me, goddamn it!* Why are you following me again?"

Rebecca is silent.

I'm so lost. *Following . . . again?* Why would my patient be following him? I feel like I might jump out of my skin as I wait for more, but there's nothing. Long seconds tick by. The anxiety inside me builds and builds. What if she's not saying anything because his hands are around her throat? What if he's snapped? After all, it's clear I don't know the real Gabriel. But this is my office, Rebecca is my patient, and I need to protect her.

I can't wait any longer. I swing the door wide. "What's going on out here?" I try to summon all my doctorly authority, but it falls flat. The two of them don't even look my way. Gabriel and Rebecca are standing four or five feet apart, glaring at one another, almost like they didn't notice my arrival.

"Don't you get it?" Rebecca says. Her hands go wild, gesturing. "We can be together now. You're finally free. You can tell me everything you couldn't tell anyone else, the way you used to. I've missed you. I keep trying to get ahold of you, but . . ." Her chin wobbles.

Gabriel growls. Actually growls. "Get the fuck out of my life! It's your fault they're dead!"

Silence fills the space again. Without warning, Rebecca sobs and runs out of the office. I watch her go, my mind spinning, trying to make sense of the situation playing out before me.

Before I can say anything—or ask Gabriel to leave—he turns and locks eyes with me. My stomach swims, seeing the fury behind his gaze.

"What kind of sick game are you playing?" he demands.

"*What?*"

"You won't answer my calls, you won't answer my messages. I come to see you, and *she's* here?"

I hesitate, because I don't want to violate doctor-patient privacy. It's not my place to say Rebecca is a patient. Except she said so, didn't she?

"I don't understand what's happening." I swallow. I'm still shaking. I want him to leave, but I'm also curious. "How do you know Rebecca?"

"She's the woman who ruined my life. Who destroyed it. We were . . . together." He hangs his head. "It wasn't my wife who was the cheater. It was me. But it was a mistake, and I tried to fix it. I ended things with her." He gestures to the door. "Rebecca. She refused to accept it was over. I wouldn't see her. I refused to talk to her. Then one night, she came to the house and told my wife everything. Ellen left. She took my daughter and ran out, and"—he exhales, a shuddering breath—"the next thing I knew, they'd been hit, killed instantly by a drunk driver."

The aggression on his face fades to desperation. Grief drips from each word, from the beaten-down positioning of his body. He extends one arm to press against the doorframe, almost as though he can't keep himself upright.

The reality of it all leaves me stunned. I drop into Sarah's chair.

"She was your girlfriend . . ." I trail off.

At his nod, I think back to Rebecca talking about her ex-*boyfriend*. The one she wanted back, the one she compared every other man to. Was that Gabriel?

"I had no idea." I shake my head. "She came in one day and made an appointment, and I had no reason to believe she was anything but a patient.

She never asked about you or anything." I stop talking, because I'm dangerously close to breaching patient confidentiality. "I'm sorry," I add.

"When did you start seeing her?" he asks.

I think back, gulp when I realize the timing. "Not long after you first came in."

I expect him to go. To take himself and his grief outside. I certainly can't be the one to help him, not after everything. But he just keeps talking, like we're in session.

"She destroyed my life. One thing at a time. When I ended it—she had been my student, but not when we were dating, before." He slides down the wall to sit on the floor, knees up, hands hanging helplessly over them. "When I ended it, she went to the other professors. My peers, my boss. She told them everything. I nearly lost my job. But she's of age, and I wasn't her professor at the time. Everything was always consensual. Then she started following me." He shakes his head. "I'd thought she stopped, but she must've followed me here."

Following him. Like I had.

My throat clenches, and I want to tell him to stop—to leave, because I don't want to know. I don't want it made any clearer to me how wrong I was all this time. But he just keeps talking.

"It got out of control. I threatened to go to the police. And for a little while I thought she finally understood things were over. But then she came to me at work, sobbing in my office about how much she missed me. She started to undress, and I said no. And that's . . ." He pauses to take a deep breath. "That's the night they died. The night she ruined my life. My wife would have never been out walking around that night if Rebecca hadn't told her what we did."

"I'm so sorry." Useless words. I say them anyway, because I don't know what else to offer.

Gabriel looks up, meets my eyes from across the room. "And that's how it happened. That's how my family ended up being killed by your husband."

I gasp. He knows. He's known all along, and now I know it for certain.

Gabriel lowers his gaze to the floor, shakes his head, and climbs to his feet like it takes great effort.

"Goodbye, Meredith." He walks out the door, leaving it open behind him.

CHAPTER 38
Now

I
t's too much to process.

Even after hours, my mind can't seem to wrap around all of the information. Can't wrap around how foolish I've been not to recognize that Gabriel was playing me all along. It doesn't help that I've started drinking. Again. *That never helps.*

I need to talk to someone. My choices are limited. There's my brother, but if I told him one-tenth of the crazy story I'm living, he'd be so worried he'd camp out on my couch and never leave. Plus, Jake has a family. I shouldn't be his problem. I *won't* be his problem. I could call Dr. Alexander, of course. But he'd want to delve into *my* psyche, try to convince me to let go. What I need is to delve into *their psyches*—Gabriel's and Rebecca's. Plus, there's the matter of doctor-patient confidentiality. Because of that, there's only one person I could really talk to about all this—Sarah. My patients sign forms allowing disclosure of confidential mental health information to my staff. After all, Sarah does the insurance billing, so she knows the diagnoses and patient histories.

But it's nearly ten o'clock already, and she has Charlie. So I feel bad calling. Though after another glass of wine, I seem to get over it.

"Meredith?" she answers. "Is everything okay?"

"No. It's not, Sarah. I need to talk to someone."

"Say no more. I'll be over in twenty minutes."

"What about your son?"

"He's with his father tonight."

"Oh." That makes me feel a little better about calling. "Thanks, Sarah. I appreciate it. I'll see you soon."

I finish my current glass of wine and have another before there's a knock at my door. Sarah takes one look at me and her face falls.

"You look like shit, Mer. Did someone hurt you?"

I shake my head and step aside so she can enter. "No. Nothing like that. I promise."

Inside, I uncork a new bottle of wine and pour glasses for both of us. "Full disclosure," I say, extending one to her: "I've had three already."

"It's okay. I had two at home by myself earlier."

I smile and we go into the living room together, taking seats next to each other on the couch. I tuck my legs underneath myself and try to figure out a place to begin. But this story is like a ball of yarn; if I cut any one string and start it rolling, the entire thing will unravel. So I decide to start at the worst place, get it over with.

I swallow. "Gabriel Wright isn't just a patient. He's the husband of the woman Connor mowed down, the woman and child he killed."

Sarah's eyes bulge. She raises her glass to her mouth and chugs half of it down.

I smile sadly. "We're both going to feel like shit tomorrow. Because that's only the beginning of this story."

"Maybe I should get the bottles and we'll just put straws in?" Sarah says.

"Don't tempt me."

Over the next half hour, I tell Sarah the entire story—from how I'd started following Gabriel, to him mysteriously showing up at the office and seeming not to know who I was, to sleeping with him during our session. Then I place the cherry on top—Rebecca's story, how she fits into all this.

Sarah's jaw hangs open when I finally stop to take a breath.

"Jesus Christ, Mer. That is so fucked-up. Are you afraid of him? Or her? Of them? Like do you fear for your safety?"

I nod. "I didn't before today. Though I've felt like I was being followed for months. I suspected maybe it was Gabriel, but I couldn't be certain. In hindsight now, maybe it wasn't that I *couldn't* be certain, but I didn't *want* to be certain. Because if I was, I'd have to stop what I was doing. And I didn't want to. I was emotionally tangled with Gabriel on so many levels." I pause. "But I do feel scared for my safety at this point. I knew Rebecca had issues, but to start seeing me as a therapist because the guy she's obsessing over is also a patient? At least, that's what I have to assume she did. That feels almost *Fatal Attraction* level. I think I might need to get a restraining order or something."

Sarah nods. "I definitely think you should get one. You can't walk around in a constant state of fear."

I drink the rest of the wine in my glass. "It will be complicated to go to the police, because of doctor-patient confidentiality."

"Isn't there an exception to that rule when someone is in danger?"

I nod. "Yes, but what if I'm wrong? What if Rebecca is just a scorned ex-girlfriend with an obsession over her boyfriend? It's really only a feeling I have that she might be dangerous to me. She's never made a threat or anything. And as far as I know, she's never made one to Gabriel, either. And Gabriel has never threatened me. In fact, I had sex with him on more than one occasion and went to his apartment!" I rake my fingers through my hair, pulling at the roots. "Sarah, what the hell have I done to myself? What have I gotten myself into? This entire thing could have been avoided if I hadn't followed Gabriel the first time I saw him. I started this. *I brought this on myself.*"

"No, you didn't. Don't you dare take that on. You might've followed him, but it all started innocently. You said so yourself—you followed him that first day to find out if he was happy, because you had so much guilt over what happened. But regardless, even if you did start the ball rolling, it's gone too far now. You shouldn't have to feel like you're in danger."

"I'm not even sure I have the whole story yet. Even with everything I know now, I feel like I have only half the pieces of a puzzle. I wish I had asked Gabriel why he came to my office, what he wants from me. And why he's been following me."

"Oh my God." Sarah's eyes go wide again. "I just thought of something."

"What?"

"A few weeks ago, you and I left the office at the same time. I was waiting across the street at my normal bus stop, and I saw Rebecca doing it."

"What do you mean? Doing what?"

"She was about half a block behind you, sort of weaving in and out of the crowd. I thought it was a strange way to walk, but hey—we live in New York City. Now it makes sense. She was keeping back from you and trying to stay hidden behind people. Mer, what if it's not Gabriel Wright who has been stalking you the last few months, but Rebecca Jordan?"

CHAPTER 39
Now

hen I blink awake, I'm not in bed.

Not even on the couch.

Disoriented, I roll onto my back, only to feel the press of cold, hard tile beneath my shoulder blades.

The bathroom. I spent the night in the bathroom again. Overhead, the bright bulbs over the sink all but blind me. I push to sitting, and then, with one hand on the edge of the counter, pull myself all the way up.

Big mistake.

My vision tilts. I lower myself back to the floor as my stomach threatens to empty itself. Something smells. Me? I smell, and I smell horrible. The remnants of already vomiting, of perhaps not making it to the toilet on time. I exhale, and hot tears stain my cheeks. I feel like one of my wineglasses, fragile, like I could shatter into a million pieces.

I try to climb to my feet again, desperate for water to quench my dry mouth, to get the acrid flavor of bile out of my teeth. I rinse, spit, and take big gulps of cool water. Eventually, I turn the faucet off and look up to meet my gaze in the mirror.

Jesus Christ.

I barely recognize myself. Smeared makeup, blotchy skin, hair awry. I'm pretty sure the speckles over my sweater are vomit. I turn the shower on hot, not bothering to strip before I step in. The burning water temperature makes me gasp, but I let it get to the point that it's unbearable before I turn it down a notch. Then I strip and reach for a body sponge, adding eucalyptus bodywash and slowly scrubbing every inch of myself.

I'm disgusting.

And I'm disgusted with myself.

Somewhere in the midst of trying to make myself feel clean again, *normal* again, I suddenly remember.

Last night. Wine. Sarah.

I told her everything.

And she said . . . I gulp back another round of nausea threatening to spill forth. She said she saw Rebecca following me. I lean on the wall, the shower beating down on me, considering the implications. Considering the relationship she must have had with Gabriel. The fact he's been stalking me. Or she has. Or maybe both of them.

I scrub at my face until it hurts.

Eventually, I turn off the water. Somewhere in my apartment, my phone chimes, then chimes again. Then a third time. I tense with each notification, heart rate climbing and climbing, wondering who's so desperate to get a hold of me. I wrap myself in a towel—a towel that smells, that needs to be washed. I toss it on the ground and open the linen closet to grab a fresh one. But it's empty. My pulse climbs higher. I don't even have a clean towel. I retrieve the dirty one and wrap it around my body, pondering what else I've forgotten to do. What else I've missed in this haze I've been living in.

My phone is hidden between couch cushions. The only reason I find it is that another text comes through. I breathe with relief when I see who it is—Sarah, checking on me. She's already sent two messages.

> Sarah: Good morning, sunshine. I wanted to check in after our late evening. Are you up?

And then

> Sarah: Listen, I'm a little worried. Be careful, okay? Call me if you need anything.

I quickly tap out a response, hating that I've made her worried when she's been so kind to me.

> Meredith: All is well. Thanks for everything last night.

Then I swipe to my email.

There are two from Gabriel.

Both empty, except for the subject line.

The first one reads:

We need to talk.

The second came in ten minutes later:

I'm serious. Call me.

In my head, his words are not kind. Are not a polite ask. They're a curt demand. Sarah's warning comes back to me. She's worried. She thinks I need to be careful.

I realize, I think I do, too. And it's time to do something about it.

———————

"Detective Green, please."

The officer at the front desk looks at me over her glasses. "Name?" she asks. "And what's this about?"

"Meredith McCall." And because the woman shows no recognition of the name, I add, "Connor Fitzgerald's wife."

At that, her eyes widen. "Take a seat, please. I'll see if he's available."

I pick a chair in the corner, putting my back to the wall. A second after I sit, I realize it's a defensive posture. Something I watch for in my patients. My eyes linger on the door. I watched behind me the whole walk here, keeping an eye out for Gabriel, for Rebecca. I glance down at my phone, and he's emailed again. Just a subject line, like before.

Can I come over?

I tense and look up, hoping to catch sight of Detective Green. A clock ticks above the front desk, that same *tick-tick-tick* of my old clock. For the briefest moment, I can understand how my patients become delusional. How they start to think even a clock is out to get them. My breath shudders as I exhale and turn away from the damn thing. I wish the detective would just get here already.

The door opens. And he stands in front of me, hands tucked in his cheap suit pockets, a patient look on his face that he probably thinks is a smile. But it's not, not really.

"Dr. McCall, how can I help you?"

I look up at him but say nothing.

His brows furrow as he stares at me. "Are you all right?"

"No."

Indecisiveness flashes across his face, but he gives a little wave. "Come on back, Dr. McCall. Coffee? Water?"

"Water, thanks."

A minute later, we're tucked into a gray cubicle. A few old photos are pinned to the wall, but otherwise it's neat, clean. A single coffee mug, a plastic bottle of water, a notepad, a pen, and a computer.

He takes the seat behind the desk and splays his palms open. "What's going on?"

My trembling fingers touch the plastic water cup. I've rehydrated and scrubbed and put on clean clothes, but the residue of last night—of these last months—still clings to me. I wonder if I'll ever feel normal, like myself again. Maybe someday. When this is all a memory. Maybe there's even still time to meet someone new. To have a family. I can almost see it, a flicker of light in a world that's felt like twilight for a long time now.

I take a slow, deep breath before looking him in the eyes. "I need to get a restraining order against someone. Him and his . . ." I search for the right word. "Ex-girlfriend? They've been stalking me. Following me out on the street. They know where I live. I think. A few months ago, I came home to my apartment door open. No one was inside, but someone had been. I know it." I try to think of how to explain that Rebecca became my patient, I assume, to get close to me. Probably Gabriel did, too. But I decide to leave that part out, at least for now. It would mean breaking patient confidentiality. I've read the American Medical Association's Code of Ethics multiple times over the last few days. A doctor may break confidentiality when a patient threatens to inflict serious physical harm on a specific, identified person and there is a reasonable probability that the patient will carry out the threat. Or when a crime is likely to occur. Neither Gabriel nor Rebecca has made any threats. I couldn't even tell Detective Green if Gabriel had told me he'd murdered his own wife, unless he also threatened my life or someone else's, and I thought he might actually do it. But they've followed me, outside of our sessions, outside of when I've treated them as a physician. And stalking is a crime. So I can report their following, but not disclose that they are patients or anything that was said during our sessions. I'm well aware how thin the line is I'm straddling.

Detective Green's frown deepens, but I can tell I have his full attention. "Who?"

I take another breath, another attempt to calm my nervous system. "Gabriel Wright."

The detective's eyes go wide. "Gabriel Wright? The man whose family . . ." He shakes his head. "When did this begin? Can you be more specific about what he's doing?" He pulls out a pad of paper and scribbles notes as I answer his questions.

"And what interactions have you had with him? Has he initiated all of them, or have you initiated any?"

I press my lips together, answering as truthfully as possible. I tell him what I can, about feeling eyes on me, hearing footsteps behind me. But again—I can't tell him he's a patient. I also won't tell him Gabriel and I slept together, because that is yet another thing that can get me in trouble. There's so much I can't say. I also realize the irony of me sitting here asking for a restraining order against a man who, a few months ago, might've had grounds to get one against me because of my stalking. But my intentions were never to harm; just the opposite, really. And I have no clue what Gabriel's intentions are.

By the time I've answered all of Detective Green's questions, he's leaning back in his chair in a way that tells me that there's probably not enough to get a restraining order. I squeeze my hands into fists, almost ready to say the rest—that Gabriel and Rebecca both *just happened* to come to me for therapy. But instead I move on and explain how Gabriel followed me on one of my dates, interrupted in the middle of it. And how I went walking the other night, and he appeared out of nowhere, stopping me. None of it is untrue. I just leave out the part where I was excited to see him, where I went back to his apartment and we had sex.

"I don't know what to say, Dr. McCall. This is highly unusual. And seeing someone around town—especially in Manhattan—I mean, of course you'll recognize him, but that doesn't mean he's stalking you."

My breath catches. I need more. I have to tell him more.

"His ex-girlfriend. Like I said, she's stalking me, too."

"How do you know?"

"My assistant has seen her following me. She's come to my workplace. She's followed me." I swallow, trying to think of what more I can say. "I don't feel safe. I want restraining orders against both of them."

"Well, we can try." Detective Green scribbles more notes. "Though I have to tell you, I'm not hearing any specific threat to your safety. And for some reason, I feel like you're not telling me the entire story, Dr. McCall."

I blow out a jagged breath and nod. "There are things I *can't* say, because I'm not permitted. If you can read between the lines . . ."

He squints at me. "*Can't* say, not *won't*? So this has to do with doctor-patient confidentiality, then?"

I try to keep my face as impassive as possible. "I can't say."

He frowns and pulls open a drawer. "All right. Well, there are some forms to fill out. I'll bring it to the DA and then a judge will review it. Can you tell me the girlfriend's name?"

Again, I hesitate, but I have a right to protect myself.

"Rebecca Jordan."

The detective writes it down, but halfway through her last name, he goes still.

"Why does that name sound familiar?" he murmurs, staring down at it. He finishes writing, blinks, and then looks up at me. "Hang on a sec." He stands, goes to a file cabinet, and pulls the middle drawer out. He skims through what looks like a hundred files. I watch, confused, wishing he'd give me the forms already so I can get this over with. I'm itching to get out of here. To get home.

Finally, he settles back in his chair, flipping through papers. He runs a finger down a form filled out in black ink, and again goes still.

He looks up.

"There obviously wasn't a trial, so the only time I came across the name was when I took the witness's statement and later when I typed it up. Which was a long time ago now. That's why it only rang a vague bell."

"Witness?" I say. "I'm confused."

Detective Green turns the paper in his hand to face me and points to the middle of the page. "Rebecca Jordan was the witness who saw your husband's car hit the Wrights."

CHAPTER 40
Now

"S eventeenth Precinct. How many I direct your call?"

"Hello. I'd like to speak to Detective Green, please."

It's my second call in two days, but it's been three since I went to speak to him. And nothing. No calls. No update. Definitely no restraining order.

"Detective Green isn't in today. Is there anyone else who can help you?"

I sigh. "I don't think so."

"Would you like to leave a message on his voicemail?"

"Um, sure. Thank you."

The woman connects me. Detective Green says something about hanging up and calling 911 for an emergency, and then there's a long, flat beep. Normally I'd organize my thoughts before I left someone a voicemail, but I don't bother to try now. I already know it's not possible to sound calm and collected, and I'm past the point of caring.

"Hi, Detective Green. It's Meredith McCall. I was hoping to get an update on the restraining order, because, well . . . I need to go to work today. I've canceled my patients the last two days, but I can't keep doing that. My patients need me. And I'm out of milk." *And wine*, though I don't say that. "Anyway, I can't stay locked up in my apartment, so I'm going to have to go out. But quite frankly, the thought terrifies me. I mean, why are they doing this to me? What do they want?" I pace through my apartment as I ramble.

When my eyes catch on the shiny new locks I had a locksmith add to my front door yesterday, I swallow. "If you could please call me when you get this message, I'd appreciate it. Thank you."

I swipe my phone off and see a new text has arrived from Sarah.

> Sarah: Morning, boss. Just checking in to make sure we're a go for today.

I want to type back *Cancel all patients until further notice.* But I won't. I need my practice as much as it needs me. Plus, the walls of this apartment are closing in around me. So instead I type back that I'll be at the office by eight and go about trying to cover some of the dark circles under my eyes. It's a futile effort, of course. Because raccoon rings are only half the problem. I've also lost weight. More than I realized. And I haven't seen sunlight in a while. So my eyes are sunken into a pale, hollow face that looks sick. Which I suppose I am.

I leave my apartment like a criminal on the run—checking through the peephole before opening the *three* locks I now have on my door, looking both ways on the street before darting to the waiting Uber. Even when I'm safely inside the car, I don't feel safe. My eyes flit around the streets looking for them. *For Gabriel. For Rebecca.*

When I walk into the office, Sarah's face falls.

"Oh, Mer. You don't look good."

"I haven't slept so well."

"Or at all . . ." She shakes her head and comes around her desk. "Are you sure this is a good idea? Maybe you should wait until you hear from the detective before trying to come back to work."

I force a smile. "I'm fine. Really. It'll be good to be busy today."

Sarah doesn't even get a chance to call me out on the lie. She doesn't have to. I prove I'm full of crap when the office door opens and I jump.

My heart is in my throat, and it's only Mrs. Radcliff. My first patient. I nod good morning and slink into my office, where I find a large cup of chamomile tea and a bagel waiting on my desk. Thank the Lord for Sarah.

She also stalls my first appointment a few minutes, which I'm certain is to give me a chance to collect myself, which I badly need.

My first session starts off rocky. I have a hard time focusing at first, but eventually I ease into it and start to settle. By the afternoon, I'm feeling a bit like myself again. A healthy lunch helped. I stop jumping every time my phone buzzes. When my last session of the day is finished, I close the door behind the patient and Sarah smiles.

"You did it."

"Thanks to you. I wouldn't have been able to muddle through this last week without you, Sarah."

She waves me off. "Eh. That's not true. You're tough as nails, lady."

I motion to the door. "Why don't you get out of here? I think I'm going to stay for a while and write up my patient notes."

"No, it's fine. I can stay until you're ready to go."

Today has given me courage, and I've already leaned on my assistant enough. "No, I insist. Go home. I'm good on my own."

She hesitates. "Are you sure?"

I smile. "Yeah, I am. I need to do this."

Sarah studies my face for a moment before nodding. "Okay. But lock up behind me."

"I will."

And I do. I lock both doors—the outer and the interior one to my office. I throw myself into typing up my notes for the day, and before I know it, more than an hour and a half has gone by, and I only have one more patient to write up.

But then I hear a knock.

And not the outer door to my office suite, which I locked.

My interior one.

Someone is inside.

It's so faint I'm talking myself into believing I've imagined it.

Until it happens a second time.

"I know you're in there, Dr. McCall."

Rebecca.

Oh God!

I stop breathing and don't move a muscle.

How did she get in? Did Sarah lock the outer office when she left and I *unlocked* it, thinking I was doing the opposite? Or did Rebecca *break in*? And *oh God*. That time my door was open at my apartment—was that her, too?

The room is so quiet it makes me wish the angry clock was back.

Maybe she'll go away.

If I stay quiet, maybe she'll go away.

The door handle jiggles.

"I just want to talk, Dr. McCall."

I reach for my cell phone and dial a nine and a one, but my hand is shaking so badly I drop the damn thing on my desk before I can hit the last number. It bangs loudly. I can't pretend I'm not here anymore.

"Go away!" I yell. "I'm calling the police."

"I'm not going to hurt you. I just want to tell you the whole story, fill in all the missing pieces. About Gabriel." She pauses. "And Ellen. And little Rose. You're still my doctor, and I trust you."

Those names—Gabriel. Ellen. *Rose.* They hang in the air, floating like the apple on the tree in front of Eve. I know it's calculated. Rebecca's trying to lure me in, just like she's done since the beginning with her stories that would feel so relatable to me—because I was treating the man she was talking about, and she knew it.

Yet I find myself walking toward the door. But I don't open it. "Say whatever you want to say and leave."

There's a long stretch of silence before she speaks again. I push my ear against the door so I won't miss a word.

"That night—the night his wife died—she was going to leave him. After I told Ellen about Gabriel and me, how in love we were, she left. His wife left with their daughter. I followed them for blocks. She had a bag with her. She called someone and told them that she was really leaving him this time. That he'd had *another* affair and she was done. She was angry, so, *so* angry. But then *he* called. Gabriel. And she started to cry. I could hear him on speakerphone apologizing and feeding Ellen all of these lies about how much he loved her and how sorry he was and how the affair meant nothing. He was going to do everything in his power to get her back. And I couldn't have that. Gabriel loves me. He just felt obligated to her."

Rebecca is quiet again, but she's right on the other side of the door now, so I can hear her breathing. Her voice is lower when she finally speaks again. "Gabriel needed to be free. Ellen was weak and would've gone back to him. So when she stopped at the light, and I saw a car swerving all over the road . . . I pushed her. I didn't mean to hurt her daughter. I didn't see that she was holding her hand and would drag her in front of the car, too."

My throat tightens, and my eyes bulge from my head.

I should finish calling 911, barricade my desk in front of the door until they arrive to save me. But instead, I find myself doing the exact opposite. I reach for the doorknob and pull open the door. I need to see this woman's face. I'm too shocked to speak. Rebecca is looking down at the floor, so I just wait. For what, I have no idea.

When she eventually raises her head, the corners of her mouth curl up and her eyes light with mirth. A chill races through my body. This woman has just admitted to murdering a woman and a small child and she's *smiling*. I've underestimated how deranged she is. She raises her index finger to her lips in the universal quiet sign.

"Remember, we have doctor-patient confidentiality, Dr. McCall."

She turns and walks out of my office.

CHAPTER 41
Now

hree more days pass, and I've still heard nothing from Detective Green. He won't answer my calls, won't return my messages. So I'm going to see him, and nothing's going to stop me, not even the damn rain.

I hug my rain jacket tighter, pull the hood down to cover my face, but fat drops collect and drip to my nose, my cheeks. I wrestle with my umbrella, but for the third time it ends up inverted, utterly useless.

"Goddamn it." The words escape before I can stifle them, and I smack the umbrella against a building in frustration. A man in a business suit stops, peers at me briefly, and hurries away like I'm one of my own patients, on the verge of losing it.

But I'm way past losing it. My sanity is long gone. I look over my shoulder when I'm locked inside my own apartment, and I stare out at the street while hiding behind my living room curtains. I check the peephole four times before I open the door, carry a kitchen knife in my pocket, and never take the same route more than once.

I can feel eyes on me. Their heavy presence makes every breath a little harder to take. Every step is like I'm carrying a backpack full of bricks.

I haven't caught sight of either of them, but knowing—*just knowing Rebecca is a murderer*—rocks me to my core. That little grin after she'd admitted it, that reminder about patient confidentiality, it sends a fresh chill down my spine every time I think about it. Not only am I sure they're following me, but the knowledge of what Rebecca's done is too much. No person should have to bear a secret like this.

Finally, I reach the police department. I stumble in, yanking off my soaked jacket and realizing it must need to be replaced, because it kept me anything but dry. I catch my reflection in a pane of glass separating the front area from the back, and I look like I've just walked out of an institution. A patient who escaped, rather than their doctor.

"Detective Green, please," I say to the man at the desk. He looks familiar, and from the way he looks at me, he clearly knows who I am. I'm pretty sure that's not a good thing.

"Have a seat. I'll see if he's available."

I hesitate. "I'm not leaving until I see him. I'm in danger."

The man nods, a faint smile on his lips. "I understand, ma'am."

I hold back a sigh. I don't just look like someone who's institutionalized, I'm being treated like that, too. Fake smiles, neutral responses. It's textbook—*don't upset the patients.*

Shockingly, Detective Green takes only two minutes to come out from the back—I know, because I'm watching the clock as it tick-tick-ticks.

"Dr. McCall? Right this way." He holds the door open, beckoning for me to go ahead of him. I already know where his cubicle is, so I head straight there. And for a moment, I'm relieved. It's safe here, within these walls. Even if it's just a few minutes of respite, that's more than I've had in days.

"How can I help you?" He takes his seat and swivels it to face me. "I actually planned on calling you later today."

Hope blooms in my chest, and for a moment, I forget I look like a drowned rat. Like a desperate mental patient.

"About the restraining order?" I prompt.

He sits there, twiddling a pen between his fingers. There's something in his gaze, something that makes me tense.

"They said no, didn't they?" I ask.

He sighs. "I'm sorry. I just heard back from the DA about an hour ago. A restraining order is a serious ask. It impinges on someone's rights. So there has to be sufficient evidence. The DA said there wasn't enough proof of a threat, and you said yourself that you're not certain who was following you most of the time." He sets the pen down and splays his hands. "I'm sorry. I tried. I wish I had better news for you."

"But . . ." I worry my hands, bite my lip, look down at the fake wood grain of the cheap desk. "But I'm in *danger*. They *are* dangerous. Dangerous to me. Rebecca especially."

The scene in my office plays on repeat in my mind. That smile. The gleam in her eyes, knowing she murdered Gabriel's wife and got away with it. Knowing I couldn't tell a soul.

"You have no proof, I'm afraid. Coincidences are not proof. The fact that she witnessed the accident doesn't sit right with me, either. But there's no evidence that she's a threat to you." He shrugs. "I'm sorry. Unless you have something more, there's nothing I can do."

I feel as though the floor has dropped out from beneath me.

I can't keep living like this.

Day in and day out, looking over my shoulder. Feeling eyes on me, then turning quickly. And of course I can't see them, because I live in New York, and there's a whole city walking the sidewalks. It's the easiest city in the world to stalk someone in.

"But she's dangerous," I repeat. Though even I hear the defeat in my voice.

Detective Green leans forward, hands clasped together. He looks right at me. "How are you so sure, Dr. McCall? Is there something you're not telling me? I imagine you deal with all sorts of patients. What makes you sure this one's a danger?"

I swallow. "I wish I could tell you. But I can't." Tears form in my eyes, helplessness washing over me.

The detective leans closer, lowers his voice, and touches a single finger to my hands, which are ice cold. "I won't lie to you. I am suspicious of Rebecca. It doesn't add up. She doesn't add up. I did a little investigating after you came in, went over to the school Gabriel Wright works. It's on record that something was going on between the two of them. Why wouldn't Rebecca have mentioned on the night of the accident that she was having an affair with the man whose family she'd just watched get killed? I was the one who took her statement. She never even indicated she knew the guy." He shakes his head and pulls back. "But there's no evidence. Of anything. So . . ." His voice trails off, and silence settles between us.

He's asking me to give him something. I can feel it.

And I could. I could tell him what Rebecca said. If I did, though . . . I squeeze my eyes shut. If I did, I could lose everything. My license, my job, my practice. I'd never work as a psychiatrist again.

I heave a sigh and get to my feet. "I guess I'll be going." I gather my sopping-wet jacket, clutch it in a single hand, and start to walk away.

"Dr. McCall, I'm sorry."

I don't reply. I just keep walking. I make it down the hall, through the door, and out to the entryway.

But I come to a dead stop when I see a woman. A mother. Maybe thirty years old. She holds the door open, reaching her hand to her daughter, a tiny version of herself. Both of them have blond hair, worn straight down. The mother's face looks weary, tear-streaked. But the daughter, she's maybe six years old, has a grin, wide eyes. She's looking everywhere, clearly entranced to be at a police station.

I picture Gabriel's daughter. She'll never smile again. Never hold her mother's hand again. Never get to experience the thrill of something new.

Rose was her name.

And Rose deserves better than this. She deserves justice more than I deserve my license, my ability to help people, which is of questionable value these days.

I turn on my heel. Go back to the man at the desk.

"Actually, I need to talk to Detective Green again. I forgot to tell him something."

"Seriously?" he asks.

"Seriously." Suddenly, I'm no longer a drowned rat, a crazy woman.

I'm a woman who knows exactly what she needs to do, finally. And it feels good.

He beckons to the door, pushes a button, and it buzzes. "I'm sure he's still in his office. Go on back."

I stride down the hall to find Detective Green staring at a case file. Rebecca's name is there, handwritten in black ink. It's *that* case file.

"I'm going to tell you something," I say without preamble. I drop back into the chair and look at him straight-on. "Rebecca Jordan confessed to me that she killed the Wright family."

CHAPTER 42
Now

*K*nock. Knock. Knock.

I grab the hockey stick that leans next to the front door. It's an improvement over the kitchen knife I kept nearby until a couple of days ago. Though I still hold my breath as I push up onto my toes and check the peephole, so I can pretend I'm not home if need be.

My eyelashes flutter against the tiny round window, blinking at the unexpected visitor, and I blow out lungsful of air as I twist all of the locks and open the door.

"Detective Green? It's good to see you."

He eyes the door, zoning in on all the gleaming locks, and frowns. "Hello, Dr. McCall. Could I come in for a few minutes?"

"Of course." I step aside.

Detective Green enters, and his eyes fall to the hockey stick I forgot I'm still holding in my hand.

"Oh." I set it next to the door and smack my hands against each other. "I was just organizing some stuff."

He offers a pacifying nod. "How are you holding up, Dr. McCall?"

"I'm okay. Well, I'd be better if I wasn't terrified to leave my apartment, if I'm being honest." I force a haphazard smile and motion toward the kitchen. "How about some tea? I was just about to make myself a cup, so the water's already hot."

"That would be great. Thanks."

Detective Green follows me into the kitchen. We both stay silent while I take a second mug down from the cupboard and steep two tea bags.

"Milk?"

He shakes his head. "Just some sugar, if you have it. My wife says I like a little tea in my morning sugar."

I smile and reach for the sugar bowl. It hasn't been used much since Connor. "My husband was the same way."

Settling into the seat across from Detective Green, I take a deep breath. "So, how's the investigation going?"

"Very well, actually. That's what I came to talk to you about. Rebecca Jordan has been arrested."

The statement hits like a needle scratching to a halt on a record. It feels like the wind has been knocked out of me. "When?"

"Last night." He nods. "She was arraigned this morning. The judge denied bail. Ms. Jordan is no longer a threat to you, Dr. McCall."

My heart races. "Are you sure?"

He smiles. "I was in the courtroom and watched the officers escort her out in handcuffs. She's not going anywhere for a long time. She confessed last night, on video, to two murders—Ellen and Rose Wright."

I cover my mouth. Relief floods through me, but it's mixed with something else—sadness, I think? Another life destroyed in this mess.

Detective Green wraps his hands around the mug in front of him. "Ms. Jordan also provided details of all the times she's followed you, said it had been going on a long time, ever since you walked out of some coffee shop in the fall of last year."

Oh my God. The woman with the long blond hair and an armful of books! I *knew* Rebecca always looked vaguely familiar. I'd just never been able to place her face. But now it's clear as day. She'd been behind me, staring at me, the afternoon I first spotted Gabriel and followed him. I'd chalked it up to being in her way. I'd been so frazzled that day. That was *months* before I'd known she existed. It's terrifying to think how unaware I was for so long. How vulnerable.

"But why? Why did she follow me all that time?"

"It was never really about you, but about your relationship with Mr. Wright. She seems a bit . . . fixated on the man. She said she followed you because you were following him." Detective Green shakes his head. "She wanted to know why and has been keeping tabs on you ever since. When Mr. Wright became a patient of yours, she did the same. Her interest in you was territorial."

"Did she break into my apartment? I came home one day and my door was open. I could've sworn I remembered locking it. And my key had gone missing a few weeks earlier."

"Not that she admitted to. Though I wouldn't put anything past her. The woman pushed a child into oncoming traffic and told us about it as calmly as if she were discussing the weather. She did send you some packages, though. A Hello Kitty doll and a book? She was trying to scare you, playing mind games. Thought it might keep you away from Mr. Wright."

I shake my head at how deeply this woman was involved in my life. I've replayed the sessions I had with Rebecca over and over in my head, trying to figure out what was truth and what was lies. The only thing I know for certain is she has unhealthy, obsessive relationships with men.

I sigh. "I hope she gets help."

Detective Green sips his tea, watching me over the brim. He's observant, not unlike a psychiatrist, who often learns more from actions than words.

"What about Gabriel?" I ask.

"We've interrogated Mr. Wright three times about his role in things. His story checks out. He was never the one following you. It was always Rebecca." Detective Green catches my eye. "Though he seems to think you were following him, too. He said you crashed into each other in an alley at one point months back, when he was leaving his storage unit."

I've never told Detective Green how things started, but the truth needs to be set free. So I nod. "I was following him for a while. It started by accident. I never set out to do it, I swear. One day, I was sitting in a coffee shop, looking outside, and there he was. The man I'd watched crumple in the emergency room on the worst night of my life. It seemed like the worst night of his, too. Only now he looked happy and I . . . I followed him. I didn't mean for it to become a thing, but somehow it did." I inhale and blow out a wobbly breath. "Am I in trouble for that?"

He shakes his head. "No. Gabriel Wright has no interest in pressing charges. He feels bad about things that transpired between the two of you. He said you were . . . more than his doctor. Is that right?"

I look down, ashamed of my actions, and nod. "We were intimate, yes."

Detective Green shakes his head. "You two have some interesting ways of grieving. But regardless, I don't think you're at risk anymore. Rebecca is off the streets, and with your testimony, she won't be back out for decades, if at all. That is, *if* you're still willing to testify. It should be an open-and-shut case with her confession, but it never is once these dirtbag defense attorneys get involved. Last night she was taking responsibility on camera, and by this morning at arraignment, her lawyer was singing a new tune."

"What do you mean?"

"Her attorney asked for a competency examination. Sounds like he's going to put up an insanity defense. Even had his client rocking back and forth in the courtroom, mumbling about Thailand."

"Thailand?"

Detective Green shrugs. "She just kept rocking back and forth and mumbling, 'Thailand, Thailand, Thailand.' When the judge took the bench, he threatened to have her removed if she didn't quiet down. Her lawyer apologized and said his client believed she should be in Thailand, not prison."

"What does Thailand have to do with anything?"

"It doesn't. That's the point. Incoherent babbling is a ploy for her defense. Vincent Gigante, one of the most notorious crime bosses, walked around the city wearing a bathrobe, mumbling nonsense to no one in particular, for years. It's what these defense attorneys do. They put on a show. So it will be helpful if you testify. The DA said it will probably cost you your license, once the medical board gets wind that you broke doctor-patient confidentiality, since she never threatened you with any harm."

I nod. "I will. I'll testify. The last few years have been nothing but secrets and lies. The truth has to come out. Gabriel's wife and daughter deserve justice. And I need to give it to them. That's the only way this can end for all of us."

"What will you do if you can't be a psychiatrist anymore?"

I shake my head. "I don't know. But maybe a fresh start is just what I need."

Detective Green finishes his tea and slaps his hands on his knees. "Well, I should get going. The DA will take things from here and be in touch. I've given him your number."

I walk the detective to the door. He stops and looks at the hockey stick. "He was one hell of a player."

I smile sadly. "He was."

"I hope it brings you some peace to know the Wright family's deaths were not his fault. He shouldn't have been on the road in his condition, but Rebecca Jordan committed murder."

"I think it will take some time to absorb, but I'm grateful you got to the bottom of things. Thank you for all you've done."

Detective Green nods. "Take care, Dr. McCall."

I lock the door behind him—one lock, not all three this time—and lean against it, looking over at Connor's stick. Tears stream down my cheeks.

"It's over," I whisper. "*You* can be free now, too."

CHAPTER 43
Now

life almost feels normal lately.

Well, a new normal. I'll never work as a psychiatrist again. Never go into my office and thank Sarah for grabbing me a coffee, then retreat to my desk to prepare for the day. A part of me misses it. But another part of me is glad to be done with having my life revolve around other people's problems. My own are enough to carry. It's still a struggle every day, but I keep putting one foot in front of the other and pushing forward.

A warm, early summer day greets me as I push out of the storage unit facility. But I'm not here to stalk Gabriel. No, I've let that go. I've stopped looking over my shoulder—mostly, anyway. Today I'm leaving with a stack of flattened moving boxes clutched in my arms. I balance them as I step off the sidewalk and cross the street, feeling the warmth of bright sunshine on my face. A drop of sweat rolls down my cheek, and I shrug my shoulder to wipe it away.

I've decided to move. I'm letting our apartment go—I think it's for the best. I think you'd agree. A small brownstone with a tiny garden awaits me in Carroll Gardens. When I went to look at it with the real estate agent, a teal wreath with Easter eggs and cartoon bunnies hung from the front door. It was so cheerful, the sort of detail that made me realize I still have a whole life ahead of me, and if I shake this one loose, I might even enjoy it.

As I take the stairs up to my apartment for one of the final times—the movers come tomorrow—I shift the boxes, reaching for my keys. But someone stands at the top of the staircase. I pause to let them go by, but they don't move, so I look up.

My breath catches.

"Gabriel."

I find my balance before taking the last step. For a moment, I think of turning and running the other way. But I don't run anymore. Not that I could, weighted down by boxes as I am, but the new me stands her ground.

"What are you doing here? And how do you know where I live?"

"Your husband's address was on the police report from . . . that night. And I came to talk to you, if that's okay?" He tucks his hands into his pockets and rocks back on his heels, trying, I think, to put me at ease.

"So talk." My words come out harshly, but he's shown up at my front door unannounced. A tiny bit of me is glad to see him. But mostly, I wish he'd waited a day. I'd be gone by then. I set the boxes on the landing, lean them against the stairwell rail, and fold my arms across my chest.

"Thank you." He presses his lips together and nods. "Thank you for agreeing to testify. Detective Green said you'll lose your license to do it, and I know that's a big sacrifice. I appreciate you doing that for me."

"I'm doing it for Ellen and Rose. Not you. They were the only innocent people in all of this. I owe them justice. It's the least I can do."

Another nod. "Fair enough."

I lean over to grab my boxes, because it seems he's done talking. But questions bubble up, and I can't contain them. I rise empty-handed.

"Why did you do it? Why did you come to my office if you knew who I was? Why did you come to me for treatment?" I demand.

Gabriel opens his mouth, then passes a hand across his face, scratches his chin. "I was angry. Not thinking straight. I wanted to make you suffer, like I was. Make you listen about my loss. I wanted you to hurt." He leans back against the wall. "But you were actually kind. You tried to help me. And . . ." He lifts his gaze for just a moment. "I found myself drawn to you, attracted to you. Which was the worst possible thing that could have happened. I had to come back again after that. For a while, you were the only thing that made me feel better. Made me feel like—like there was something more to life." He sighs. "It doesn't make sense, does it? I don't make sense. Grief doesn't make sense." He eyes me. "You should know, that part was real. I really did like you."

Silence stretches between us. I meet his eyes to gauge his sincerity, and I find nothing but truth reflecting back at me.

"I really did like you."

That shouldn't warm me in the way it does. I shouldn't feel anything. But I do. Some soft spot inside me unfurls, and I relax a little.

"Here." He holds something out, tucked into his fist, and waits until I give him my hand so he can fold it into my palm. "Gotta go." He smiles ever so slightly and motions to the boxes. "Good luck with whatever's next."

I don't stop him as he hurries down the stairs. When I open my hand, it's Connor's keychain, the one I saw in Gabriel's storage unit.

"Wait!"

Gabriel turns.

"Why did you go to the storage unit so often?"

He smiles sadly. "I put my daughter's things in there because they were too painful to look at. Then I went to visit them every day anyway." He shrugs. "Don't ask me to make sense of it."

I know a thing or two about self-punishment.

I hold up the keychain. "How did you get this?"

"Found it hooked to my coat pocket the day we crashed into each other near the alley. You must've dropped it when you fell, and my coat caught it."

"Did you know who I was that day?"

"I knew you looked familiar. Probably wouldn't have made the connection if that keychain didn't have number seventeen on it. But once I saw that, I placed the face. You were at the hospital the night . . ."

I take a deep breath and nod.

"Any more questions?" he asks.

I shake my head. "Take care of yourself, Gabriel."

"You, too, Doc."

I watch him walk down the block, and I keep staring long after he turns the corner. Then I look down at the keychain in my hand.

"It's just me and you again," I whisper. "The last little bit of *you* I have left."

CHAPTER 44
Gabriel
—One year later

"Hi. What can I get you?" A bubbly blonde with glossy lips tilts her head with a smile. She's cute—my type. My old type, anyway. Probably no older than twenty-three, wide-eyed, and eager. There's a familiarity to her. I briefly consider whether she might be a student of mine, but it doesn't really matter.

"I'll take a small coffee and . . ." I lean down and look in the glass case. "One of those nice-looking crumb cakes, please."

"Coming right up."

I swipe my credit card. Shuffle down the line. Stand with four strangers all staring down at their phones as they wait for their orders.

"Gabriel? Order pickup," a voice rings out a few minutes later.

I take my coffee and the paper bag. Out of habit, my eyes slide back to the cute blonde. She smiles, waits for me to break our gaze. Or maybe she's waiting for me to walk back over, flirt a little. Ask for her number, perhaps. But the new me isn't interested. My tastes have changed. Grown and matured.

I take my usual spot, sitting in a tufted leather chair toward the front of the shop. It gives me the perfect view of the house across the street, the one with the cheery flower boxes and the seasonal wreath that hangs on the front door. Brooklyn has grown on me the last few months, especially this neighborhood in Carroll Gardens with all the inviting brownstones. Who knows, maybe I'll move here. Maybe I'll leave Columbia and teach at Brooklyn College, like a certain new adjunct professor I know.

Speaking of which, the door opens across the street. The new puppy runs out first, pulling its owner with it. I smile as Meredith barrels down the stairs, yanking the leash and trying to stop the beast. But the animal probably weighs almost as much as she does already. It's all gangly and leggy, with drool hanging from its wrinkly face. Neapolitan mastiff, not exactly the ideal breed for New York City, but somehow it suits Meredith.

She gets control of the dog at the bottom of the stairs, makes him sit for a treat. Then she starts her daily walk. Sometimes her friend joins her, the one married to the hockey player I pretended not to recognize that night at Sunny's. But today she's alone. I'm glad. I don't like too many distractions during the limited time I get to spend with her each day. I wait until they're almost at the corner before I exit the coffee shop and follow. Brooklyn doesn't have the same shield of people to hide behind as Manhattan. I need to be careful.

I follow for six blocks. At the corner of Third and Smith, she stops and digs her phone out of her pocket. A gust of wind blows, almost taking my baseball cap with it. There's a storm coming later tonight. I stand behind a tree on the opposite side of the street, pull the brim of my hat down, and watch her side-eyed. Her hair flies around in the breeze, and it makes me smile.

Meredith looks good, great even. She's gained a few pounds, which she needed. And put some highlights in her dirty-blond locks, let them grow past her shoulders. But it's her smile that rocks me. I wait for it each day, my own version of the sunrise to remind me there's hope—a new start, a new promise, a new life. She's halfway through her morning dog walk, so I begin to grow concerned that maybe today I won't see it. But then it happens. Meredith says something into the phone and her head bends back in laughter. Warmth blooms inside my chest.

She's happy.

Really happy.

I wonder if whoever is on the phone makes her feel that way.

I wonder if it's a man.

I wonder if maybe someday *I* could make her smile.

She teaches now. I looked her up on the college's website while I waited for her to come out the other day. Adjunct professor of psychology. We have a lot in common. Our jobs, our history, our curiosity about people and what makes them tick.

She's on the move again. Finished with her call, Meredith continues her morning walk. Left, then left, back up for six blocks before the final turn. When she rounds the corner, returning to her block, I wait, staying a good distance behind. Another dog on a leash approaches and the two animals can't resist—they jump all over each other, even as their owners try to get them to stop. They play, standing on hind legs with open mouths and swatting each other in the face. Meredith is too busy trying to gain control of her dog to notice something fall to the ground. But I'm not.

A few minutes later, the dogs are finally separated, and Meredith walks the last quarter block to her house and goes inside. It's Tuesday, so it'll be another hour or so before she comes out to head to class. I have school myself today, so I can't stay, but I am curious about what she left behind on the ground. So I pull my hoodie up and over my hat, bringing it forward as much as I can to shield the sides of my face, and jog across the street.

A small silver charm gleams in the sunlight. It's shaped like a bone, a dog tag that broke free of the collar. I lean down and scoop it up for a closer look. But as I do, the dollar bills I have tucked in the pocket of my hoodie slip out. I catch all but one that the wind steals, and the lone bill goes tumbling down the street with dirt and sand and everything else in the path of the brewing storm. I let it go, more interested in seeing what little treat Meredith has left behind for me than in chasing a dollar. Nothing is on the front of the tag, but I flip it over to the other side and my heart stops when I read the name engraved.

Romeo.

She named her dog Romeo.

From Shakespeare.

The subject I teach . . .

Is that a coincidence?

I want to believe it's not, that Meredith still thinks about me. Or maybe she doesn't, but it's a sign. A sign I should keep waiting.

Waiting for *you.*

I fold the tag into my palm with a smile and start to walk away. But a voice from behind me catches my attention.

"Sir!"

I turn.

The man holds something out. "I think you dropped this." He smiles. "I thought it was Monopoly money at first. But it's a baht, right?"

"Yes, it is."

"I went to Thailand on my honeymoon. That's why I recognized the currency. Beautiful country. Did you just get back?"

I shake my head. "Leave next week."

"If you're going with someone, check out Koh Yao Noi. Gorgeous beaches. Secluded. They do these candlelight dinners on the sand. It was my wife's favorite part of the trip."

I smile. "Thanks for the tip. I was supposed to take someone, a reward for a job well done. But as it turns out, she won't be able to make it, so I'll be going alone."

ACKNOWLEDGMENTS

Thank you to Emily Bestler and her publishing team for believing in this book from the very start. And to Hannah Wann and Becky West for bringing *The Unraveling* on a fabulous journey to the UK.

To my agent and friend, Kimberly Brower—thank you for always being there to support me and steer the ship to new adventures.

Behind every woman who succeeds is a tribe of successful women who cheer her on, have her back, and encourage her to do scary things. Thank you to my tribe leader, Penelope Ward, who is always by my side, and to Cheri, Luna, Julie, Elaine, Jessica, and the 26,000 smart ladies in my amazing Facebook group, Vi's Violets.

To my family—Chris, Jake, Grace, Sarah, and Kennedy, who never doubted I could, even when I questioned it.

To you—the *readers*. Thank you for your support and excitement. Whether we are meeting for the first time, or you've been with me for more than a decade reading my romance novels, I'm so grateful you took a chance on this story.